Praise for these bestselling authors

Jane Graves

"Graves is a solid storyteller with
a confident, convincing voice."
—*Publishers Weekly*

"Graves's ready wit and charismatic characters are
an abundant source of comic relief. Readers looking for
a strong hero and a feisty heroine who face off against
each other will enjoy this fast-paced tale."
—*Publishers Weekly* on *I Got You, Babe*

Dorien Kelly

"Kelly is an author who delivers first-rate reads."
—*The Oakland Press*

"Warmly appealing thanks to its assured prose and
deft characterizations. Dev is especially winning as a
charming but conflicted romantic hero, while the quirky
folks who populate Ballymuir create a funny, affectionately
drawn world to which readers will eagerly return."
—*Publishers Weekly* on *Hot Nights in Ballymuir*

Tanya Michaels

"Tanya Michaels employs first-person narrative
to excellent effect, taking the reader on a
joyous, sexy and heartbreaking ride."
—*Romantic Times BOOKclub*

"Tanya Michaels turns up the heat in *Going All the Way*,
a spirited, spicy story that will leave readers wanting more."
—*Romantic Times BOOKclub*

»»»»»THE BOYS ARE BACK »»» IN TOWN

JANE GRAVES
DORIEN KELLY
TANYA MICHAELS

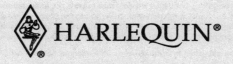

HARLEQUIN®

TORONTO • NEW YORK • LONDON
AMSTERDAM • PARIS • SYDNEY • HAMBURG
STOCKHOLM • ATHENS • TOKYO • MILAN • MADRID
PRAGUE • WARSAW • BUDAPEST • AUCKLAND

ISBN-13: 978-0-373-83713-7
ISBN 10:   0-373-83713-5

THE BOYS ARE BACK IN TOWN

Copyright © 2006 by Harlequin Books S.A.

The publisher acknowledges the copyright holders
of the individual works as follows:

FALLING FOR YOU
Copyright © 2006 by Jane Graves.

FORWARD PASS
Copyright © 2006 by Dorien Kelly.

READY AND WILLING
Copyright © 2006 by Tanya Michna.

www.eHarlequin.com

Printed in U.S.A.

CONTENTS

FALLING FOR YOU
Jane Graves

PROLOGUE

12:01 a.m., June 2, 1991

IT WAS BARELY JUNE, BUT THE summer heat had already settled in the Texas hill country. The night air felt damp and oppressive, wrapping itself around Kirk like a shroud. He sat leaning against a tree, staring into the campfire, listening to the crackle of kindling. The fire only made the night hotter, but it was a tradition he shared every year with Caleb Tanner and Matt O'Connell. They sat alongside him now, drinking beer and reminiscing about the year gone by. But the last thing Kirk wanted to do tonight was remember.

Down the road was Trehan Point, a favorite destination for the kids from Prescott High. They'd nicknamed it Trojan Point for a reason. And Kirk would have been there with Amanda right now if not for what had happened last night. Just thinking about it made anger and humiliation churn inside him. He took another swig of his beer, even though he knew that no matter how much he drank tonight, nothing could wash those feelings away.

Caleb pulled a second beer from the six pack and popped the top. "Another year done."

"Our last," Matt said.

"Good thing," Caleb said. "I don't think we could have come up with anything better than moving that junkyard for next year's stunt. The Pick 'n Trade is unbeatable, O'Connell. Your best idea yet."

"Right up until I got caught," Matt said.

"Come on, man," Caleb said. "You're a freakin' *legend!* Did you see the look on people's faces when they saw all that crap on the high school lawn? Who cares if you ticked off that crazy Delisle guy? And thanks for not ratting us out."

"It was no big deal," Matt said.

"Wouldn't have worked that way if it had been me they'd caught," Kirk said. "The last thing my old man would have done was save my ass with the sheriff."

Matt looked away, probably because he knew it was true. Of course his old man had bailed him out. Matt was a jock, after all, and in small-town Texas, football was number one in everybody's book. On the other hand, Kirk felt nothing but the utter worthlessness that came from having a father who couldn't stay away from drugs and alcohol long enough to hold a job, a mother long gone, and not a solitary person in his life who truly gave a damn.

Matt turned to Kirk. "So I heard that after what happened last night, Amanda broke up with you."

Kirk took a swig of beer, then gave Matt an offhand shrug. "It was just as well. I was going to break it off with her after graduation, anyway."

That was such a lie that it made him sick to his stomach just to say the words.

Last night they'd taken a drive. And suddenly

Amanda was talking about how hard it was going to be for them to see each other while she was in college, particularly if she was in Austin and he wasn't, so they were going to have to really think about their relationship. But he knew what she really meant. She wanted to get him out of the way so she could hook up with one of those rich frat boys at the University of Texas, a guy her hard-ass father would actually approve of.

Kirk had gotten angry. They'd had a fight. He'd driven faster. Then he'd lost traction around a sharp curve, and before he knew it, he'd lost control and side-swiped a tree. The police had shown up, and they'd both ended up in the emergency room. They'd just gotten a little bruised, but still Amanda was shouting at him, telling him she never wanted to see him again.

To hell with her, he'd thought last night. *She always thought she was too good for you, anyway. What do you need with a woman like her?*

But now that the reality of losing her had finally hit home, it was all he could do not to go back and beg her for another chance. His pride, though, was the only thing he still had left, and he had no intention of giving that up.

Matt turned to Kirk. "So, when you taking off?"

"Tomorrow night. I'm going to California."

"Yeah? Why California?"

"Because it isn't Prescott."

"I'm leaving tomorrow night, too," Caleb said. "I've already told my grandmother I've got a friend in Austin who thinks he can get me a job. She's so thrilled at the thought of my being employed she barely said a word. How about you, Matt? You gonna work at the golf club again this summer?"

Matt shook his head. "I'm moving up to Oklahoma to live with my uncle and get in shape before the season starts."

Caleb grinned. "Are you gonna remember us when you make the NFL? Seriously, you know hanging out with you guys was the only thing that made this shit town bearable for the past two years."

The NFL. Kirk thought about his own hazy future and felt a stab of jealousy. Matt might be a bad-ass when it came to high school pranks, but at least he knew where he was going in life and had the talent to get himself there.

Kirk had nothing.

Matt raised his bottle. "To Jim Morrison, James Dean and all the rebels who knew when to die. You went out big, and we salute you."

Kirk lifted his beer and chugged the last of it, knowing he should feel a little nostalgic since he'd spent the past few years running wild with Caleb and Matt. The Dead Rebels, they'd called themselves, in honor of Dean and Morrison and all those guys who lived fast and died young. But he didn't feel anything right now but the urge to get out of there.

Kirk rose and tossed his beer can into the bushes. "I've got to go."

"So soon?" Caleb asked.

"I have things to do. I'll see you guys tomorrow."

He walked down the moonlit road to where he'd left his father's car. It had been easy to make off with it tonight with his father passed out drunk. Truth be told, Kirk preferred him that way. At least when he was sleeping, he wasn't shouting or swinging.

He opened the car, reached into the glove compartment and took out a small velvet box. He walked to the edge of the cliff that sloped into the valley below. Opening the box, he stared at the tiny round diamond glinting dully in the moonlight.

He told himself it was a good thing Amanda had never seen it. She probably would have laughed at it, anyway. A girl with plans to become a doctor wouldn't even think of marrying a guy who didn't even have a job lined up after graduation. How stupid had he been to think she might?

He snapped the box shut and hurled it as far into the valley as he could. It fell so far that he didn't hear so much as a faint thud when it hit.

There. It was over and done with.

Now that Amanda was officially out of his life, it was time for him to address the only emotion he was allowing himself to hang on to, and that was the burning desire he felt to blow out of the crappy little town that had hated him almost as much as he had hated it.

"I'm getting the hell out of this place," he said through clenched teeth. "And I'm never coming back."

CHAPTER ONE

THE PROBLEM WITH GREAT exit lines was that they had a way of making a liar out of a man.

Kirk stood on the edge of the cliff and gazed out over the valley below. The countryside was just as he remembered it—dry limestone slopes dotted with cedars and scrub oaks, dropping down to shady bottomland intersected by shallow creeks. In the distance lay Prescott, a little newer and shinier than it had been fifteen years earlier, but with enough of the old landmarks still standing to remind him of what life there used to be like.

He peered over the edge of the cliff to the bottom of the ravine, where the second-unit crew had finished inflating an air bag big enough to catch a grown man falling from a great height with a minimum of bodily injury. The average person in his right mind wouldn't consider taking a six-story dive with nothing but a glorified balloon to break his fall, but for Kirk it was all in a day's work.

He loved the rush of that heart-pounding moment right before a stunt, whether he was flying across a gorge on a motorcycle or hurling himself off a ten-story building. Of course, a gust of wind at the wrong time could knock him inches off course, which could be deadly.

And that made the rush even better.

Off to one side in a cordoned-off area stood several townspeople who had come out to witness the excitement of making a movie, and the irony of it wasn't lost on Kirk. In that crowd were undoubtedly some of the very people who at one time would have stood in line to give him a one-way ticket out of town. He dropped his forehead to his hand to rub away the twinge of pain he felt there, amazed at how just thinking about Prescott's narrow-minded citizens was enough to give him a headache.

When the producer said they were investigating the possibility of shooting in the Texas hill country, Kirk hadn't thought a thing about it. Texas was a big state, and the hill country covered a lot of acreage. Then the scout returned with the news that he'd found the perfect location—Prescott—and memories Kirk wished had stayed buried forever had come flooding back.

No. That wasn't completely true. There had been one good thing. Someone he'd never been able to forget.

"You okay?"

Kirk looked up to see Andy approaching, walkie-talkie in hand. "Yeah," he said with a sigh. "Just a little headache."

"One too many beers last night?"

"Not unless one is one too many."

"Then it must have come from sleeping on one of those mattresses at that dinky little place we're staying. Just once I'd love to work on a big-budget picture. You know. The kind where they put you up somewhere besides the No-Tell Motel."

"I believe they call it the Bluebonnet Inn."

"Whatever."

"Is everything set up?" he asked Andy.

"Yep. As soon as the doctor's on site, it's a go."

Kirk came to attention. "What? She's not here yet?"

"No, and she'd better arrive in a hurry. We're losing the light, and Dan's screaming that he doesn't want to set up the shot again tomorrow. The budget is already so tight it squeaks."

Dan Pederson was one of the tougher directors to work for. It took nothing to piss him off, and the lack of a mandatory doctor on site when the producer insisted on one would certainly do it. But all Kirk could think about was the doctor herself. If she didn't make it for some reason…

At the bottom of the ravine, a red SUV swung around in a semicircle and came to a halt. The door opened, and a pair of long, jeans-clad legs appeared. A woman emerged from the car, pulling off her sunglasses to survey her surroundings.

It was her. No doubt about it.

Even at this distance, there was no mistaking that lithe body, that graceful walk as she approached Becky, the production assistant. As they exchanged a few words, a soft breeze picked up her dark, shoulder-length hair and stirred it around her face, and when she threaded her fingers through it and tossed it back as he'd seen her do a thousand times before, it was as if the past fifteen years had melted away.

Becky's voice crackled through Andy's walkie-talkie. "Okay. The doctor's here."

Andy turned to Kirk. "The wind's up a little."

"It's nothing. I can adjust."

"Okay, then. On with the show."

Kirk had never believed in fate. He believed a man made his own way in the world with no influence from unseen forces that moved people around like chess pieces. But when he'd discovered a week ago that the woman he was sure had gone on to a place much bigger and better than Prescott was living there again, he had to wonder if cosmic forces hadn't conspired to bring them together one more time. Now all he could think about was going back to that fork in the road he'd stood at fifteen years ago and finding a way to explore the path he hadn't taken.

And as soon as he threw himself off this cliff, that was just what he intended to do.

WHEN AMANDA SAW THE HEIGHT of the freefall the man was about to take, she decided either he was minus a few brain cells or had a death wish. Likely both. A good psychiatrist could probably sort out those problems, but she treated bodies, not minds. Her job was simply to be prepared to care for any injuries that occurred. And all for a stunt to jazz up some low-budget biker flick with B-grade actors that would probably go straight to video.

She scanned the set, which included a couple of trailers, camera equipment, a crew milling about and a gigantic air bag at the foot of the cliff designed to cushion a fall from a very long way up. She hadn't wanted to be there in the first place, and the unnecessary risk she was getting ready to witness only made matters worse. Unfortunately, she'd had no choice.

They need a doctor, Louise had said, *and you need*

some time off. That means you'll be spending a relaxing week on a movie set whether you like it or not.

When the chief of staff of Prescott Medical Clinic had pulled rank on her, she'd had no choice but to agree. Most of the time, Amanda appreciated Louise's no-nonsense approach. This was not one of those times.

Amanda admitted she was a workaholic, and it had always amazed her that some people thought that was a bad thing. The townspeople gathered here to watch the action wouldn't have believed it, but she would much rather have been back at the clinic. A week of sitting around a movie set twiddling her thumbs just wasn't her idea of a good time.

She'd arrived today with a trauma bag over her left shoulder stuffed full of emergency equipment and drugs. In her other hand she held a portable defibrillator, which would come in handy for any heart-stopping injuries. It was only because she came so well equipped and the hospital was so close that the producer hadn't insisted on having an ambulance on the set.

She looked up to the top of the cliff and the man standing at the edge of it, then turned to Becky, the production assistant who had greeted her.

"Sure is a long way up there," Amanda said.

"Here," Becky said, handing her a small set of binoculars. "You can see better with these."

Amanda lowered the bags she held to the ground and put the binoculars to her eyes. "That air bag has to look like a postage stamp from up there."

"He's done this kind of fall before."

"It's a little windy, isn't it?"

"He's a pro," the woman said as she scribbled

something on her clipboard. "He knows how to deal with that."

The woman might have been talking about an accountant crunching numbers for all the tension in her voice. And the man at the edge of the cliff seemed equally relaxed, apparently scoping out the fall he was about to take. He stood there with the kind of assurance that said he was indeed the pro Becky said he was. And what a body. Long, lean legs, broad shoulders, biceps bulging beneath a dark T-shirt. Hmm. *Very* nice. And his face…

Amanda froze. His face. It looked familiar.

She fiddled with the binoculars to sharpen the view, then focused on the man again. By then, though, he'd turned his back to speak to someone behind him, and in that view he could have been one of a thousand other thirtysomething men with the kind of body that would make any woman do a double take.

Then slowly he turned around again, and recognition struck her like a hammer blow.

She whipped around to Becky. "What's his name?"

"What?"

"His name. The man doing the stunt."

"Kirk," she said. "Kirk McKenzie."

Suddenly Amanda felt as if all the oxygen had been sucked out of the atmosphere. She gasped with disbelief. God in heaven, it really was him.

Of all the places in the world Kirk could be right now, he was standing on a cliff ready to jump, which meant he was still pushing his luck, still defying anything and everything in his way, up to and including gravity itself. In spite of what had happened between them, the feelings she'd once had for him surged through her again, practically knocking her to her knees.

He walked to the edge of the cliff, checked his position, then turned around backward. The wind gusted again. He seemed to teeter slightly, and Amanda's breath caught in her throat.

Then he fell backward over the edge.

The wind caught his shirt and billowed it up. He seemed to fall forever, like a hawk taking a nosedive. He hit the air bag, and for a moment Amanda thought everything was fine.

It wasn't.

He'd landed too close to the edge, the bag barely cushioning his fall. He tumbled off of it onto the rocky ground, his head slinging hard against it.

Everyone on the set froze, a few interminable seconds ticking away as they grasped what had happened. Then there was shouting. People surging toward him. And in the next few seconds, Amanda realized the worst. He wasn't getting up.

Her heart beating wildly, she dropped the binoculars, grabbed her equipment and took off toward Kirk, shouting for somebody to call 911. Shoving a few people aside, she finally reached him and knelt beside him. When he still wasn't moving, dread welled up inside her. But as she reached for his wrist to find a pulse, he began to stir and his eyes fluttered open.

Thank God.

He inhaled. Coughed. He tried to rise, but she put her hand against his shoulder. Until she could get the paramedics out here with a back board, he was staying down.

"Kirk? Can you talk to me? Tell me what hurts."

"Nothing," he said. "Just need to...catch my breath."

She didn't believe a word of that. Even if he didn't have broken bones or contusions, he'd landed so hard that he had to hurt like hell.

Amanda pulled out a penlight and checked his pupils, relieved to find them equal and reactive.

"Do you remember what happened?" she asked him.

"Hit the bag wrong," he choked out.

"Do you know where you are?"

"Prescott." After a few more labored breaths, he turned to look up at her. "Both of us here again. Imagine that."

She couldn't believe it. After all these years, even after a blow to the head, he knew her in an instant.

Just as she'd known him in an instant.

Amanda pressed her fingertips to his wrist to feel his pulse. "Do you have any numbness? Can you move your arms and legs?"

"Yeah," he said. "And I'll get up—" another deep breath "—if everyone will just get out of my way."

He tried to rise, only to grit his teeth with pain. Amanda held him down.

"Kirk. You've had a bad fall. Just lie still."

Grimacing, he lay back against the ground, drawing in a few more deep breaths. "I told you I'm fine."

"Don't listen to him," a man said as he crouched down beside Kirk. "He once walked on a broken ankle for a week." He looked at Amanda. "An ambulance is on the way."

"Andy," Kirk said. "Call it off."

"No," Amanda said, giving Andy a sharp stare. "I want an ambulance here right now."

"We've got a tight budget on this film," Kirk said.

"I'm not concerned about the budget on this film."

"You've checked me out. No need for the hospital."

"You had a short period of unconsciousness. That means that at the very least you have a concussion, which means you're going to the hospital for a CAT scan."

"No. No hospital."

She leaned in close, her eyes narrowing in warning. "Now, Kirk, I know it's been a long time, but you should *still* know better than to mess with me."

Kirk closed his eyes in resignation. Andy glanced back and forth between them. "You two know each other?"

Amanda looked back at Kirk. He opened his eyes again and stared at her, and suddenly it was as if fifteen years melted away in the evening light.

"We did," she said.

She heard a siren growing closer, but she couldn't take her eyes off Kirk. He had the same dark eyes she remembered, and the same dark, thick hair, though he wore it shorter now. An inch-long scar cutting through one of his eyebrows hadn't been there before, and a few creases at the edges of his eyes and mouth hinted at the passage of time. Even so, she couldn't imagine not recognizing him wherever they'd happened to meet.

She saw some sand on his face, and when she reached down to brush it away with a soft sweep of her fingertips, it tripped a long-ago memory.

Galveston. Their senior trip. The two of them lying on the beach. She'd reached down to brush the sand from his cheek then, too. Only that time he'd pulled her down until her lips met his, and for the next few hours they'd forgotten anyone else existed. As she thought about that now, all her professionalism seemed to evaporate, and she became the girl she'd been so long ago, staring at the boy she'd loved beyond all reason.

The siren wound down. Amanda rose to her feet and stood by as they loaded Kirk into the ambulance, then tossed her equipment into her car and hopped in.

As she headed to the hospital, the irony of the situation struck her. She wasn't just seeing Kirk again. They were heading for an emergency room. She still remembered how he'd walked out of Prescott Community Hospital all those years ago before walking out of Prescott itself, swearing he would never return.

Famous last words.

For all the times that she'd thought about what it would be like to see Kirk again, not once had she imagined it happening anything like this.

TWO HOURS LATER, AMANDA was at Prescott Community Hospital reading the report of Kirk's CAT scan. At first she felt hopeful. There was no intracranial bleeding. Neurological-function tests had already ruled out a spinal injury. He had a concussion, but otherwise he'd escaped relatively unscathed. But as it turned out, this injury wasn't the problem.

It was the injuries that had come before.

Hoping the radiologist had gotten something wrong, she dropped the report and pulled out the X rays. She slid them into the light bank and examined them, but they only confirmed what she'd already read in the report.

"My God," she said under her breath.

"Problems?"

Amanda turned to see her colleague Louise walk into the room. As always, her steel-gray hair was pulled into a knot at the nape of her neck, and she held a cup of coffee she'd bought from the coffee bar in the lobby. The sugar and extra shot of espresso it contained probably didn't matter. At age sixty-four, she had the kind of annual physical results women half her age would kill for.

"They told me at the nurses' station that Kirk's films were back," Louise said. "I take it the results aren't good."

Amanda sighed heavily, still reeling from the whole experience. "Take a look at these."

Louise set down her coffee. Grabbing the glasses dangling around her neck, she put them on and leaned in close to study the films, her mouth turning down in a worried frown.

"Hmm. Scar tissue."

"Two places. Here—" she pointed "—and here. He's had at least one intracranial bleed before."

"Have you ordered his records from California?"

"He has to authorize it, and he refused. He's as bullheaded as ever. Thinks he's invincible. I almost couldn't talk him into coming to the hospital."

"I assume he wasn't exactly forthcoming with his history."

"He kept telling me he was fine. That the fall was no big deal. And then I saw these films."

"He can't afford to get hit in the head again."

"But what are the odds of it *not* happening? He throws himself off cliffs for a living. Can you believe that?"

"Of course I can believe it," Louise said, taking off her glasses again. "Now, if he'd turned up as an insurance agent or an accountant, *that* would have surprised me."

"Right. Kirk wearing a suit and sitting behind a desk, pushing paper. That'll be the day."

Louise flipped off the light and faced Amanda. "With that kind of history, he was lucky to walk away this time."

"I know. He needs time to heal. And I have a feeling he's going to give me a hard time about that."

"I talked to the producer on the film before the crew came down here," Louise said. "He's a fanatic about safety on the set. Use that if you need to in order to bench him."

Amanda nodded.

"So…how did it feel to see Kirk again?" Louise asked.

She frowned. "Frustrating."

"And?"

"If you're thinking there could still be something between us, you're wrong."

Louise gave her a noncommittal shrug, but as always, Amanda could tell she was thinking more than she was saying.

Amanda's mother had been Louise's secretary for more than twenty years before she'd died from breast cancer when Amanda was twelve. Never married, Louise lived for her job, but she had been the one who had filled in the blanks in Amanda's life. Over the years, Louise had been like a mother to her. She knew almost everything about Amanda there was to know, including more of the details about her relationship with Kirk than her father ever had.

"I need to go talk to him," Amanda said.

"Are you okay with this? It's tough treating someone you're close to."

"I'm not close to Kirk," she said, sliding the X rays back into the envelope.

"So he's just one more patient?"

"Yes. He's just one more patient."

Liar.

She remembered those seconds of fear she'd felt when he'd tumbled off that air bag, and she knew just how much she was deluding herself.

Forget all that. You're his doctor now. Act like it.

Yes, she'd been in love with Kirk. Or, rather, she thought she had been. But with the rationality of adulthood to put everything into perspective, she knew it had been nothing more than teenage romanticism coupled with hormones gone wild, and she'd do well to remember that now.

Amanda left the room and strode toward the ER. There she found a flurry of activity—the click and clatter of orderlies wheeling patients, phones ringing, people talking. Her heart was beating faster than usual, which irritated her to no end. Sparring with him as a teenager had been one of the more entertaining things she had ever done, but it wasn't something she looked forward to now.

She stopped for a moment when she reached the curtained-off area where Kirk lay, then pushed back the curtain.

He was gone.

CB's ROADHOUSE WAS ONE of those tacky little dives on the outskirts of town that everyone except the hardest of drinkers would pass right by. A rusty jukebox played everything from Toby Keith to Willie Nelson, music to move to if a person wanted to venture onto the tiny dance floor. Enough neon beer signs hung on the walls to light an airport runway.

The crowd was sparse tonight. Kirk didn't know if that was because it was a weeknight, or because the majority of the people in Prescott were good southern Baptists who wouldn't be caught dead in a place like this.

The bartender set a beer down in front of him, then rested her forearms on the bar, giving him an inviting smile.

"So you're one of those movie guys? That's *so* exciting. I love action/adventure movies. That's what you're making, right?"

"That's right."

"So who's in it? Anybody I've heard of?"

"Hard to say, since I don't know who you've heard of."

The woman laughed, then looked at him suggestively. "Hey, I get off in an hour. If you want to hang around till then, maybe we can hook up."

She was pretty. Natural blond. Unnatural breasts. She wore low-slung jeans and a baby blue shirt that showcased every curve. The way she smiled at him said she'd probably get horizontal fast, and the way she moved her hips when she walked told him it would be a satisfying experience for all concerned.

But he just wasn't interested.

He tried to tell himself it was because his head was still pounding from the accident, but his apathy had nothing to do with his headache and everything to do with another woman he couldn't get off his mind.

He remembered opening his eyes and staring up at Amanda, right into those beautiful brown eyes that were so dark her pupils got lost. Her skin still looked so soft and unblemished it was as if she hadn't aged a day. Even the determined set of her jaw as she checked him over reminded him of the Amanda he'd known back then. She'd always refused to let anyone get in the way of something she intended to accomplish.

"Tonight's not a good night," he told the blonde.

"Oh, baby. You just leave it to me. I can turn your bad night into a good one in no time."

"Maybe another time."

Disappointment flashed across her face. Then she gave him another smile. "Well, there's always tomorrow night. You be sure to come back around, you hear?"

As she sashayed off, he thought about how Amanda was going to hit the ceiling when she found out he'd left the hospital, and tomorrow she'd give him hell for it. Doctors. They were all about negativity, about all the terrible things that might happen rather than the not-so-terrible things that were likely to.

He sighed. Oh, hell. Maybe he should have just stuck it out, gotten the test results and let her discharge him. Then maybe he could have invited her along tonight, and they'd be sitting together right now instead of him being alone with nobody but a chatty bartender for company. Why hadn't he just stayed at the hospital?

Because you were afraid of what you were going to hear.

He grabbed his beer bottle and drained it, then ordered another. But no amount of alcohol in the world was going to hide the truth: if he injured himself badly enough, he'd be forced to quit the job that made him feel alive in a way nothing else did.

"Kirk?"

He turned at the sound of the woman's voice and felt a start of surprise. Then he wondered why he was surprised at all. Knowing Amanda the way he did, he should have seen this coming.

She slid onto the bar stool next to him, skewering him with a disapproving stare.

"We need to talk."

CHAPTER TWO

"APPARENTLY THERE WAS SOME confusion at the hospital," Amanda said. "You're supposed to stay until your doctor says it's okay to leave. But here you are. Can you tell me why?"

"How did you know I was here?"

"You asked one of the nurses where you went in this town these days if you wanted to have a good time."

"And the best answer to that question is still CB's. Guess nothing ever changes, does it?"

"How's the headache?"

"All gone." He lifted his beer bottle. "Self-medication does the trick every time."

"It's not a good idea to drink after a concussion. Alcohol will mask changes in your neurological status."

"Sorry. I heard there was a bar stool here with my name on it. Can't ignore that."

"Don't you want to know the results of your CAT scan?"

"I have a feeling I'm going to get them whether I want them or not."

"Actually, it's good news. I didn't see any new damage."

"Then why are we having this discussion? If nothing's wrong—"

"I didn't say nothing was wrong. I said you don't appear to have any *new* damage."

He stared at her a moment, his face impassive, then turned away and took another sip of his beer.

"Kirk? How many times have you gotten hit on the head?"

He set the bottle back down on the bar and signaled the bartender to bring him another one.

"Never mind," Amanda said. "You don't have to tell me. I can see it on your films. You have extensive scarring from at least one previous intracranial bleed. I'm surprised you don't have residual neurological damage."

"Big words, Doctor. You're taxing my vocabulary."

"I don't have to dumb this down for you. You know exactly what I'm talking about."

He said nothing.

"Even with a clear CAT right now, your short loss of consciousness ups your concussion to a grade three. That means you need to take it easy for at least a week."

"That's not going to be possible."

"If you hit your head again, you risk second-impact syndrome."

"Everything I do is risky."

"It could be fatal."

"Live for today, I always say."

"No. Take care of yourself today, or you might not have a tomorrow."

He shrugged and took another sip of beer. His nonchalance was driving her absolutely crazy. "You haven't changed a bit, have you?"

"Why? Because I want to do my job?"

"No, because you'll do your job even if it's dangerous."

He laughed a little. "If I sat out every time I banged my head, I'd never work again."

"Don't you understand? If you keep getting hit, sooner or later the damage will be permanent. Is that what you want?"

"Kirk?"

Amanda turned to see a man slide onto a bar stool beside Kirk, and she realized it was Andy, the man who'd called the ambulance earlier. He was a big, brawny man with a furrowed forehead and a disappearing hairline that placed him somewhere in his early fifties, and an expanding waistline that said this wasn't the first bar stool he'd ever sat on.

"Hey," he said. "What happened? I went down to get something to drink at the hospital, and when I came back, they told me you'd already left. One of the nurses said you were coming here."

Kirk turned to Amanda. "Chatty little thing, isn't she?"

"So what's the diagnosis?"

"I'm fine," he said, then shot a glance at Amanda, daring her to disagree. But if he thought she was letting this go, he was sadly mistaken.

"I figured as much," Andy said. "It takes a lot to hurt that hard head of yours." He offered his hand to Amanda. "I don't think we were properly introduced before when Kirk was lying down on the job. I'm Andy Durrell."

"I remember," she said, shaking his hand. "You're the stunt coordinator."

"That's me," he said. "The man behind the magic."

Kirk grimaced. "The man behind the magic? You're kidding, right?"

"Hey! Can't you see I'm trying to impress a lady

here?" Then he smiled again at Amanda. "He's used to that handsome face of his doing all the work for him. Me, I've got to rely on what's up here." He tapped his temple.

"Rocks?" Kirk said.

"Brains, pretty boy." He turned back to Amanda. "See, any idiot can throw himself off a cliff. That's the easy part. The real guts of stunt work is in the planning, the preparation, the execution. The vision, if you will."

Kirk turned to Amanda. "Just so you know, Andy's harmless. He's got a wife at home he's crazy about and a baby due in the next few weeks. And yeah, he's way too old to be a daddy, but love makes a man do strange things."

Andy gave a sigh of mock frustration. "Kirk blows my cover every time."

"So you're Kirk's boss?" Amanda asked

"On this shoot, you bet I am. I say jump, he says how high. Or how far down, to be more exact."

"Good. Then you're just the man I want to talk to about Kirk's injuries."

Andy's smile evaporated. "Huh?"

"He has a grade-three concussion. That means he's at high risk for permanent damage, maybe even death, if he hits his head again before it heals."

Andy turned to Kirk. "Is that right?"

"He needs at least a week off," Amanda said. "And he needs to be aware of any mental status changes. Of course, depending on how much alcohol he's had—" she cast a sidelong glance at his beer bottle "—that may be hard to tell."

Kirk turned to Andy. "Do you know anybody in this business who hasn't gotten knocked in the head a time or two? Comes with the territory."

"But not all of them have a history of an intracranial bleed," Amanda said.

Kirk let out a breath of irritation. "Amanda—"

"After that blow to the head today, he's lucky to still be walking and talking. One more head injury too soon could make him an invalid, or worse."

"She's overreacting," Kirk muttered.

"From what I'm told," she went on, "there's only one thing the producer on this film hates worse than a blown budget, and that's his people pushing the envelope on safety. All those lawsuits waiting to happen put him in a really bad mood."

Andy looked at Kirk. "Hoo, boy. She's got you there."

"So here's the bottom line. If I see Kirk doing anything that risks a head injury for at least another week, I'll be on the phone to the producer so fast neither of you will know what hit you. Now, do I make myself clear?"

Andy looked a little shell-shocked. "Yeah, honey. I hear you."

"Good. I'll see you on the set in the morning." She slid off the bar stool and headed for the front door, looking back over her shoulder at Andy. "And don't call me honey."

She heard Kirk's footsteps behind her. "Amanda, wait."

She continued to walk. He caught up with her at the door and grabbed her arm.

"It's my life," he said, his voice low and angry, "and you don't have any right to get in the middle of it."

She pulled her arm from his grasp. "That's true. I don't. Unless you happen to injure yourself on the job. And then I'm *all over* your life."

"Don't do this, Amanda."

"Don't do what? Save you from yourself? God knows somebody has to."

With that, she spun around, opened the door and left the bar.

KIRK WENT BACK TO THE BAR, slid onto his bar stool and picked up his beer. He started to take a sip, then set it back down again. Damn it—he couldn't even have a beer now without feeling guilty.

"Wow," Andy said. "She's kinda touchy, isn't she?"

"Try calling her 'honey' again. You'll find out just how touchy."

"So how did you say you know her?"

"We went to high school together. Right here in Prescott, if you can believe that."

"No kidding? So were you two…close?"

"Yeah. We were close."

"So did you dump her? Is that why she's pissed at you?"

"No, Andy. I didn't dump her."

"She says you have a concussion. That's not a good thing. And what's this about an intracranial bleed?"

God, this was turning into a mess. Kirk had never intended for anyone to know about that.

"I was doing an overseas job a year ago," he said. "I got knocked in the head pretty badly. But I haven't had any trouble since. She's overreacting."

"But she released you from the hospital."

Kirk was silent.

"She didn't release you?"

"You know how doctors are. They love to keep you

hanging around so they can run up the bill. I felt fine. There was no reason to stay."

"I don't like the sound of this."

"Amanda's like a bulldog with a bone. If she says she'll contact Dixon, she's not bluffing. We need to figure out a way to keep her from doing that."

Andy shook his head. "Sorry, buddy. You heard the doctor's orders. I don't need the producer to call you off. I'm doing it myself."

"What?"

"Have you seen what happens to guys who get hit too much? Boxers? Quarterbacks? It's not pretty. Some of them are lucky to be able to feed themselves."

"I told you I'm fine."

"Not according to the doctor. And she's right about Dixon. He might be a tightwad about the budget, but he's also a stickler for safety."

"So what are you going to do for the next week? It's hard to get stunts on film when you don't have a stunt man."

"Murphy and Giles are here."

"Yeah, they're fine for the fight scenes and the motorcycle stunts, but what about the high falls?"

"I'll find somebody."

"On this short notice?"

Andy blew out a breath. "Look. You're the best man for the job. There's no doubt about that. But I don't want you ending up a vegetable. If the doctor says she wants to pull you for a week, then you're gonna stay on the bench. You'll still be earning a paycheck, though. I need your help blocking the action sequences."

Kirk pulled out his wallet and threw a few bills down on the bar. "It's not about the money, and you know it."

"Kirk—"

"I'll see you tomorrow."

He left the bar, got into his car and stuck the key in the ignition.

And wondered what the hell to do next.

A couple of hours later, he was walking out of a movie theater, barely able to remember the movie he'd spent two hours watching. It was some character-driven flick without a stunt in sight. Good thing. If he'd had to look at somebody else doing what he wasn't going to be doing for the next week, he'd have gone crazy.

Reaching his car, he sat behind the wheel, thinking about just heading back to the bar and taking that bartender up on her offer. At least it would beat sitting alone in his room at the inn, where the only thing he'd be thinking about was how cutthroat his business could be, and how it wouldn't take much for somebody else to start getting the jobs that had always been his.

Then he thought about one night a few months ago, when he'd woken up in the middle of the night and looked down at the woman lying next to him. He didn't know her name. He didn't know the name of the motel where he was staying. And only by looking at the phone book on the nightstand did he know what city he was in.

No. He didn't want to spend time with some nameless, faceless woman he wouldn't even remember the next day.

He wanted to see Amanda.

He dropped his head back against the headrest and let out a sigh. No. Not smart. She was feeling pretty unkindly toward him right now. Why would he want to stir things up all over again?

Two-twenty-four Laurelwood Drive.

The address popped into his mind, the one he'd managed to track down before he left California. It hadn't taken much to find out Amanda was living in Prescott again and working at the clinic. With a few clicks of a mouse, he'd been able to find her home address.

If he were a reasonable, rational man, he would simply go back to the inn and try to stop thinking about her. Unfortunately, he'd never been particularly reasonable or rational.

He started the car, put it in gear and headed for Laurelwood Drive.

CHAPTER THREE

AMANDA HUMMED ALONG WITH A song on the radio as she surveyed the hideous green walls of her living room. Finally it struck her where she'd seen this color before—in a hospital psychiatric ward built in the 1950s. If the people there hadn't already been insane, that color would have driven them to it.

She had already taken down the blinds, masked the woodwork and poured paint into the pan. Now she rolled on the first swipe of taupe, thrilled with the transformation from puke green to a nice, serene color. For the past fifteen years, she'd lived in college dorms and cookie-cutter apartments with colors and fixtures that were somebody else's idea of attractive. Now that she'd finally returned home, it was time to settle into a place that was hers.

She rolled the paint onto the wall, masking the green paint swipe by swipe, trying to put the day she'd had behind her. Actually, the day had been relatively normal, right up to the moment Kirk had shown up, acting so stubborn and bullheaded.

No. He can only make you crazy if you let him.

She jacked the radio up, then dipped the roller again and smacked it to the wall, swaying her hips back and forth to the music as she painted. *Focus,* she told herself. *Listen to the music, roll on the paint, dance your ass off, and pretty soon you'll forget all about him.*

She rocked and rolled her way through most of one wall, letting the music and thoughts of a livable house drown out everything else. *Great music. Pretty walls. Kirk who?*

Then she heard the song.

She froze, the roller still against the wall, squeezing her eyes closed in silent protest. Good Lord. Did they have to play that song right *now?*

She reached over to flip the station. When her fingers touched the button, though, she froze, listened to a few more bars, then slowly backed away.

"Never Tear Us Apart."

Music was such an insidious thing, triggering memories she would have sworn she'd long forgotten. Finally she gave up trying to ignore them. She tossed the roller to the pan and sank to the floor beside it. Leaning against a section of unpainted wall, she pulled her knees up and rested her elbows on them, closing her eyes with a heavy sigh. For the next few minutes, she let herself drown in the music, remembering what she knew in her heart was best to forget.

Kirk had been a dark, mysterious boy who could lurk in shadows on a sun-filled day, the kind girls stared at on the sly and talked about in hushed whispers. When he'd scoffed at Amanda's good-girl reputation and told her he'd be happy to help her lose it, she'd asked him why he thought she'd want to get laid by a future prison inmate. When he'd asked her how it felt to walk around with her panties in a knot, she'd told him it appeared that he had an unnatural attraction to women's underwear.

But while the surface confrontation was there for all to see, something else had churned beneath it. She'd accused him of being a moron because his grades sucked, even though she could feel intelligence radiate from him like heat off a summer sidewalk. He'd told her prissy honor students were about as sexy as ninety-year-old nuns, then had looked at her with a gaze so hot it made her sweat. But it was only because of a chance meeting on a deserted stretch of state highway their senior year that the sparks between them had finally caught fire. Her car had broken down, leaving her stranded at sunset miles from home.

Then Kirk had driven by.

When he'd seen her, he'd hit the brakes, then backed up his car until it sat in front of hers on the shoulder. He'd stepped out slowly, leaned against his car and surveyed the situation.

Oh, God, she thought. *Why him? Anybody but him.*

"Well, now," he said with a smirk of amusement. "What's a nice girl like you doing in a place like this?"

She walked toward him, gravel crunching beneath her shoes. "My car's broken down. I'm pretty sure it's the transmission."

"Transmission, huh? Yeah, that can be a real problem."

Jerk. "So are you going to offer me a ride, or what?"

"No, I don't think I am."

"Why not?"

"Because if your father sees you getting out of my car, chances are I'll end up looking down the barrel of a shotgun."

"Not a problem. My father doesn't even own a shotgun."

"I was speaking metaphorically."

"Metaphorically?" She raised her eyebrows. "Hmm. Looks as if somebody's been listening in English class after all. What's next? Personification?"

"Yeah. I'm planning on becoming a poet. I hear that pays really well."

"Great. Personification it is. We can talk about it all the way home."

But he just stood there staring at her, his dark eyes taunting her, telling her just how much he enjoyed having the upper hand.

"Look, I'd really rather not walk home in the dark," she said. "No telling what's roaming around out there."

"Whatever it is, I bet you could beat the hell out of it."

"Hey, if you're not going to give me a ride, tell me now. I need to start walking if I'm going to make it home sometime before midnight."

The next few moments dragged on endlessly, and she was actually afraid that he intended to leave her out there. Finally he shoved away from the car.

"Get in."

She circled around and got into the passenger seat. He jammed the car into gear and hit the gas.

"I live on the west side of town near—"

"I know where you live."

They drove in silence. She could feel the tension in the car even though neither of them said a word. She couldn't decide which was worse—fighting with him or listening to the silence.

She was relieved when he finally pulled up to the

curb in front of her house. As she reached for the door handle, he finally spoke.

"Why are you so uptight all the time?"

She slumped with a sigh of irritation, then glared at him over her shoulder. "Why do you ask? One last insult for the road?"

"You're avoiding the question."

"I'm *not* uptight."

"Sweetheart, you're so uptight you squeak when you walk. Do you ever have any fun?"

"Of course I do."

"How could you? You spend all your time studying."

"So what are you going to do with your life? Huh? Oh, wait. I forgot. You're going to be a poet."

"You're so damned self-righteous. *God,* that pisses me off."

"No, what pisses you off is that I refuse to take any crap from you." She moved around to face him directly. "What I want to know is why you have to be so confrontational about everything. Basically, you're just not very nice."

"Nice?" He laughed a little. "Is that what you're looking for? A guy who's *nice?*"

"I'm not looking for *any* guy."

"Sure you are. All women are. It's human nature."

"Human nature? Now you're into philosophy?"

"I'm into a lot of things. I'm not as dumb as you think."

"Oh, yeah? You're always screwing off in class, or skipping class altogether. Sounds pretty dumb to me."

Slowly his gaze became sharp and penetrating, and she wondered whether she'd pushed one too many of his buttons.

"Maybe," he said, "I have other things on my mind."

A strange lilt had entered his voice, different from his usual tone. And why did he keep looking at her like that? Quietly, intently, as if he could see right inside her?

"Then you need to get those other things off your mind," she told him.

He leaned toward her, running his hand slowly and deliberately along the top of the passenger seat behind her. "There's not much chance of that."

Oh, God.

She should have been telling him to stay away, but instead she sat there motionless, strangely aware of every breath he took. He seemed to be searching her face. For what, she didn't know, until his gaze wandered to her mouth and locked on to it.

"See," he said, easing closer, "in spite of everything, I just can't help thinking about…"

"What?"

"What it would be like to kiss you."

Amanda's pulse pounded inside her head. But she held her gaze steady, even as thoughts of all things sexual clouded her mind.

"So you want to know what it would be like to kiss me?"

"Oh, yeah."

She waited one beat. Two. Then she came closer, her lips hovering over his.

"It would be *spectacular.*"

She put her palm to his chest and pushed him away. As she turned to open the passenger door, though, he grabbed her by the wrist. She started to yank her arm away.

"Amanda."

Something about the way he said her name—quietly, almost tenderly—transfixed her, and she couldn't move. His grasp faded to a feather-light touch she could easily have shaken off.

She didn't.

He turned her around slowly until she was facing him again, and for some unfathomable reason she let him do it. His cockiness had disappeared, replaced by an expression of pure desire.

"Spectacular, huh?" he whispered.

She swallowed hard. "That's right."

"You let me be the judge of that."

With that, he pulled her to him and dropped his lips against hers, kissing her in a way that was exciting and forbidden and made her hot all over. But it wasn't just that he knew how to kiss. It was the fiery attraction behind the kiss that they'd tried to ignore but now neither one of them could deny.

Then suddenly she came to her senses, jerking herself away, breathing hard. "We can't do this."

"We can't *not* do this."

"You and me? Are you kidding?"

He leaned away, some of that cockiness edging its way back in. Slowly he released her. "Try to stay away. Just try it."

She opened the car door and got out, feeling hot and shaky and trying like hell not to show it. She swore she could feel his gaze boring into her all the way to her front door. And in the ensuing days, it turned out that Kirk had been right.

Staying away from him had been impossible.

Even now, years later, just thinking about what had

happened between them in the months that followed
that night sent her heart into overdrive. Even when her
father had forbidden her to see him, for the first time in
her life she'd defied her rigid upbringing and had seen
Kirk on the sly as often as she could. He had a way of
making only one thing seem important, and that was
being with him.

Then she thought about how it had ended. How the
fantasy she'd lived with Kirk had been shattered on a
hot May night on that same dark, deserted road outside
Prescott. She couldn't believe how foolish she'd been
to think she could have anything lasting with an aimless,
thrill-seeking boy who would never be anything else.

The music trailed off and she opened her eyes again,
secure in the knowledge that Kirk's denial of his medical
condition was a sign—a sign that her decision all those
years ago never to see him again had been the right one.

Then she heard a knock at her door.

CHAPTER FOUR

AMANDA ROSE FROM THE FLOOR, flicked off the radio and went to the door. Looking out the peephole, she was startled to see Kirk standing on her front porch.

She closed her eyes for a moment, then swiped a strand of hair out of her face with the back of her hand and opened the door.

He gave her a smile. "Hey, Amanda. Nice evening, isn't it?"

"Kirk? What are you doing here?"

He shrugged. "I was in the neighborhood."

"Oh, really? And how did you know where I lived?"

"Lucky guess?"

Getting a straight answer out of him when he wanted to be obtuse had always been a tall task, and right now she had no desire to beat her head against that wall.

"I'm in the middle of painting right now."

He nodded down at her clothes. "The walls, or you?"

Suddenly she realized just how awful she looked in her paint-spattered shorts and oversize T-shirt. Why had she even opened the door?

A better question, though, was why it mattered to her what Kirk thought about her. And she didn't have an answer for that.

"Look, Kirk. If you've come to try to make your case again—"

"No. I'll sit out for a week, just like you said."

Amanda looked at him skeptically. "No stunts?"

"No stunts."

"I'm not sure I believe that."

"I'm not sure I blame you."

"You could have told me tomorrow on the set."

"But now you can sleep easily, knowing I'm taking your advice."

"I hadn't planned on losing any sleep."

"Uh-huh." He nodded thoughtfully. "So...do doctors generally go to bars to chase down difficult patients who don't know what's good for them?"

Suddenly Amanda felt like a fool. Why had she done that? If he didn't care about his medical condition, why should she?

Another good question she couldn't answer.

"No, that's not standard procedure. But when a patient doesn't want to go to the hospital when he clearly should, and then he leaves against medical advice—"

"Amanda? Just for a little while, can we forget the doctor-patient thing? What's wrong with old friends just getting together to catch up?"

"That's hardly all we were to each other."

"Well, then," he said, stepping inside and pushing the door shut behind him, "all the more reason for us to catch up."

The sound of the door closing set her nerves on edge. "I told you I'm right in the middle of something. I really need to get back to work."

"Good idea. I love watching you paint."

"What?"

"I've never seen anyone dance and paint at the same time. You put on quite a show."

She whipped around to look at her curtainless windows. Good Lord. Everyone on the block could see right into her living room.

She walked to the window and looked out. Across the street, Mrs. Taggert's drapes suddenly fell shut.

"Damn," she muttered. "I swear Mrs. Taggert spends her whole day peeking out her drapes, trying to get dirt on her neighbors."

"Betty Taggert? The city councilwoman?"

"She hasn't been on the council for a long time. She has to be eighty by now."

"I don't suppose she's mellowed in her old age?"

"Nope. If anything, she's even more nasty. Wasn't she the one who said that you and the Rebels were the root of all evil?" Amanda held up her palm. "Never mind. Most of the time she was right about that." She glanced out the window again and sighed. "Now she's taken to peeping in my windows. I give her twenty-four hours before she's spread this all over town."

"What? That you're still hanging out with one of the town bad boys?"

"Like I said, you've forgotten what it's like to live here."

"No, believe me, that's not something you easily forget."

"I have to do something about these windows."

She disappeared into the kitchen and came back with some newspapers and masking tape, dragging a four-foot stepladder behind her. She set it up in front of the window and handed Kirk the tape. Then she took two steps up the ladder, where she lay a sheet of newspaper over the window. She felt his gaze trained intently on her the whole time. He'd always had the ability to focus every ounce of his concentration on whatever caught his attention. It had just been a long time since the object of his attention had been her.

She held out her hand. "Tape."

He ripped off a piece and gave it to her.

"You didn't tell me where you're living," she said. "Is California home for you?"

"That's where I have an apartment and pick up my mail once in a while. I spend a lot of time on location. How about you? How long have you been back in Prescott?"

"About six months." She stuck that piece of tape down and he handed her another one.

"Where were you living before?"

"Dallas. Then Louise offered me a staff position at the clinic, and I took it."

"Louise Metzger. I remember her."

"Yes," she said, securing the opposite side of the newspaper. "You know we've always been close."

He stared at her with confusion. "Still, I guess I'm surprised to see you back here. You couldn't wait to leave."

"I couldn't," she said, taping the lower corner of the newspaper. "But you know what? I found out that the big city isn't all it's cracked up to be. The more I thought about it, the more I missed Prescott. Louise offered me a staff position, and when she retires, she wants me to take over the clinic. With my father gone now, she's really the only family I have left."

"Your father died?"

"About three years ago." She glanced at Kirk. "How about your father? Where is he now?"

"Gone from here. Where, I don't know, and I don't care."

Amanda sighed. "That's a shame."

"Not really. You know what he was like."

Amanda nodded. "If you'll remember, my father was a little difficult, too. But in other ways."

"A little overprotective?"

"Oh, yeah. After my mother died, he overcompensated. He made sure I hung out with the right kids. That I toed the line academically. Got on the fast track for college. I was born being a little driven already, but he still made me crazy sometimes." She sighed. "But I guess he just wanted the best for me."

"And I wasn't it."

Amanda smiled. "No. You weren't." She flattened another sheet of newspaper against the window beside the first one and took pieces of tape as he handed them to her. "Didn't you also say you'd never step foot back in this town again?"

"I go where the work is."

"So did you go to California right after you left here?"

"Graduation night."

"But you had no car."

"I bought a bus ticket. When I got to L.A., I found a junker for sale. That's how I got around."

"Did you know you wanted to go into stunt work?"

"Not at first. I just worked dead-end jobs for a while, and then I started hanging around a gym where there were a lot of guys who did stunt work. I liked the sound of it, so I scraped for the money to go to a stunt school. I made some connections and started getting jobs."

"A stunt performer. Why does that not surprise me?"

"I'm a better one than you saw today. I don't like screwing up."

"So why did you?"

"What?"

She turned around and looked down at him. "Screw up."

He looked puzzled for a moment, as if he wasn't sure how to respond. "It was the wind," he said finally. "It happens."

"Hmm. There was a little breeze, but…" Then it struck her. She'd seen him teeter just a little before he'd jumped. "Kirk? Were you feeling dizzy up there?"

"Of course not."

"Maybe I just assumed you had no residual neurological damage. But if you do—"

"Amanda? Can we talk about something else? We've just about beat my medical condition to death. Surely we can find a more entertaining topic than that."

She started to press the issue, then decided there would be plenty of time in the coming week to find out exactly what had happened to him in the past that might affect his future.

"Sure, Kirk. Let's talk about something else. Uh… let's see. How about those Cowboys?"

"Sorry," he said. "I've become a Raiders fan."

"Doesn't matter. I don't know much about football, so it would have been a short conversation, anyway."

"But you always liked going to the games in high school."

"I liked hanging out with my friends. I guess I still do. Lorna Jacobs still lives here, and she and I usually go to the high school games together. She has a nephew who plays."

Amanda stepped down off the ladder to tape more newspaper beneath the first two sheets so the window would be totally obscured. She grabbed a piece off the floor, and when she rose again, Kirk's smiling expression had melted into a more thoughtful one.

She froze. "What?"

Slowly his gaze grew more focused and intimate, until he was looking at her not as the boy he'd been then, but the man he was now. A man who had more on his mind than a little sports talk.

"God, I've missed you."

She closed her eyes. "Kirk—"

"Fifteen years," he murmured. "And then all at once, there you were today, looking as beautiful as you did back then."

No. She didn't want to hear that kind of thing from him. She didn't want him unearthing old feelings that needed to stay buried.

"Tell me," he said, his voice falling into a lower register. "Have you thought about me since high school? Have you ever wondered what it would be like to be together again?"

Yes. More times than you can count.

"No," she said. "Not really."

"You never could lie worth a damn."

"Don't flatter yourself. What happened back then was all wrong, and we both know it. So I haven't bothered thinking about it since."

He nodded thoughtfully. "While I was sitting in your driveway, I heard something on the radio."

She froze. Surely he hadn't...

"A song we listened to in high school all the time. And when it came on tonight, you stopped dancing."

Her face heated up again. She hated having a fair complexion. It turned her cheeks into a perfect canvas for any blood that happened to rush to them whether she wanted it to or not.

"Tell the truth, Amanda. That song made you remember a lot of things." He paused. "Like Trojan Point."

God, yes.

"I remember one night when we were sitting in my car," Kirk said. "I'd stuck in a tape with that song on it. You had your hair up, just like you do now."

"I always wear it up."

"Which I didn't like in the least," he murmured. "I wanted to see it loose around your face. So I leaned across the console and slipped the band right out of your hair."

"You always were pretty presumptuous," she said.

"That's right. I told you never to put it up again." His gaze shifted to her ponytail. "Apparently you weren't listening."

He reached for the band that held her hair. She dropped the newspaper and put up her hands to stop him, but she was too late. The band was out, and her hair fell from its ponytail to cascade around her shoulders.

She pulled the band away from him. "Now, why did you do that?"

"I believe I already told you that."

"Whenever I'm working—"

"Leave it down."

She sighed, tossing the band to the top of the ladder. "You just love making all kinds of demands, don't you?"

He ran the backs of his fingers along a strand of her hair, easing it back over her shoulder. "When it comes to you incarcerating this gorgeous hair, you bet I do."

His voice was exactly as she remembered it—enticing, provocative and very, very sexy—a voice that could make a woman lose any conviction she might be trying to hold on to.

"It wasn't as if you had the last word on that," she said.

"Oh, yeah?"

"If you'll remember, I told you my hair was my own business, and that I'd put it up whenever I damn well pleased."

His lips eased into a faint smile. "You didn't much like being told what to do."

"At least one thing we had in common."

"But you did it, anyway. Not once after that did I see you with your hair up."

Because she'd known how much he liked it when she wore it down. She remembered how he used to stroke his hands through it. Brush it away from her face with his fingertips.

Crush it in his fist as he kissed her.

"Do you remember what happened next?" he murmured.

Of course she did. How could she not? It had been a pattern with them—thrust and parry, back and forth, push and pull.

Kiss and make up.

She held her gaze steady, even as her heart was beating madly. "Yes. I remember. But that's not going to happen now."

He slid his hand along her cheek and lowered his lips toward hers. "I'm sorry, Amanda. But I'm afraid it is."

Before she could react, his mouth met hers, and instantly she felt overwhelmed with sensation—his scent, his touch, his taste—and as he tilted her head and kissed her deeper, the memory of all of those things came flooding back.

"Never Tear Us Apart."

The song she'd heard earlier filled her mind, and that was exactly what it felt like, as if nothing could tear them apart, as if she was going to fall limp in his arms, as if…

Then she came to her senses. She pulled away suddenly, pressing her palm to his chest. "What do you think you're doing?"

"I thought that was pretty obvious."

She shimmied out of his arms. "Is this why you're here? To pick up where we left off? Because if it is, you can get it out of your head right now."

He blew out a breath of frustration. "Come on, Amanda. What's wrong with taking a little trip down memory lane?"

"What *isn't* wrong with it?"

"We're adults now, aren't we?"

"That has nothing to do with it."

"Do you have a boyfriend you're not telling me about?"

"No, I don't have a boyfriend."

"Then what are you so afraid of?"

After what had happened today, it was pretty clear he hadn't changed one bit, and she refused to be dragged right back into the most ill-advised relationship she'd ever had in her life.

"I'm not afraid of anything," she said. "It was wrong then, and it's wrong now." She put her hand on the door-knob. "I think you'd better go."

She opened the door. He stared at her for a long time, as if he could see right inside her, as if he knew what she was thinking, and she sure didn't want that.

"You wanted me to kiss you," he told her. "You wanted it as much as I did. If you think I couldn't feel that, think again."

She met his gaze squarely, resisting the urge to blink or look away. Otherwise he might know just how right he was.

"Don't expect what's between us to go away," he told her. "It was there fifteen years ago, and it's still there now. And I have no intention of ignoring it." He opened the door. "I'll see you tomorrow."

He left the house, and Amanda closed the door behind him. She turned around and leaned against it, her eyes closed, her fingertips against her lips.

No. She shouldn't be doing this. She shouldn't be having these kinds of feelings for a man she was so totally incompatible with. A man who took nothing seriously, even a medical condition that could eventually sideline him forever. A man who would be gone in a week without so much as a backward glance.

But that didn't stop her from wanting him.

Lately she'd been thinking about things she'd never really considered before, like having a husband and a family along with her career. She'd had several relationships with men, some pretty serious, but eventually they'd all fallen by the wayside. And now, the older she got, the more afraid she was that the man she married would be someone she was settling for rather than a man who set her heart on fire. And when it came to blazing hearts, right now only one man came to mind.

No.

Having a relationship with Kirk had been the single most ill-advised thing she'd ever done in her life, and going there again would only cause her the kind of grief she wanted nothing to do with. But since he was still the kind of man who could make her do inadvisable things, the best thing she could do from now until he left town was to stay as far away from him as possible.

CHAPTER FIVE

AT EIGHT O'CLOCK the next morning, Amanda walked into Prescott Medical Clinic, went straight to Louise's office and sat down in one of her chairs. Louise looked up from the file spread across her desk, her brows pulled together with confusion.

"Aren't you supposed to be on your way to the movie set?"

"That's what I want to talk to you about. I want you to send somebody else."

Louise sat back in her chair. "Oh, you do?"

"Yes. I've already talked to Donald, and he said he'd be happy to go. He's got a light patient load right now that I can absorb. Plus, he's a movie freak. For this opportunity, he'll kiss your feet."

"Hmm. Never much liked men kissing my feet. There's something very unsanitary about it."

Amanda closed her eyes. "Think figuratively, Louise."

Louise tapped her pen on the desktop. "Tell me the real reason you don't want to go back."

"If you'll remember, I didn't want to go in the first place."

"What happened between you and Kirk?"

"Nothing."

"Try again."

Louise continued to stare at her with those lie-detector eyes, and Amanda decided that having a friend who knew her so well was both a blessing and a curse.

Finally she let out a sigh. "He came to my house last night."

"And?"

"And Betty Taggert was peeking out her blinds. I know she saw Kirk at my house, and now everybody in Prescott is going to know we were together."

"So what's wrong with catching up?"

"You know, that's what Kirk keeps saying. Just two old friends catching up. But then he—"

Amanda stopped short.

"What?"

"Nothing."

"No. It was something. Ah, there go your cheeks. Nothing like a good blush to tell the tale."

Amanda hated her skin and its autoblush feature. *Hated* it.

"Just how far did things go between you?" Louise asked.

"He kissed me. That's all."

"So now you feel uncomfortable around him and you want to bow out."

"Yes."

"Sorry. You're staying. The pay's good, and you need a vacation."

Amanda slumped with frustration. "You know, I really don't get that argument. Vacations are supposed to eliminate stress, not cause it."

"Uh-huh."

"Send me to the Bahamas. Now, *that's* a vacation."

"If I thought you'd actually go, I might. But being out of cell phone range of the hospital would make you crazy. But you *do* need to get away, even if it's only to a movie set for a week."

This was getting her nowhere.

"Can I give you some advice?" Louise said.

"What?"

"Instead of coming up with a thousand reasons why you shouldn't have anything to do with Kirk, maybe you should be coming up with a few reasons why you should."

With that, she dropped her gaze again to the file spread out on her desk, which was Louise-speak for *case closed.*

Amanda could continue to argue, but she knew Louise. Once she had her mind set one way, there was no changing it. What Amanda didn't understand was why Louise gave a damn whether or not she and Kirk had anything to do with each other.

With a heavy sigh, Amanda got up and left the clinic, wishing they were still filming in the wide-open spaces today rather than that old lumber warehouse on State Street. No matter how big it was, just being inside four walls with Kirk was going to feel too close for comfort.

At eight-thirty, Kirk pulled up in front of the warehouse, and when he spied Amanda's car, a smile came to his face. Kissing her last night had been every bit as good as he remembered, and now all he had to do was find a way to get her alone tonight, and he was sure they could pick up where they left off.

Becky stuck her head out the warehouse door and called to Kirk. "Andy's in the trailer. He needs to talk to you."

Kirk walked across the gravel parking lot and went into the trailer, where he found Andy on his cell phone. Listening to Andy's end of the conversation, Kirk was surprised to hear him making plane reservations. A few minutes later, he hung up and made a few notes in his planner.

"What's going on?" Kirk asked.

"Deidre went into early labor. I'm going back to L.A."

"Is she all right?"

"The doctor says everything's going to be okay. But I need to get back there as soon as I can." Andy took a deep, calming breath, then smiled. "I'm going to be a father. Me. At my age. Can you believe it?"

"I guess good things come to those who wait."

Andy's goofy smile got even bigger, and Kirk wondered just where along the way his friend had lost his mind. He'd be almost seventy by the time his kid graduated from high school. How was he going to feel about taking the daddy track then?

"Okay," Kirk said. "What about the shoot?"

"I know you hate dealing with Dan, but can you take over for me?"

"Sure. Whatever you need." He pointed at Andy. "But you owe me one."

"I'll add it to the list."

Andy grabbed his clipboard. "Murphy and Giles are ready to go on the ambush by the front door, but the sequence on the ladder still needs work." He paused. "And you'll also need to set up the fight sequence on the catwalk along with the fall so we can move on to the next location."

"I take it you found somebody to do those falls since I can't?"

"Uh…yeah."

"Who?"

Andy paused, and Kirk felt a twinge of foreboding.

"I called Colley," Andy said.

Kirk's eyes flew open wide. "Brandon Colley?"

"You know another Colley?"

"Are you out of your *mind?*"

"He's the right size to double for the character. And he wants the job."

"Of course he does. He has almost no experience."

"But a lot of natural talent. He's trained in high falls. And right now, he's the only guy I can get here on short notice."

"Assuming he decides to show up."

"He caught the red-eye last night. He's in the warehouse right now."

Kirk couldn't believe this. Brandon Colley? A kid with an overabundance of ego and zero discipline, who made it his life's mission to rub people the wrong way?

"You know if he gives Dan any crap, all hell's going to break loose," Kirk said.

"You know I'd use somebody else if I could," Andy said. "But my back's against the wall here. Tell me now if it's going to be a problem."

Kirk sighed. He didn't think much of Brandon Colley, but he'd walk over broken glass for Andy.

"Nope. I'll make sure everything runs smoothly."

And he meant it. No matter what he had to do, he was going to make sure Colley did his job, the stunts came off without a hitch, and the director was a happy man.

Andy made a few notes for Kirk, and then they left the trailer. After Andy drove away, Kirk took a deep

breath and went into the warehouse. He spied Amanda
pouring herself a cup of coffee from a pot that had been
set up along the far wall. She was dressed down in jeans,
sneakers and a sweatshirt, and just the sight of her made
a smile steal across his face. Unfortunately, at least one
other man there had noticed her, too.

Brandon Colley was heading in her direction.

AMANDA TOOK A SIP OF coffee and gazed around the interior of the warehouse. The cavernous structure was
downright spooky, crisscrossed with age-worn beams and
cluttered with rusty machinery and stacks of rotting lumber. Rays of morning light filtered through grimy glass
windows, highlighting dust particles swimming in the air.

Because of the relatively tight quarters, the director
had closed the set to onlookers, so the only people present
were the crew members. They scurried around, placing
props, moving cameras into position, and in general
doing whatever it was they did to get a scene on film.

"Well, hello there."

She turned around to find a man standing behind her.
He appeared to be in his early twenties, with sandy-brown
hair, stunning green eyes and a body that said he hit the
gym on a regular basis. He offered his hand to her.

"I don't believe we've met. I'm Brandon Colley."

She shook his hand. "Amanda Stevens. I'm the doctor on the set."

"Ah," he said. "You're the one who benched McKenzie." He shook his head sadly. "Those old guys. Can't
count on them not to fall apart on you."

Amanda had to smile at that. Old at thirty-three?
Clearly he had no idea she and Kirk were the same age.

"But don't worry," he continued. "As long as I'm here to fill in, you won't have to play doctor again." He gave her a provocative smile. "Unless you really want to."

In her younger days, Amanda would have beat a hasty retreat from a man like him. Now she was merely amused.

"So you're from Prescott?" he asked.

"Yes, I am."

"Then maybe you can tell where you go in this town for a good time. I gotta tell you—I'm not really seeing the possibility of much night life."

"Now, there's where you're wrong. The night life here is second to none. There's a lovely bowling alley, and tonight they're playing bingo at the VFW Hall."

He rolled his eyes. "Just my luck. I landed in Mayberry."

"Oh, and I almost forgot—Thursday is singles night at the First Baptist Church. The girls would go crazy if a new man showed up."

He gave her a dazzling smile, one she pictured him practicing every morning in his bathroom mirror. "Well, I can't say I'd mind the women, but church isn't exactly the atmosphere I'm looking for." He winked. "A little too much of the devil in me, you know?"

"Yeah, Colley. You're full of all kinds of things."

Colley swung around and came face-to-face with Kirk, who stared down at him with a face as rigid as stone. Amanda's heart leaped into a crazy rhythm. She couldn't help it. Not with the kiss he'd given her last night still hot on her mind.

"Hey, McKenzie!" Colley said. "Heard you took a nasty fall. That's too bad. But don't worry, old man. You'll be up and at it again in no time."

Kirk's face remained impassive. "Did Andy tell you what's going on?"

"Sure did. He's going to play daddy, and you're in charge. But don't worry, buddy. I'll make you look good."

"Go see Becky," Kirk said. "She'll take you to costuming. Then come back and we'll start rehearsing."

Colley turned to Amanda. "Gotta go. Duty calls." Then he leaned in and spoke confidentially. "But if I do happen to get hurt, you will be there to kiss it and make it all better, won't you?"

"Beat it, Colley," Kirk said.

He gave Amanda one last wink, then sauntered off.

"My goodness," Amanda said. "Is this warehouse big enough for both him and his ego?"

"Was he hitting on you?"

"Why, yes. I believe he was. I imagine he also hit on the woman sitting next to him on the plane, the flight attendant and the girl at the rental-car counter."

"Don't worry. I'll keep him in line."

"It's okay. He's just one of those guys who has to make sure every woman within the sound of his voice is lusting after him. It's insecurity, plain and simple."

"Colley? He's about as insecure as a rattlesnake."

"So how does a guy like him end up in a profession like this?"

"He played football in college but bombed as a pro athlete, so he went to stunt school. Basically, all he's doing is looking for something to impress women."

"So stunt work impresses women?"

"You're the exception to the rule. Most women don't get to see my X rays."

"So Andy had to leave?" Amanda said.

"His wife went into labor early, so I'm stunt coordinator for the next several days. Unfortunately, that means I'm going to be really busy."

"Busy is good."

"Not when I'd rather talk to you."

"Kirk—"

"Nothing's wrong with two old friends socializing."

"Unless one of them wants to pick up where things left off last night."

He gave her knowing smile. "I think both of them do. One of them just hasn't admitted it yet."

With that, Kirk turned and walked away, and as the day went on, Amanda realized that keeping him at arm's length for the next several days was going to be a far more difficult task than she'd realized. He looked her way every chance he got. Smiled in that way that said he could see right inside her. She'd always heard the phrase "he undressed her with his eyes," but only now did she know precisely what it felt like to be on the receiving end of that. She'd never felt more uncomfortable in her life, even as Kirk's attention generated all kinds of hot, sexy feelings she was having an awfully hard time ignoring.

Fortunately, at the end of the day she managed to get out of there without coming into contact with Kirk, but she knew that sooner or later he was bound to show up at her house again and insist on seeing her. If he did, she had no idea what she was going to do. The smart thing, of course, would be to keep her door locked and her lights off, because if she opened that door, there was an excellent chance she'd say to hell with it, drag him inside by his shirt collar and head straight to her bedroom.

THAT EVENING, AMANDA MET Lorna at Panther Stadium, one of those places steeped in town history that was a source of pride for every red-blooded citizen who lived and died for the thrill of high school football. A tide of black and orange undulated through their side of the stadium as the cheerleaders warmed up the fans awaiting kickoff.

"Okay," Lorna said after they got settled on the bleachers, "explain to me why I had to hear from Betty Taggert that Kirk McKenzie was at your house last night."

Oh, great. If Betty had told Lorna, she'd also given an earful to the other ladies at the Cut Hut, where Lorna worked as a stylist. With embellishments, of course.

"I wish everyone would stop gossiping altogether."

An excited buzz ran through the stands as the other team kicked off, followed by a roar when the Panthers returned the ball for a thirty-yard gain.

"Okay, now they're cooking," Lorna said, shoving her hands deeper into the pockets of her coat. Amanda shivered a little in the cool evening breeze, finally untying her sweatshirt from around her waist and putting it on.

Being in this football stadium always brought back memories. Right now, too many memories. She'd spent a lot of time in high school sitting on these bleachers, at least until she and Kirk had started seeing each other. Then football games consisted mostly of time spent *under* the bleachers.

"So did you sleep with him?" Lorna asked.

"God, no!"

"Are you going to?"

"No!"

Lorna raised an eyebrow. "So there's nothing between you two anymore?"

"That's right."

"Oh, come *on!* There has to be something still there. You two generated enough heat in high school to set off fire sprinklers. So why did he come by?"

"Just to catch up a little."

"Hmm. Right. Just to catch up. So what did you talk about?"

"You know. The usual stuff you'd talk about with somebody you haven't seen in years."

And right now, Amanda could barely remember any of it. She did, however, remember that kiss.

Another roar rose from the crowd.

"Okay," Lorna said. "First and goal. They've got to hold them here. Everything crossed."

Amanda dutifully crossed her fingers, her legs, then crossed her arms over each other in a reprise of the good-luck system they'd had in high school.

"Hot damn," Lorna said when the Panthers managed to hold their opponent. "We can only call on the good luck fairies every once in a while, but it works every time."

In so many ways, this town hadn't changed at all. Amanda never would have thought it before she returned here, but something about that put a smile on her face.

Two hours later, the Panthers had won by twenty-two points. Amanda had tried to concentrate on the game, but her mind was on Kirk the entire time, and the only reason she knew the final score was because she glanced at the scoreboard when she and Lorna made their way down out of the stands. After they stopped by to congratulate Lorna's nephew on a game well played, they went to the parking lot to find that most of the cars had already left.

Lorna stopped short, her eyes flying open wide. "My God. That's him, isn't it?"

Amanda glanced to where her SUV was parked. Kirk was leaning against it. Her heart stuttered, then settled into a hard, thudding rhythm.

"Wow," Lorna whispered. "Does he look good, or what?"

God, yes.

He wore faded jeans, a navy cotton sweater over a T-shirt, and a pair of athletic shoes that had definitely seen better days. Clothes like those would have looked shoddy on any other man, but they merely made him look confident and carefree. He stood with one ankle crossed over the other, his arms folded. When their eyes met, he went totally still, focusing on her like a laser locking on to its target.

"Lorna," Amanda whispered. "Go away."

"But—"

"Seriously. Just let me talk to him by myself."

"Hey, I just want to say hi. It's been a long time."

"Make it just a little longer. Please?"

Lorna sighed. "Okay. But you'd better call me later."

She reluctantly headed for her car, and Amanda turned toward hers.

CHAPTER SIX

AMANDA WALKED TO HER CAR, coming to a halt a few paces from Kirk. The night wind lifted a few strands of her hair and whisked them across her cheek. She pushed them away, then turned her gaze to meet his.

"Okay," she said. "How did you know I was here?"

"You said last night that you and Lorna go to the football games."

"So why are you hanging out in the parking lot?"

"I would have had to buy a ticket to hang out under the bleachers."

"Why not sit in the stands?"

"Old habits die hard."

She took her keys from her purse. "I have to get home."

"You still see me as that same kid I used to be, don't you?"

She stopped and stared at him. "I haven't seen a whole lot of evidence to the contrary."

"Take a drive with me."

"A drive?" She laughed with disbelief. "You actually expect me to get into a car with you after what happened?"

"I won't be speeding tonight. I promise you that."

"I assume you wouldn't be speeding any night."

"You know what I mean."

"Yes. I do. And it isn't going to prove anything."

"No, it probably isn't. But to tell you the truth, it's the only place I know where to start."

"Start what?"

"Making you understand that time has passed. And that people change."

He seemed so sincere that for a moment she actually considered saying yes. Then she remembered who she was dealing with. She hit the remote, and the driver's door clicked open.

"We're still attracted to each other," Kirk said. "You can't deny that."

She opened the door.

"Come on, Amanda. It's not like I'm asking you to run away with me. I gave up on that fifteen years ago."

She turned back. "Then what are you asking me to do? Finish what you started last night? We never had sex back then, so you're taking one more stab at it now?"

Kirk's gaze hardened. "You meant a hell of a lot more to me than that, and you know it."

"If so, you had a funny way of showing it. After what happened that night—"

"I don't want to talk about it."

"Of course you don't. You nearly got us killed."

His jaw tightened. "It was an accident."

"No, Kirk. It was no accident. You caused what happened, by your recklessness, your impulsiveness—"

"I never meant to go that fast. I just…I just wasn't thinking straight."

"You can say that again. You must have been doing eighty on a two-lane highway."

"If you knew how I felt—"

"You felt the need for speed. That much I knew. You went crazy on me."

"It wasn't like that!"

But it had been. She still remembered their argument, and then the strange light that had entered his eyes. He'd jammed the key into the ignition of his car, yanked the gearshift, slammed his foot down on the gas, and in moments he had been speeding down the dark, deserted state highway.

"I begged you to slow down," Amanda said. "But you wouldn't listen. It was as if I were talking to a stranger. I asked you to take me home. You said, 'What if I don't? What then? What if I keep you in this car with me and just keep on driving?' You scared the hell out of me."

"But I never meant to—"

"Never meant to what? Take a curve too fast? Slide off the road and into a tree? Put us both in the hospital?"

"It's been fifteen years," Kirk said. "Isn't it time you got over that?"

"Got *over* it?"

"I'm not that kid anymore!"

"Sure you are. You're still taking chances, pushing your luck, risking your life—"

"It's my *job* to do that!"

"Yes. But it's also part of who you are. It's why you can't accept the truth about your medical condition. You need that rush like you need air to breathe, and to hell with anything that gets in the way of that. And as long as you're still taking chances with your life, I can't trust you not to take chances with mine."

Kirk's face fell into an angry frown. "You have no idea how many times I regretted what happened that night," he said. "But I can't take it back now. I was just hoping that somehow we'd be able to get past it, and that maybe there would still be something between us. But that's not going to happen, is it?"

She just stared at him.

"You tell me I haven't changed," he said. "Look in a mirror, Amanda. That eighteen-year-old girl is still looking back. The one who can't forget what happened that night. Or forgive it."

He turned and strode to his car. He got in, slammed the door and left the parking lot. He said he was a changed man, but not one thing about him said there was any truth to that at all.

THE NEXT MORNING AMANDA went by the clinic to pick up some work to take with her to the set, thinking if she just distracted herself, then maybe she could get through the next few days without thinking about Kirk and the fight they'd had last night. She just wanted to get through the next few days without any more confrontations, then have him go home to Los Angeles and have it all be over with.

She had just stuffed several file folders into the briefcase on her desk when Louise came into her office.

Amanda held up her palm. "Don't worry, Louise. I'm on my way to the set. I'm just picking up a little work to take with me so I can at least get something done while I'm sitting there."

Louise folded her arms. "You know, you're the only person I know who would rather work than watch a movie being filmed."

"Does that really surprise you?"

"It does, considering who's part of the crew filming that movie."

Amanda zipped the briefcase shut. "I don't want to talk about him."

"Oh, boy. What happened between you two? And don't say it was nothing. I want to know."

Amanda sighed. "He showed up at the football game last night. We ended up talking about the accident."

"And?"

"And he doesn't seem to think it was a big deal."

"I might be inclined to agree with him. After all, it was a long time ago."

"But it showed me exactly what kind of person he is. It was right to break it off with him then, and it's right to stay away from him now."

With a heavy sigh, Louise walked into Amanda's office. She closed the door behind her and sat down.

"I worry about you, you know," Louise said.

"Me? Why?"

"Because you're a workaholic. If you can't find enough to do at the clinic, I've actually seen you arranging the magazines in the waiting room. I thought coming back here where life is a little more slow-paced would loosen you up a little, but it hasn't worked out that way."

"So you think I should hook up with Kirk again? A man who is bad for me in so many ways I can't even count them?"

"I don't think that's true."

"That's up to me to decide, isn't it?"

"Yes. Of course it is. But…"

"What?"

"There's something I never told you. About the night of the accident."

Louise's face had turned somber, and Amanda felt a tremor run down her spine. What other awful thing about that night didn't she know?

"Kirk probably wouldn't want me telling you this," Louise said.

"Which is all the more reason to."

"I was working in the ER the night they brought you in. You both had short admissions to the hospital, so they bagged up your belongings. Kirk was carrying something unusual with him."

"What?"

"A little black velvet box with a diamond ring."

Amanda was stunned. She couldn't mean...

"He was going to ask you to marry him."

"Did he tell you that?"

"After I saw the ring, he couldn't deny it. He swore me to silence about it, saying it was over between you, so it didn't matter. But I'll never forget the look on his face. It wasn't over for him. Not by a long shot. That boy loved you. More than you ever knew."

"But he was so angry that night—"

"Because you started talking about going to college before he could talk about anything else, and that was when it became real to him. You were both graduating the next day, and then in a few months you were going off to the University of Texas. As soon as you did, he knew he'd never see you again."

"He could have gone to college, too," Amanda said. "I told him all the time that if he'd only apply himself—"

"Come on, Amanda! Back then the closest Kirk

was likely to get to the University of Texas was barhopping on Sixth Street. He didn't have the grades. He didn't have a family to encourage him. He didn't have a damned thing. All he had was you."

Amanda put her hand to her throat, a breathless feeling overtaking her. She'd never once stopped to think about that night from Kirk's point of view, but now that she did...

"He lost you that night," Louise said. "And it was tearing him up."

"I can't believe this. He never even told me he loved me. Not once."

"You know where he came from. Those words wouldn't have come easily. He was going to let that ring do his talking for him."

And they'd gotten into that argument before he could give it to her. Now she knew why he'd reacted the way he had when she insisted he take her home.

What if I don't? What then? What if I keep you in this car with me and just keep on driving?

It was true that he'd never said the words. But sometimes, amid all the joking and the banter and the hotter-than-hell interludes at Trojan Point, he'd stop and look at her as if the world turned only because she was in it, his eyes so adoring that it made her breath catch in her throat.

"You were very close once," Louise said.

"We're adults now. Things change."

"So you feel nothing for him now?"

She paused, amazed at how hard it was to deny it. "No, I don't. Not like that. And I don't think he does, either. Just because he thought he wanted to marry me back then doesn't mean he has any of those feelings for me now. You're really going out on a limb with this."

"Back then," Louise said, "did you love him?"

Amanda blinked, then looked away. "No. Of course not. What does an eighteen-year-old girl know about love?"

"You were eighteen going on thirty. I expect you knew quite a lot."

Amanda closed her eyes. "Louise—"

"It's up to you. Go back to the set if you want to. If not, I'll send Donald. Feet kissing and all." She got up and went to the door, then turned back. "When you came back here six months ago, I was thrilled. But the more I watched you, the more I saw what a workaholic you'd become. Then I realized something."

"What's that?"

"You were turning into me."

"What do you mean?"

"I'm sixty-four years old. Most of my life has been about work. I've had my share of relationships with men, but never in all that time has a man felt about me the way Kirk felt about you. I know you were just kids, but…" She sighed. "If something's still there, just don't let it go, okay?"

As Louise walked away, Amanda sat back in her chair, feeling absolutely miserable. The one thing she hated was not being able to sort things out, categorize them, put everything in order so she could make sense of it.

You meant a hell of a lot more to me than that, Kirk had told her last night, *and you know it.*

Yes. She did know it. Even back in high school, if all he'd been after was sex, he'd have left her and moved on. Even when he had begged her for it the way most eighteen-year-old boys did, it had never once turned into the kind of coercion she couldn't deal with, and she'd never once doubted that he cared for her. She'd just never known how much. And now that she did, she was questioning everything else about him she'd thought to be true. What else about Kirk was still hidden beneath the surface, waiting to be discovered?

CHAPTER SEVEN

AMANDA LEFT THE CLINIC, and fifteen minutes later she arrived at the warehouse. Kirk was already at work with the stunt men, blocking out a fight sequence, and he didn't even acknowledge that she was there. She told herself that was a good thing, because she wouldn't have had a clue what to say to him if he had spoken to her. She'd brought her briefcase full of work along, but she quickly realized that concentrating on it was going to be impossible.

Instead, she watched as Kirk walked the men through part of the sequence in slow motion, and gradually she began to realize that a fight scene wasn't simply a few guys turned loose to start swinging. Every move was carefully scripted. Kirk went over every movement with the men multiple times so it could be executed properly, consulting with the director to take into account prop placement and camera angles.

Then he turned to Colley. "And the whole time you're up there, you're going to be holding on to something. After every punch, you need to grab the railing. Where there's no railing, we've got cables rigged to look like part of the structure."

"Why do you want me to hold on? I'm fighting. What kind of guy fights with one hand?"

"Colley—"

"My grandmother can fight up there if she holds on!"

"That's not the point."

"Then what is the point? You think I don't have the balance to throw a punch without—"

Kirk held up his hand. "Stop."

He said the single word so authoritatively that Colley shut his mouth instantly, but his sigh of disgust wasn't lost on anyone in the building.

"Listen to me, kid. You've got balance in spades. What you don't have is a handle on the character."

"Huh?"

"It's not about what you can physically do. It's about what the character would do. You're not the hero. You're a secondary character with very little fighting experience who finds himself face-to-face with the bad guys two stories above the ground. He's going to hold on every chance he gets."

Colley's belligerent expression faded. He looked up to the catwalk, then back at Kirk again, finally giving him a reluctant nod. Then Kirk showed him ways to fake a loss of balance to make it seem as if he was going to fall, yet be perfectly safe. Colley went through the motions, and then Kirk said, "Okay. Let's run through it up there."

The men climbed the ladder to the catwalk, where they rehearsed the sequence at least half a dozen times. When they finally filmed it, Colley did exactly what Kirk had instructed him to do, and it came off without a hitch, including Colley's face-first fall from the catwalk. The director gave Kirk a thumbs-up, and he nodded with satisfaction. When Colley came back down to the ground, Kirk clapped him on the shoulder, leaning in to say something to him that put a smile on his face.

Amanda couldn't help noticing similar characteristics between Colley and a few Dead Rebels she'd once known. But while shadows of those qualities still lingered in Kirk, she was beginning to realize just how much he had matured. Watching him take charge of the crew and keep things running smoothly and, above all, hold his temper with Colley, told her just how disciplined he was. Any risks he took were the deliberate, calculated risks of a skilled professional, not the impulsive actions of a hotheaded boy.

I'm not that kid anymore.

He was right. He wasn't. And the thought of that made Amanda even more miserable than she already was. Because as much as she'd been attracted to the boy she remembered, she found herself even more attracted to the man he'd become.

And no matter how hard she tried, she couldn't get that ring out of her mind. He'd been in love with her. So much so that he'd wanted her to marry him. She had no delusions that those feelings had survived intact all these years, but it gave her an overwhelming need to know just what *had* survived. Even though she could come up with all kinds of reasons she shouldn't be with him, maybe Louise was right. Maybe it was time to start looking for reasons she should.

AT SEVEN O'CLOCK THAT evening, Kirk was sitting at CB's with Dan and Colley and a few of the other guys from the crew. The other men were drinking hard, eyeing the waitresses and talking about the events of the day. Kirk wasn't particularly interested in any of that. He just settled back in his chair with a beer in his hand, telling himself this beat sitting in his room in the Bluebonnet Inn, staring at the TV, bored out of his wits. He needed something to take the edge off, and maybe a little alcohol would do the trick.

Dan had driven him nuts all day, and Colley had been a pain in the ass. Kirk had barely been able to concentrate on anything with Amanda sitting on the sidelines, knowing she was thinking about the argument they'd had last night.

As well as the argument they'd had fifteen years ago.

He felt bitter about that, but could he really blame her? She was right. He'd almost gotten both of them killed. He knew it was something a woman like Amanda would have a hard time letting go of, but he'd just hoped that after all these years she'd be able to put it aside and see him in a different light.

No such luck.

She'd left the warehouse as soon as Dan called a halt to today's shooting, and that was just as well. If her grudge was still intact, how could he expect her even to want to speak to him, much less anything more?

"Well, well," Dan said. "Look who just came in."

Kirk turned around, shocked to see Amanda walking up to the bar. He came to attention immediately, watching as she settled onto a bar stool.

"Hmm," Colley said. "Kinda surprised to see a woman like her in a place like this."

Kirk was, too. The only reason she'd come in here the other night was because she was looking for him.

"I think I'll invite her over," Colley said, rising from his chair.

"Sit," Kirk snapped.

Colley slowly lowered himself back to his chair. "What's the matter?"

"She's an old friend of Kirk's," Dan said.

"Yeah? Then why doesn't she come over?"

Good question.

Amanda spoke to the bartender, probably ordering a drink. Then she turned around to look at the table where Kirk sat. She caught his gaze, held it for the count of three, then slowly turned back. The men all looked at Kirk.

"Ah," Colley said. "I get it. She's *that* kind of friend."

No, she wasn't. At least, not anymore. Particularly after last night. So why was she looking at him like that?

It was time to find out.

Kirk grabbed his beer, went to the bar and slid onto the empty stool next to her. The bartender put a beer down in front of Amanda. She picked it up and took a sip.

"I'm a little surprised to see you here," he said.

"Really? Why?"

"This isn't your kind of place."

"You're right. It's not."

"Then why are you here?"

"I overheard the crew talking about coming here. When you weren't at the Bluebonnet Inn, I took a shot that you'd be with them."

His heart skipped. "You went to the hotel to see me?"

"Yes."

"Why?"

"Because I wanted to talk to you. I—" She paused, turning back to her drink. "I didn't like the way things were left between us last night."

Kirk didn't, either. He hadn't been able to think about much else since. But he'd never expected Amanda to come to the same conclusion.

"You're very good at what you do, aren't you?" she asked.

He gave her an offhand shrug. "It's my job."

"I watched you today. I never knew that much planning went into a fight scene."

"That was a short one. I've worked on ones that took days."

"You even held your temper with Colley."

"I had to get the stunt on film," Kirk said. "You blow up at somebody like Colley, he sulks. I didn't need that. He'll probably wash out sooner or later."

"If he checked his ego at the door, would he be any good?"

"Yep. The kid definitely has what it takes."

"But his personality's a problem."

"Yeah. I could teach him a thing or two, if only he'd listen."

"He seemed to listen today." She smiled briefly. "Every once in a while, anyway."

Amanda turned back to her beer, running her finger along the side of it, sweeping a finger's breadth of condensation away. Somebody had plugged the jukebox, and a particularly twangy country song poured out over the sound system.

"This has been really strange for me," she told him. "The last thing I expected was to see you on top of that cliff a few days ago getting ready to jump."

"Strange," he said, "and not particularly welcome?"

She faced him. "I didn't say that."

Even in the dim light of the bar, he could see that the accusation from last night was gone from her eyes. He didn't know why. Maybe it wasn't even good right now to wonder why. Maybe he should just be glad she was here.

"After what happened last night," he said, "I thought you'd never want to speak to me again."

"Actually, I wondered if you'd want to speak to me." She sighed. "I said some things I shouldn't have."

"No," he said. "You were right. That accident was my fault. After what happened that night, you had every right to tell me to go to hell."

"And I've wondered ever since then what might have happened between us if I hadn't."

Kirk froze. "But you told me you hadn't thought about me since high school. That what happened back then was all wrong, so you hadn't bothered thinking about it since."

"I lied."

Kirk couldn't believe she was saying this. Couldn't believe that all this time, she'd been thinking about him, just as he'd been thinking about her.

The song on the jukebox changed, and it turned out to be even worse than the one before it.

"Bad song," Amanda said.

"Really bad," he agreed.

"It's too loud in here."

"Yes, it is."

"You know that drive you wanted to take last night?"

"Yeah?"

"Let's do it now."

Kirk paused only a moment before grabbing his

wallet to pay the tab. Amanda reached for her purse, but he held up his palm and tossed down a twenty. They rose together and walked out of the bar. He had a vague sense of the other men staring at them as they left, but all he could think about was Amanda. He had no idea where they were going, and he didn't care, as long as they were going there together.

They walked through the parking lot, the cool night air swirling around them. Amanda fished out her keys and hit the remote to unlock the car. Kirk reached for the passenger door.

"Kirk."

When he turned back, she slipped the keys into his hand. He looked at them with surprise. "But last night—"

"Forget about last night."

I trust you, she was telling him, and in that moment he swore he would never speed on a public roadway again as long as he lived.

He opened the passenger door for her, then got into the driver's seat and started the car. "Anywhere in particular you'd like to go?"

"When you leave the parking lot," she said, "take a right."

He did as she asked, and to his surprise, what used to be cow pastures lining the state highway had become the newer part of Prescott. They passed a brand-new bank, a new convenience store/gas station, then a couple of housing subdivisions sprawling to the west. With essentially nothing the same in this part of town, Kirk felt totally disoriented.

"Take a left here," Amanda said.

"A dirt road?" Kirk said as he swung the car onto it. "Where are we going?"

"Don't you recognize it?"

No. Nothing looked familiar. He steered the car through the trees, then emerged from the woods and hit a dead end. Ahead was a rocky valley, lit only by the last muted rays of a red-gold sunset.

Trojan Point.

Kirk was stunned. With all the new construction leading up to it now, he hadn't even recognized where they were. And now memories came flooding back of all the hot, steamy nights he and Amanda had spent up here.

Kirk killed the engine, leaving them in silence. The daylight had almost disappeared, replaced by a three-quarter moon rising over the valley. Amanda settled back in her seat and let out a comfortable sigh. She wore a pair of jeans and one of those fuzzy sweaters that felt so good to touch, particularly if there was a body underneath it like hers. And her hair. Soft and silky, flowing over her shoulders like rainwater. He hoped she'd worn it down because she knew he liked it that way.

"It's pretty, isn't it?" she said, staring at the moon.

Just the sound of her voice in the near darkness kicked his heart up a notch.

"Yeah," Kirk said. "Not much activity up here these days, is there?"

"It's a weeknight. I hear it's still busy on the weekend."

Silence again.

"I have a confession to make," she said softly.

"What?"

"When I looked up that first day and saw you at the top of that building, my first thought had nothing to do with the accident in high school. All I could think about was how I felt about you then. I've been thinking about that all day. How much I cared about you."

She shifted a little and rested her hand on the console between them. Long, slender fingers. Flawless skin. She had the kind of hands that could instantly soothe a sick patient.

Or drive a man wild.

"Back in high school," Kirk said, "you were always so out of my league."

"What?"

"I acted so tough, talked so big, but the truth was that I couldn't believe you even gave me the time of day. You spent most of your time getting good grades and trying to make something of yourself. About all I ever did was drink and smoke and play stupid pranks with my friends."

"Oh, yeah," Amanda said with a little eye roll. "The pranks." Then she smiled. "But I have to say that the last one was pretty inspired. I still can't believe you and the Rebels pulled it off."

She was right. It had been a pretty big undertaking to tear down a good portion of a junk yard and reassemble it on the front lawn of the high school. But it was the kind of thing boys like them did—boys with too much time on their hands and nobody who cared enough to set them straight.

"Yeah," Kirk said. "A lot of people were pissed off about that. I remember wishing a few times that my father would smack me senseless for some of the crap I pulled with my friends."

"Really? Why?"

"Because then at least I'd have known that he gave a damn."

Amanda nodded. "So have you seen anything of Matt or Caleb since high school?"

"Nope."

"Kinda surprises me. You guys were pretty close."

"When I left here, I left everything." He paused. "There was only one thing worth remembering."

A soft smile lit her face, only to fade away again. "I'm sorry things were so hard for you back then."

"Being with you made it easier."

"That was because I knew there was a lot more to you than where you came from. I know you pretty much ignored academics, but you were still one of the smartest guys I knew. And you were fun, too," she said with a smile, "once you got rid of some of that attitude."

And she was the reason he had. She'd taken zero attitude from him when attitude was all he felt he had to give—a rotten attitude about the hand in life he'd been dealt, that horrible feeling of nobody giving a damn whether he lived or died. But she had. For those few precious months, he'd found out what it was like to be the center of somebody's life, and he'd loved her so much he'd ached with it. But in the end, he'd hurt her. And then he'd found out that it was possible that all the love he wanted to give her might never be returned.

Kirk slid his hand over hers where it lay on the console, giving it a gentle squeeze. "I'm sorry about what happened that night."

"It was a long time ago," she said. "And you're not that kid anymore."

She looked down at where their hands met. She

turned hers over and laced her fingers through his, then brought her gaze up again, stopping momentarily to hover over his lips before meeting his eyes again.

"Your trip to Prescott wouldn't have been complete without coming up here," she murmured.

"It does bring back memories."

She stared at him in silence for a moment, her green eyes shimmering in the pale moonlight. "And coming up here wouldn't have been complete without this."

With that, she leaned in slowly and met his lips in a soft, lingering kiss.

CHAPTER EIGHT

KIRK WAS STUNNED. After last night, he couldn't have imagined that she'd bring him here tonight, much less that they would be doing this. When she finally pulled away from him, he slid his hand along her cheek, staring at her for a moment, gauging her reaction, and when she looked back at him expectantly, he kissed her. Then he kissed her again. And before long they were making out like teenagers, engulfing each other with hot, wet kisses, each one more sizzling than the last.

He had no idea how much time passed. It could have been minutes, or it could have been an hour. At one point he pulled away just long enough to turn on the radio to an oldies station, and when he heard that music, he was sure that one of those warm, dreamy nights he remembered so well had come to life again.

"Listen," Amanda said, when a certain sappy love song came on the radio. "If I remember right, that was playing the night you finally got past first base."

Kirk laughed softly. "Yeah. I remember that." He sighed. "You were a *very* good girl back then."

"Yes. I was."

He leaned in and kissed her neck. "Are you still?"

"Why don't you find out?"

He slid his hand beneath Amanda's sweater, wrapping his hand around her waist. When she responded with a soft sigh of satisfaction, he inched his hand up to trace his fingertips over the underside of her breast, then across her nipple, feeling it tighten beneath the silky fabric.

"More," she whispered.

He unhooked the front clasp of her bra and swept the cups away, curling his hand around her breast as he leaned in and kissed his way along the column of her neck. She tilted her head back and closed her eyes, moaning softly, her breathing heightened, her face flushed. He strummed back and forth across her nipple, feeling it tighten even more beneath his thumb. She shuddered with pleasure, then skimmed her hands along his shoulders and downward to his collarbones, searching for his shirt buttons.

He backed away a bit, and she unfastened three of the buttons and slipped her hand inside his shirt to stroke his chest. Her hands felt so soft and sure, tormenting him with thoughts of what it would be like to finally make love to her. It was probably growing colder by the minute—the weather report said it might slip into the forties tonight—but Kirk felt as if every molecule of his body was searing hot.

"This was about as far as we went back then," Amanda whispered, her hands still moving over him.

"I know," Kirk said. "Believe me, I remember every painful moment."

"Painful?"

"Oh, yeah. Frustration is painful for a teenage boy. You have no idea how much I wanted you."

"No. I knew."

"And you wanted me."

A shaky sigh escaped her lips. "You know I did."

"But you said no."

"Good girls always say no."

"And that drives bad boys crazy."

When he leaned in to kiss her again, her hand crept to his thigh, moving in small, tantalizing circles. Forget teenage boys. He'd just discovered that a grown man's frustration was even worse.

"There's always the backseat," she murmured.

His heart jolted hard, and it was all he could do not to leap out of this car, dive into the backseat with her and make every teenage dream he'd ever had come true. But he wasn't a teenager anymore. He was a grown man with a burning desire to make love to the woman he'd never forgotten, and to do it in a way that she'd remember from now on.

"Sorry, Amanda. I haven't thought about making love to you all these years to settle for a quickie in the backseat."

She smiled. "Then how about a nice, warm bed at my house?"

Just when he thought this night couldn't get any better, it had.

THEY TALKED VERY LITTLE on the way home, but Amanda could practically feel the air quivering between them. Kirk was right. Back then she'd wanted him with a desire bordering on obsession, but she had never expected to feel that way now, as if she'd die if she didn't have him.

A few minutes later, she unlocked her front door and she and Kirk went inside. He clicked the dead bolt shut with one hand and reached for her with the other, and after a long, leisurely kiss, she took him by the hand and led him to her bedroom.

She found a condom in her nightstand drawer and tossed it down beside the clock. Then they undressed each other, stopping along the way for a kiss, a caress, and more than once Kirk whispered things in her ear that made her heart thud with anticipation. He lay her gently on the bed, bracing himself on one elbow beside her and leaning in for a deep, blistering kiss. Then he opened his eyes and brushed a strand of hair away from her cheek.

"Every time I kissed you back then," he murmured, "I wondered what in the hell I'd done right in my whole lousy life to deserve a girl like you."

Lit by moonlight alone, his face was barely illuminated, but still she saw it—that look in his eyes she remembered so well, the one that said he worshipped the ground she walked on. She thought about the ring again, about how painful it must have been for him that night when she told him she never wanted to see him again. Suddenly it was as if that boy was looking back at her, the one who wanted so desperately to love and be loved.

She could feel how much he wanted her. He was practically trembling with it. But the urgency of youth had been replaced by the slow, deliberate, passionate touch of a grown man in complete control of himself.

Kirk eased his hand between Amanda's legs to stroke her. The darkness seemed to heighten every one of her senses, making her feel as if every nerve ending was waiting for his touch. He used his mouth and his hands and his soft-spoken words to excite her in ways she had only dreamed of before, until there was no way she could be hotter or more ready for him.

Finally he rose above her, putting on the condom and then parting her thighs, and with one firm thrust he was inside her. He began to move, gradually increasing his pace, and Amanda could barely breathe for the sheer intensity of it. It felt so good to give in to this kind of desire, to be with this man, this night, this way. The air was cool around them, but she felt hot, so hot, as they filled a need together that neither one of them could deny any longer. And by the time they reached the peak of pleasure, Amanda felt as if she were finally fulfilling a long-held fantasy. The reality of it was far better than she ever could have imagined.

AMANDA WOKE THE NEXT morning when the alarm went off—the one she almost hadn't remembered to set. It was six-thirty now, and she and Kirk were due on the set at eight.

Kirk stirred beside her. Only the smallest bit of sunlight was filtering in through her blinds, but she saw him blink his eyes open. Then he reached for her under the covers, pulled her into his arms and kissed her.

"Good morning," he said with a smile, then rolled her to her back and kissed her again, making it clear exactly what he wanted. As he made love to her again, Amanda slipped back into the same dream world she'd been in last night, relishing every moment of being with him. Later, as she lay in his arms, she felt so warm and contented that she wished they could spend the day in bed.

"That was good," he said with a sigh of satisfaction.

She smiled. "Very good," she murmured, stroking his chest. "But the bad news is that now we're running late. We still need to get your car from CB's, assuming it hasn't been stolen or vandalized."

He glanced at the clock. "Good point."

"Why don't you take a shower, and I'll make us some breakfast? Then I'll get ready."

"Sounds good."

As she started to get up, her fingers tripped over an irregular patch of skin along his rib cage. She'd felt it a moment ago while they were making love, and she remembered feeling it last night, too, but both times it had been too dark to make out what it was. But as he threw back the covers now, the sunlight made it visible for the first time. A large, irregular patch of skin maybe six inches across. She knew what it was. A scar from a burn.

But that was the least of it.

As he sat up in bed, she saw a jagged white scar that ran along his upper chest from a wound that had to have been closed with at least a dozen stitches. On the front of his shoulder was a purplish scar the size of a silver dollar she couldn't tell the origin of, and there were three or four other smaller ones that had probably been lacerations.

"My God," she murmured, staring at his chest.

"Not exactly pretty, is it?"

"I'm sorry. I just didn't expect…"

"Hazards of the business." He gave her one last kiss and rose from the bed.

That was when she saw the scars on his back.

As he disappeared into the bathroom, Amanda dropped her head back to the pillow, every fear she'd ever had about Kirk's profession suddenly striking her full force. Last night she'd forgotten all about it, concentrating instead on the undeniable fact that even after all this time, they couldn't stay apart. All the old emotions were still there, burning just as brightly as they had back then, emotions neither one of them could hide. But one look at his body this morning brought her right back around to the hard truth. Every day he went to work was one more day he could hurt himself permanently, and the apprehension she felt about that told her she cared even more about him now than she had fifteen years ago.

THE CREW HAD MOVED THE SET out to a nearby ranch, where they filmed some motorcycle stunts that involved a chase through rugged hill country. The sequence culminated in the character getting shot, losing control, and causing a crash that took out two other riders beside him. All day long, Amanda's stomach flip-flopped with apprehension as she watched them. She could only imagine how she would have felt if one of those men was Kirk.

When they finished shooting for the day, she felt obligated to be pleasant and tell him how wonderfully the stunts had come off. He nodded, then leaned over and told her with a wink and a smile that he could have performed them better. And by the look in his eyes when he said it, he was eager to hop on a motorcycle and back up that claim, which made her stomach twist all over again.

When they left the set, Amanda suggested that they go to Hanson's for dinner, and Kirk had really warmed up to that idea. Men rarely forgot great barbecue, and Hanson's had some of the best.

Sitting in a booth by the window, Amanda discovered she didn't care about the prying eyes of townspeople who recognized Kirk and talked behind their hands, clearly speculating what the two of them were doing together. It hadn't even bothered her when Betty Taggert had planted herself in a chair on her front porch that morning, clearly waiting to see if Kirk had indeed stayed all night. Amanda had merely smiled and waved and watched the old bat's mouth drop open.

After they finished dinner, they sat in the booth and talked, filling each other in on their lives. Kirk had been a lot of places and seen a lot of things, which made Amanda feel as if her own life was pretty mundane. She'd always told herself she wasn't sure why she'd ever been attracted to him when everything about her personality was dead opposite. But now she knew that was exactly *why* she was attracted to him—because he was everything she wasn't.

In high school, she loved the way he'd brushed aside all her good-girl tendencies and taken her for a walk on the wild side. It had been fun and exhilarating at a time in her life when the pressures of school, along with the pressures she'd put on herself, were so intense that she'd forgotten what it felt like to step off the straight and narrow, even for a moment.

And now, getting to know Kirk all over again made Amanda feel that same kind of exhilaration, reminding her of why she'd once been so in love with him.

They left Hanson's after dinner and dropped by CB's, where they sipped a few beers and talked some more. After a while, Amanda got up to go to the ladies' room, and when she came back, Kirk was standing at the juke-box. Then a song came on that put a smile on her face.

"Never Tear Us Apart."

Kirk took her by the hand and led her to the dance floor. Other people were in the bar drinking, but because nobody else seemed inclined to dance, Amanda felt a little conspicuous. But when Kirk pulled her into his arms, all that self-consciousness seemed to evaporate, and all she could think about was him.

"I thought there was only country and western music on that jukebox," she said.

"Nah. There's all kinds of music. Country and western is just the only stuff that gets played." Kirk ran his hand up and down her back. "Wish I could have brought you here with me in high school."

"Just how often did you go to places you weren't old enough for?"

"As often as they'd let me in."

He enveloped her hand in his and rested it against his chest. Then he dipped his head and kissed her on the neck. She sighed.

"I'll be leaving soon," Kirk said.

Amanda closed her eyes. The words she didn't like hearing. "Yeah. I guess so."

"I don't want fifteen more years to pass before I see you again."

"I don't, either."

"Then come to Los Angeles with me."

She stopped and leaned away from him. "What?"

"I know it's sudden, but we need to talk about it. I'm leaving day after tomorrow."

"But I can't leave here! The clinic—"

"There are hospitals and clinics all over Los Angeles. You'd have no trouble finding a job there."

"But Louise expects me to take it over when she retires."

"Are you telling me she couldn't find somebody else?"

"Well, I suppose she could, but—"

"Now, I know you'd have a lot to wrap up here before you could move out there, so you couldn't come right away. Just tell me you'll come eventually."

"Wait a minute," she said, slipping out of his arms and backing away. "Slow down. This is just a little too much for me right now."

She left the dance floor and walked back to their table, where she sat down again, took a deep breath and tried to get a grip, which was hard to do with that damned song still playing on the jukebox. Kirk was telling her he thought she should give up everything and move to Los Angeles. How crazy was that?

He slid into the chair next to her, resting his forearms on the table and leaning in to catch her eye.

"Amanda? Am I being presumptuous again? Am I wrong in assuming you feel the same way about me that I feel about you?"

She couldn't lie. Something had happened in the past few days, something she hadn't expected.

She'd fallen in love with him all over again.

"No," she told him. "You're not wrong."

A look of relief passed over his face. "Then why waste time? I have a nice apartment. Well, the decorating isn't so hot, but you can do anything to it you want to. Or we can move somewhere else. Buy a house—"

"Kirk! You've got to slow down here. Seriously."

He leaned away dutifully, but she could still see the enthusiasm in his eyes.

"You're crazy," she said. "You know that, don't you?"

He smiled. "I never claimed to be completely sane. I know that doesn't help my case very much where you're concerned, but there you go."

She shook her head with disbelief. "You showing up…all this happening between us…I could never have imagined—"

"You couldn't?"

"What?"

"I think somewhere in the back of your mind, you imagined all of this."

He was right. In spite of everything that had happened between them, and in spite of all the men she'd had relationships with, it was still Kirk's face she saw when she closed her eyes at night. She couldn't deny wanting to be with him. But she just wasn't the sort of person who leaped first and looked later.

"I just want you to think about it," Kirk said. "That's all I'm asking right now. Just tell me you'll think about it."

She'd come back to Prescott to get away from the big city. She liked it here. It felt like home. The idea of leaving her practice behind and going to a city the size of Los Angeles overwhelmed her.

But Kirk disappearing from her life was equally overwhelming.

"Yes," she said, as the last few bars of the song faded away. "I'll think about it."

He smiled. "That's all I wanted to hear right now."

Kirk drained the last of his beer and signaled the

waitress for their check. As Amanda watched him, she realized something else was eating at her, something he wasn't even taking into account.

In the end, it wasn't really about where they lived. That was one of those practical problems that had to be sorted out in any relationship. It was about the fact that if he kept up his profession, she'd be worrying every moment that the next job he took would be his last. If he had another head injury, he could end up with permanent neurological damage. Or in a coma.

Or dead.

Before they could take this any further, she knew that somehow, some way, she had to convince him to get out of the profession he loved so much, because the last thing she intended to do was sit by and watch him do the one thing that could take him away from her forever.

CHAPTER NINE

THE NEXT DAY THEY FINISHED shooting another motor-cycle sequence, and Kirk could feel the adrenaline pumping through his veins just watching it unfold. He'd be on the ground in Los Angeles tomorrow afternoon, and the next day he had another job waiting for him. His medically imposed sentence would be up, and he couldn't wait to get back to the action.

That evening Amanda fixed dinner at her house, and Kirk realized it was the first home-cooked meal he'd had in months. Maybe longer. As he sat in her kitchen and watched her stir a potful of pasta, he thought about how it would feel to be with her every evening like this. To go to bed with her every night and wake up with her in the morning. In the past few days, he'd done the kind of soul-searching he thought he never would, wondering what his life was all about. Wondering what the future was going to bring. Now he realized how lonely he'd felt for the past few years, and how much he needed a woman like Amanda to fill up that emptiness.

But first he had to persuade her to come to Los Angeles.

After they finished eating, Kirk took her by the hand, drew her into his lap and whispered in her ear. "Ever do it on a kitchen table?"

She laughed softly. "We might want to do the dishes first."

"Nah. In the movies the hero always just sweeps the dishes away, hurls the heroine down on the table and has his way with her."

"You break my dishes," she said, moving in to kiss him, "and you're toast."

As her lips met his, her hair fell along her cheek, that gorgeous dark hair that he could spend hours just running his fingers through. He wrapped his hand around her thigh and gave it a gentle squeeze, sighing with satisfaction, wondering how he'd survived without this woman.

"Forget the table," he said. "Bed."

She laughed as he swept her into his arms and carried her to the bedroom, where he spent the next hour making love to her. For a long time afterward, they lay in silence. Kirk should have felt relaxed, but every moment that passed made him more and more edgy. This was their last night together. He'd be flying out of here tomorrow afternoon. They needed to talk about where they went from here, but the later it got, the more afraid he was to ask.

"I've been watching you for the past several days," Amanda said suddenly.

"What?"

"You're very good at coordinating the stunts. Have you ever thought about doing that all the time?"

Why was she asking about that? "Nope. I'm just filling in for Andy as a favor. It's not something I want to do for the rest of my life."

"Why not?"

"Because a stunt coordinator is under everyone's thumb. He has a lot of responsibility to make things happen, but he rarely has the time he needs to do it really well."

"You seemed to do it pretty well to me."

"Yeah, with Dan on my back the whole time. Producers and directors pop antacid like candy and take out their frustrations on everyone else. Where I'm at now, I take the jobs I want, leave the rest behind and let guys like Andy deal with all the crap. He's good at that. I'm not."

What he'd just told Amanda was true. Every word of it. But it wasn't the whole truth. It wasn't just that being a stunt coordinator meant dealing with men in authority.

It meant he'd never feel that rush again.

As a kid, he'd climbed the tallest trees. Dived into lakes when he was told not to. Skateboarded down hills that would have terrified the average kid. And when he'd gotten his driver's license, the street racing had started. He'd been arrested four times, but it never stopped him from doing it again.

He'd stumbled into a career as a stunt performer and knew he'd found his own brand of paradise. Not only did it give him the rush he craved, for the first time in his life, he was good at something. Growing up, he'd always been told he'd never amount to anything, but people respected his ability as a stunt performer. And he wasn't about to give that up.

Come tomorrow, he'd be back in Los Angeles, ready to get going again. He only hoped Amanda would eventually be coming with him.

"Amanda?" he said.

"Yes?"

"I can't leave tomorrow until you give me an answer. Will you come to California with me?"

She didn't answer right away, and every second that passed made him that much more apprehensive.

"I don't know if I can," she said.

Disappointment surged through him. "Okay. I know you're not crazy about the idea of moving back to a big city, but—"

"Kirk," she said. "Geography is the least of our problems."

"What do you mean?"

She rose on one elbow. To his surprise, she sat up in bed and flipped on the lamp. Picking up the covers, she pulled them slowly down to his waist, baring his chest. Then she ran her fingertips over one of his scars. "What happened here?"

He paused, wondering why she was asking. "A piece of burning debris fell on me during a battle sequence."

"What's this?" she asked, touching the long scar on his upper chest.

"I went along with a stunt coordinator's bad judgment on a motorcycle stunt."

"What are the others?"

"To tell you the truth, Amanda, I'd have to think a while to remember."

"You've had a lot of injuries."

"Most of them are old. I don't do fire anymore, and I've learned who to trust."

"There's hardly a place on you that hasn't been hurt. I can't even imagine what your X rays look like."

"They're no big deal. Just a couple of broken bones."

"If they're no big deal, then why wouldn't you authorize your doctor in Los Angeles to release them to me?"

He looked at her skeptically. "Amanda? Why are we talking about this?"

She sighed. "Look, I know you don't want to hear this. But I just don't think you know just how dangerous what you're doing is. One more blow to the head—"

"Amanda—"

"Will you listen to me?"

"Will you stop playing doctor for five minutes?"

"I'm not *playing* anything! I'm telling you what you're doing is dangerous. You could die!"

"You benched me for a week. I'm staying on the bench for a week. You told me I was good to go after that."

"I was speaking as your doctor. With no residual neurological damage, and with rest from the concussion, no doctor would keep you from working. He would explain the risk, then leave the decision up to you."

"Then there you go."

Her eyes began to glisten. "But now I'm speaking as somebody else. As somebody who cares about you. Who doesn't want to see you hurt. If I go to Los Angeles with you, I'll wonder every day if that's going to be the day you don't come home. And I don't think I can handle that." She lay back down again, her head on his shoulder. "Give it up, Kirk. Give it up before it's too late."

Give it up before some tragic accident happens. But she was also relaying another message. *Give it up before you lose me.*

"Amanda," he said, reaching over to stroke her hair. "We can work this out."

"I just wanted you to know that it's a problem."

"One that'll keep you from coming with me?"

She paused. "I don't know."

"I can probably cut back on the most dangerous stuff," he told her. "Take fewer jobs. Money's not a problem."

"But you'll still be doing it."

"I can't really believe that you'd ask me not to."

When she didn't respond, he felt a trickle of uneasiness. Was she trying to tell him it was over, but she just didn't want to come out and say it?

God, he hoped not.

Amanda flipped out the lamp and lay back down, but she still didn't say anything, and after several minutes, he realized she'd fallen asleep. He continued to lie there in the dark, staring at the ceiling, seized by the most terrible feeling that when he left for Los Angeles tomorrow, it would be the last time he'd see Amanda.

AMANDA WOKE IN THE MIDDLE of the night. The air was chilly, the room dark. Disoriented for a moment, she looked at the clock. It was three-twenty. She turned over.

Kirk wasn't there.

She looked toward the bathroom, but the light wasn't on, so she rose from the bed and walked into the living room to see light streaming in from the kitchen. When she came around the doorway, she saw Kirk sitting at her breakfast table, his head in his hands. A glass of water and a bottle of aspirin sat next to him.

"What's wrong?"

Startled by her voice, he glanced up, looking at her through weary eyes. "Just a headache. It'll pass."

She sat down next to him. "Have you been having other headaches?"

"Every once in a while, just like everyone else."

"This one drove you out of bed."

"I just happened to wake up. Came in here to grab some aspirin."

"Okay, then. Come back to bed."

He nodded and rose from the chair. But as he started to take a step, he stumbled to one side, putting his hand against the table to steady himself.

"Sit down," Amanda said, grabbing his arm.

He shook off her hand. "I'm fine."

"Is the dizziness worse since this recent accident?"

"It's three in the morning," he said sharply. "I'm half asleep. That's what the problem is."

"You're lying."

She stared at him a long time. He looked back with a rigid, uncompromising stare. Then slowly that expression gave way to one of resignation. He sat back down in the chair and dropped his head to his hands again.

Amanda felt a tremor of apprehension. "Has it happened other times since this most recent accident?"

He sighed. "Once."

"I'm worried about you," she said.

"I know."

"Stunt work," she said quietly. "You have to quit."

"Maybe. Someday."

"Someday may be too late."

Kirk was silent.

"What if you start to do a stunt, and then suddenly you feel as dizzy as you did just now? Or you hit your head again? What then?"

"It won't happen."

. "I want you to stop, Kirk. Completely."

He snapped his head up. "You already said I could start work again in a week."

"That was before I knew about this."

"Don't take this away from me, Amanda. Don't you *dare.*"

"Somebody needs to. If you keep on like this—"

"Stop it! Just *stop!*"

She drew back, stunned by his angry words and the look of defiance on his face.

"What if the tables were turned?" he said. "What then? Would you want to quit being a doctor?"

"If it threatened my life, yes."

"Well, then. I guess that's the difference between you and me."

She didn't know what else to say. She knew it would be pointless to get into another argument with him, because he knew. He knew the dangers, yet he insisted on ignoring them.

"I can't live like this, Kirk. I know too much about your condition, and I'll always worry that every stunt you do will be your last."

"So are you telling me it's over?"

She stared at him, tears welling up in her eyes, heartbroken that it had come to this. She opened her mouth to say something, only to close it again and look away, because there was nothing left to say.

Kirk dropped his head again, rubbing his eyes with the heels of his hands. Then he let out a heavy sigh. "I think maybe I should just go back to a room at the inn."

Those words cut Amanda right to the quick. She knew now that the divide between them was so huge that they'd never be able to bridge it.

He stood up and walked to the doorway leading to the living room, his gait a little shaky, only to stop and turn back.

"I need to know," he said. "Are you going to tell anyone about this?"

Amanda knew now that Kirk was like the man with a family history of lung cancer who refused to quit smoking, or a diabetic who kept eating sugar. People who knew something was bad for them, but they refused to stop doing it no matter what their doctors said. And there came a time when a doctor had to let a patient go. Let him do things that might be bad for him as long as he'd been informed of the consequences. And if she were only his doctor, she might be able to do that.

But she also happened to be in love with him. And that changed everything.

"I haven't decided yet," she said.

"I never thought you'd do this to me."

"Don't you understand? It's not something I'm doing *to* you! It's something I'm doing *for* you!"

His expression grew hard. "I'll find a way to work, Amanda. No matter how much you try to stop me."

He left the room. She sat at the table for the next few minutes, listening to Kirk in her bedroom as he got dressed and gathered up his things, and then his footsteps in the living room. The front door opening and closing.

Then...silence.

CHAPTER TEN

THE NEXT MORNING, KIRK arrived at the new location on the outskirts of Prescott, where they were going to shoot a fall from an old water tower. The crew had blocked off the area and then inflated an air bag to catch Colley's fall. As soon as Colley was ready, they could roll.

It looked to Kirk as if half the town had turned out to watch, but he hadn't seen Amanda yet. He'd barely gotten any sleep after leaving her house last night, and his head was pounding unmercifully. Almost nothing had gone right since the moment he arrived in Prescott, and now he felt as if his whole world was crashing down around him.

"McKenzie?"

He turned to see Dan behind him, and he wasn't a happy man. "We've got a problem."

"What?"

"Colley. He's refusing to do the stunt."

"Refusing? Why?"

"I don't know. But you'd better go talk to him."

"Where is he?"

"In the trailer."

In that moment, Kirk would cheerfully have shot Andy. Hadn't he told him Colley was going to be trouble? Hadn't he *told* him?

"Don't worry," Kirk said. "One way or the other, Colley's going off that tower in the next ten minutes, even if I have to throw him off myself."

AMANDA UNDERESTIMATED THE number of people who would turn out to watch this final day of shooting, and when she arrived at the water tower, she was forced to park two blocks away. But within a few minutes, she found Becky and checked in so they'd know she was on the set and the filming could start. Then she looked up at the tower, thanking God it wasn't Kirk who would be taking that dive.

She chatted with a few of the people in the crowd whom she knew, but the whole time she was furtively scanning the crew members, wondering where Kirk was. Part of her said it was best if she never saw him again, but another part of her was desperate for one last glance.

Finally she spotted him. He stood near the foot of the tower, wearing a black leather jacket, jeans and boots, which struck her odd, until she realized that he was dressed exactly like one of the biker gang members in the movie they were filming, complete with heavy silver chains around his neck. When she looked around and didn't see Colley, slowly it dawned on her.

Colley wasn't doing this stunt. Kirk was.

"Amanda?"

She turned to see Becky approaching her. "Kirk needs to see you."

"Me? Why?"

"He just told me to find you and bring you over."

Amanda's heart was beating like crazy as she followed

Becky, ducking under the rope that held the crowd at bay. Kirk took her by the arm and pulled her aside.

"What's going on?" Amanda said.

"Colley's refusing to do this stunt. And that means I have to. Dan's champing at the bit, but since the week you benched me isn't up until tomorrow, he needs your permission before I can do it."

She couldn't believe this. "Forget the week, Kirk. You have a much bigger problem than that."

"Dan doesn't know that. Not unless you tell him."

"If Colley's refusing to do it, just how dangerous is it? I mean, it has to be at least ten stories to the top of that thing."

"Nine. But that's not the problem. It involves going off backward, and apparently he's never done that before. But trust me. It's as straightforward a stunt as they come. I'll walk away, no problem."

"What if you don't?"

Kirk's expression grew hard. "It's my responsibility to make sure the job gets done. And I can't do that if you get in my way."

"I'm trying to *help* you!"

"Listen to me, Amanda. This profession is all I have. Growing up, I was told over and over what a rotten kid I was and that I would never amount to anything. Well, I have amounted to something. I finally have a little bit of self-respect, and I'm *not* going to let you take away the thing that gave that to me."

"I understand that," Amanda said. "I really do. But if I say nothing today and you end up dead because of it, how am I supposed to live with that?"

"I'm out of here, Amanda. In three hours, I'm gone.

So what possible difference could it make to you if I live or die?"

Oh, God, how could he not know the answer to that question? "The difference is…" She swallowed hard, fighting tears. "The difference is that I love you. I loved you fifteen years ago, and I love you now. And I'm *not* going to let you do something that might get you killed."

With that, she spun around, spied Dan standing by a camera and made her way toward him. Kirk called after her, but she ignored him, weaving around the crew members who were waiting for the shooting to start. Dan turned around, his face so strained with tension that his blood pressure had to be going through the roof.

"So what's the verdict?" Dan asked. "Is McKenzie good to go?"

She started to say it. She started to tell him what she'd witnessed last night, and that it was her professional opinion that not only should Kirk sit out this stunt, he should sit out every stunt for the rest of his life.

Then she looked back over her shoulder.

Kirk had sat down in a chair, his elbows on his knees, his head in his hands. He looked like a man who had lost everything.

She turned back. Tried to get herself to say it. But in that moment, she knew she couldn't do it. He wanted this profession more than anything. It was so tightly wound up with his personality and his self-image that he thought he'd be nothing without it. He wanted it so desperately that she couldn't take it away from him. And it wasn't in spite of the fact that she loved him.

It was because of it.

"Yeah, Dan," she said. "He's good to go."

Dan turned immediately and began to rally the troops. Amanda ducked back under the rope, got lost in the crowd and prayed that somehow, some way, Kirk would come to his senses and decide not to do it. She watched at a distance as Dan went over to talk to Kirk. And when he turned around, went into the tower and started up the stairs, her heart shattered.

KIRK STOOD ON THE LEDGE of the water tower nine stories above the ground, his mind so full of conflicting emotions that he felt dizzy from that alone.

He looked down with no fear at all. Anticipation, yes. Excitement, definitely. He craved the feeling of his stomach swooping up to his throat, followed by the high he always felt from knowing he'd pulled it off, the high that came from doing the only thing in his life he'd ever been good at.

As much as Colley was scared to jump, Kirk was scared not to. The idea of going back down the tower terrified him, because if he did, that would be it. The end. The acknowledgment that his career was over.

Then he thought about Amanda.

How they'd ended up at such cross purposes, he didn't know, but the moment she told him she loved him, he'd wanted to drop everything, take her in his arms and tell her he loved her, too. But he knew that even though she'd backed off today, in the future she would never let up. Eventually she'd insist he quit, taking away the very thing that made him who he was.

He put his hand to his forehead, feeling the blood pulsing through his skull, thinking about how things had changed in recent months, how he'd created a whirlwind of activity around himself—drinking too much, sleeping with a different woman in every city, driving hard and fast, all of it in an attempt to drown out the truth: if he miscalculated just a little one day on the job, or his head started swimming again, it could all be over in a matter of seconds.

But now he knew another truth. It wasn't dying he was afraid of. Living. That was what frightened him. Living with the knowledge that if he were gone tomorrow, not a solitary soul on this planet would truly give a damn.

But now that wasn't true. Amanda cared. She loved him.

Somewhere in that crowd below, she was watching. Waiting. Wondering what he was going to do. Praying, he knew, that he'd change his mind and come down off this water tower, no matter what she'd told Dan.

But the thought of that terrified him. What would he do if he couldn't do this?

For a moment, he saw nothing in his mind but a void, an emptiness he couldn't fight his way out of. And then it was as if a veil slowly lifted, revealing something good and strong and wonderful in his life that would take away the emptiness forever.

Amanda.

He closed his eyes, her face becoming clear in his mind. When he'd arrived in Prescott, he'd needed this, because he had nothing else. Now he did. Amanda had said she loved him. *She loved him.*

Instantly everything became clear. He still couldn't fathom why she'd wanted him as a teenager and even less why she wanted him now, but she did, and he'd be a damned fool to turn his back on that. He had no clue what he was going to do from now on to support himself. But as long as Amanda was in his life, he had the feeling that everything was going to be uphill from here.

He stared down at the people gathered on the ground, looking so tiny from nine stories up. He smiled a little at the thought of what he was getting ready to face. It wasn't going to be pretty, but he couldn't have cared less.

He backed away from the ledge, ducked back inside the tower, and hurried back down the circular staircase. When he emerged at the bottom, Dan was waiting for him.

"Will you cut out the crap and just do the stunt? You're a pro. Act like one!"

"You're right. I am. And there's one thing a pro always knows."

"What's that?"

"When to quit."

Kirk started walking toward the trailer. Dan shouted after him. "Quit? What the hell are you talking about? I need to get a stunt in the can! Now, am I going to get it, or not?"

"Oh, you'll get it, all right," Kirk said over his shoulder. He climbed the steps and yanked open the door. Colley looked up from where he sat and glared at Kirk.

"Get the hell out of here, McKenzie. I don't need you riding my ass about this."

"You did falls like this one at stunt school, right?"

"Not hanging backward off a water tower nine stories up!"

"A fall's a fall. It's all the same."

"But—"

"No buts. Get up, kid. You're coming with me."

"I'm not going anywhere."

Kirk leaned in and gave him a no-nonsense stare. "If you don't get out there and do that fall, you're finished in this business. Word of mouth will kill you. And most of those words will be coming from me."

"I can't go back out there! I just made an idiot of myself!"

"Do it now, or you never will."

Colley folded his arms and glowered at him. Kirk blew out a breath of disgust.

"Okay, kid. It chokes me to say this, which means you're only going to hear it once, so listen up. You've got talent. If you get your head on straight and your attitude in the right place, you can be a superstar in this business."

Colley blinked with surprise. "Really?"

"Yeah. Unless you let nerves get to you, in which case you can kiss it all goodbye. Is that really what you want? To give up?"

Colley bowed his head for a moment, his eyes closed. Finally he looked up again. "No. I don't."

"Good. Now, I want you to walk right out this door. Hold your head up and go right for the tower. No hesitation. I'll be right behind you."

Colley took a deep breath and did as Kirk said. They went inside the tower and started up the staircase. When they reached the top, the kid was so pale Kirk wondered if he was going to faint dead away. Colley grabbed the iron railing so tightly his fingers turned white. But at Kirk's direction, he climbed over it. Kirk gave Dan the okay sign. The cameras rolled, and Colley fell.

It was a beautiful landing.

Everybody applauded, complete with whistles and

catcalls. By the time Kirk made it back down the stairs, Colley was standing beside the air bag, looking a little shell-shocked.

Kirk grinned and clapped the kid on the shoulder. "Now, that," he said, "is the way it's supposed to be done."

Finally he coaxed a smile out of Colley. "Actually," he said, his voice a little shaky, "it was kinda fun."

Kirk let out a long, cleansing breath, then turned to look for Amanda.

AMANDA WAS OVERCOME BY the most profound sense of relief she'd ever felt in her life. Thank God Kirk had listened to her. He'd told Dan he was quitting, and he'd never be in that kind of danger again. Thank God—

"Amanda?"

She turned to see Kirk holding out his hand. "Come with me."

Confused, she took his hand, and he led her into the trailer, where he shut the door behind them and locked it. He took her by the shoulders and stared down at her.

"Tell me again," he said.

"What?"

"Tell me what you told me before."

She swallowed hard, knowing what he meant, but it had been hard enough to say it the first time.

"I love you," she said.

The moment the words were out of her mouth, Kirk dragged her into his arms and kissed her, a kiss so hard and determined that it took her breath away, gradually winding down into a kiss so slow and dreamy that she felt as if she were melting in his arms.

"I love you, too," he said. "And if you'll have me, from now on I'll never do anything more dangerous than walk down a flight of stairs, and if you ask me to, I swear to God I'll take the elevator."

"I know you're only quitting because of me. Are you sure it's what you really want to do?"

"If you only knew how I felt when you told me you loved me, you'd never even ask that."

She looked away, still unsure. He touched his finger to her chin and pulled it back until she was looking at him again.

"I felt this swooping sensation in my stomach," he told her. "A feeling that I was totally in the moment and nothing else on earth mattered. I crave that kind of feeling, Amanda. I always have. When I was a kid, I got it by skateboarding and street racing. As an adult, I got it by jumping off buildings. And now…" He smiled. "I get it when you tell me you love me."

Finally she understood the boy he'd been all those years ago, acting so wild and reckless in an attempt to fill the emotional void he'd always felt, but everything he did was nothing more than a pale substitute for the love he was really looking for. So from now on, she was going to love him so much he would never feel empty again.

"That was a good thing you did with Colley," she said.

"I had to do something before Dan had a heart attack."

"It was more than that. He could have left here humiliated, and you made sure that didn't happen. And considering he pulled it off without a hitch, it looks as if you're a pretty good teacher, too."

"Yeah. Maybe I am."

He leaned in to kiss her again, only to stop short. He looked away, and for a moment she could practically see his wheels turning.

"Kirk?"

A smile spread slowly across his face.

"What?" she asked.

"I'm not sure. I have an idea, but…"

"What is it?"

"I may not be able to do the dangerous stuff anymore, but nothing's stopping me from teaching it."

"Teaching it?"

"What if I open a stunt school?"

"A stunt school?"

"Okay, it's a little crazy, and I'm going to have to check into some things, but…" He smiled. "I just might be able to make it work."

Amanda felt herself caught up in his enthusiasm, but at the same time she couldn't help but feel a little down. She thought about Prescott, about the clinic, about Louise, and the life she had wanted to build here.

"What's wrong?" Kirk asked.

"Nothing," she said. "Nothing at all. It'll take me a while to settle things here, but…" She forced a smile. "I've never been to Los Angeles. I imagine it's a great place to live."

Kirk blinked with surprise. "Are you telling me you'd move there for me?"

"You're giving up the stunt work you love. Moving to Los Angeles is the least I can do for you."

He smiled and gave her a hug. "That's good to know, sweetheart. But it's not necessary. You don't have to come to Los Angeles. I can open a school here."

"Here? But aren't most stunt schools based in Los Angeles?"

"Actually, they're all over the country. Most of them offer intensive courses that are only a few days long to learn a specific skill. That's exactly what I can do here. And Austin is nearby. All kinds of films are being shot in the hill country now, so that proximity will help. With the referrals I can get from Andy alone I should be able to get things rolling."

"Kirk, you realize you're talking about staying in Prescott."

"Yeah," he said with a dramatic sigh. "I know. But love does funny things to a man. Let's go get a cup of coffee, and I'll tell you more about what I'm thinking."

TWO DAYS LATER, KIRK AND Amanda were sitting in a booth at Hanson's with a real estate agent and the owner of the old lumber warehouse where they'd shot several scenes. Kirk had taken another look at it and knew it was the perfect place for the school. There were flights of stairs. Catwalks. Plenty of room to get mats in there to teach stage combat. All they had to do is get utilities in there and pretty the place up a little, and it would be the perfect location. And the owner was more than ready to sell.

Kirk had already started asking permission of a few local ranchers to use vacant land to teach car and motorcycle stunts. He'd told Andy about his plans, and he said he'd start spreading the word immediately, so when Kirk was ready to open, he could get off to a flying start. And Kirk started putting together a list of stunt performers whom he was sure he could persuade to come to

Texas to teach a few workshops. As each detail came together, Amanda could see his enthusiasm growing.

"You're going to miss doing stunts, aren't you?" she asked him that evening when they were curled up on the sofa together.

"I'd be lying if I said I wasn't."

"I'll tell you what. We'll go to amusement parks once a month so you can ride the roller coasters."

"You'd ride roller coasters with me?"

"God, no. I'd wave to you from the ground, though."

He laughed and hugged her, then pushed her down to her back on the sofa and kissed her until their laughter died away. When she opened her eyes again he could see *I love you* there as plainly as if she'd said it, and he felt that rush all over again.

"When I saw you up there on the water tower, ready to jump…" She brushed a lock of hair away from his forehead.

"Yeah?" he said.

"I thought about losing you again, only this time forever."

And he was going to thank God every day of his life that he'd made the decision to take the long way down off that tower rather than the short one.

"Wait until everyone in town hears that you're staying in Prescott," Amanda said with a smile. "Think of the gossip we're going to cause."

"Yeah, we are, aren't we?" Kirk gave her an evil grin. "Why don't we get it started right away?"

He took Amanda by the hand and pulled her over to the window.

"This one's for you, Mrs. Taggert."

He ripped the newspaper off the window, then took Amanda in his arms and kissed her long and hard. With luck, the old lady would get an eyeful, and before the day was out, the news would spread to the Cut Hut and beyond, and everybody in Prescott, Texas, would know that this boy was back in town to stay.

FORWARD PASS

Dorien Kelly

PROLOGUE

12:01 a.m., June 2, 1991

BUDDIES, BS AND BEER should have been three of the best things in a guy's life. Should have been, but on this warm June night, they weren't doing much for eighteen-year-old Matt O'Connell. He was feeling angry and restless, wishing for a gust of wind to cut through the heavy air and carry him straight out of Prescott, Texas. But he'd be leaving soon enough, anyway.

Matt stood close to the edge of the campfire he'd built with his friends, Kirk McKenzie and Caleb Tanner, wondering what kind of an ass he was to be this unhappy when from the outside his life was perfect.

Team quarterback.

Plenty of money.

Enough girls wanting to go up the road to Trehan Point and get naked with him that he had no right to complain.

Next to him, Caleb opened a beer. "Another year done."

"Our last," Matt replied.

"Good thing," Caleb said, echoing Matt's thoughts. "I don't think we could have come up with anything better than moving that junkyard for next year's stunt. The Pick 'n Trade is unbeatable, O'Connell. Your best idea yet."

"Right up until I got caught," Matt said. And the only ones who knew that he had been were Caleb, Kirk, the sheriff, the Delisles and Matt's parents.

"Come on, man," Caleb said. "You're a freakin' legend! Did you see the look on people's faces when they saw all that crap on the high school lawn? Who cares if you ticked off that crazy Delisle guy?" He took a swig of beer, then added, "And thanks for not ratting us out."

Matt shrugged. "It was no big deal."

"Wouldn't have worked that way if it had been me they'd caught," Kirk said. "The last thing my old man would have done was save my ass with the sheriff."

Though it was stupid to feel this way, Matt was mightily sick of having his ass saved. Just once he wanted to play by the same rules that everyone else did. But he was an O'Connell, and his dad had the local system greased.

Tired of thinking about his own problems, Matt turned to Kirk. "So I heard that after what happened last night, Amanda broke up with you."

Kirk downed a swallow of his beer, then answered. "It was just as well. I was going to break it off with her after graduation, anyway."

By the sound of Kirk's voice, he didn't want to talk about yesterday's car accident...or Amanda. Matt felt bad for his friend, since Amanda was the only girl who'd ever been able to make Kirk a little less of a hard-ass. Hell, he'd even laughed when he was with her.

"So, when you taking off?" Matt asked.

"Tomorrow night. I'm going to California."

"Yeah? Why California?"

"Because it isn't Prescott."

Which made sense to Matt. Kirk and Caleb both had it way rougher than Matt ever had, but where Caleb just shrugged a lot of it off, Kirk didn't. He wasn't the kind of guy to share details, and Matt wasn't the sort to ask, but he knew it wasn't exactly smooth living at the McKenzie house.

"I'm leaving tomorrow night, too," Caleb said. "I've already told my grandmother I've got a friend in Austin who thinks he can get me a job. She's so thrilled at the thought of my being employed she barely said a word. How about you, Matt? You gonna work at the golf club again this summer?"

Matt shook his head. "I'm moving up to Oklahoma to live with my uncle and get in shape before the season starts."

He'd be trading the Prescott Panthers' orange and black for the same colors at Oklahoma State. The way he was feeling, even that was too much sameness. But at least he'd go back to being a freshman grunt on the team, and his father would be too far away to show up at every damn practice.

And he wouldn't have to wake up every morning wondering if he'd cross paths with Jamie Delisle, either. He'd known her forever, and until the last time he'd been alone with her, she'd been the sweetest girl he'd ever met. Smart as a whip, too. Then she'd kind of made a pass at him. Okay, more than kind of...she'd made a full pass, complete with a box of rubbers waved in his face. Not sweet and not smart.

He'd freaked out, and not so many nights later, freaked out her dad by moving the junkyard. Matt's dad had made sure that the stunt was kept quiet, so

Matt wouldn't lose that full-ride scholarship up in Stillwater.

Caleb grinned. "Are you gonna remember us when you make the NFL? Seriously, you know hanging out with you guys was the only thing that made this shit town bearable for the past two years."

Matt didn't see much point in answering. No way would Caleb believe that at the moment Matt didn't give a dead armadillo's rump about the NFL. That he was sick of all the hometown hero ass-kissing. That he was pissed off at everyone in Prescott and he didn't know *why* he felt like that.

So instead, Matt raised his beer and gave the toast that had become their tradition. "To Jim Morrison, James Dean and all the rebels who knew when to die. You went out big, and we salute you."

The toast to the Dead Rebels did nothing. Matt felt as hollow as he had since the night they'd moved the Pick 'n Trade.

Kirk stood and tossed his beer bottle into the scrubby bushes outside the glow of their fire. It hit against another bottle with a sharp clink. "I've got to go," he said.

"So soon?" Caleb asked.

"I have things to do. I'll see you guys tomorrow."

Kirk left, Caleb drank and Matt sunk back into his thoughts. Tomorrow. Graduation. Shit. He wondered if Jamie's dad was going to be there.

Or even Jamie.

Last night, he'd eavesdropped on his dad and mom talking in low voices. His mom had said that Mr. Delisle had been admitted to the hospital for some long-term help. And the way she'd said that word—*help*—had sounded so full of pity that Matt had felt sick.

He knew there was stuff going on that he was being spared, but he couldn't even get them to talk about the Delisles to his face. He'd tried again tonight, and had gotten so pissed off that he'd busted one of his mom's dishes right at the supper table. And then he'd left before he could see more of the disappointment on his mother's face...or hear more of his father's warnings that he should just shut up and keep his act together until it was time to leave for Stillwater. And how one day Matt would know just what a lucky boy he was.

Like he didn't already. He was so lucky that he hated himself. He drained his beer and then raised the empty bottle in farewell to Kirk, who was as usual, peeling out like a maniac on the road below. Each of them was going to leave Prescott in their dust, and Matt O'Connell couldn't wait.

CHAPTER ONE

A warm November morning, fifteen years later…

A WISE MAN ONCE SAID THAT you can never go home again. As Jamie Delisle drove into Prescott, she was having a tough time locating the downside of that piece of philosophy. Though the Prescott Pick 'n Trade had been replaced by a strip mall, she averted her eyes from its former site. Fifteen years might have passed since she'd lived in the shabby little house hidden behind the Pick 'n Trade's stacks of junk, but time hadn't done much to blunt the embarrassment. Old habits died hard, and old memories even harder.

Gripping the steering wheel tighter with hands already tense from nerves, Jamie reminded herself that she wasn't just the junkman's daughter any longer, and that her days of trying to be invisible were in her past. She hadn't even yet hit thirty-five and already she had a waiting list of interior design clients in her adopted hometown of Chicago, where she was known for her sleek, almost minimalist style. She had enough money that she would never have to wear secondhand clothes again. Of course she still did, but these were vintage chic, and not embarrassingly time-worn relics chosen out of the Community Giving Closet in the back room at church.

Still here she was, the Tuesday before Thanksgiving, feeling totally thankless about being back in town. She'd given up on believing that she'd enjoy her fifteenth high school reunion on Friday night. Jamie aimed for mere survival. No matter how hard her best—and pretty much only—high school friend, Crystal, had begged, Jamie had refused to attend reunions five and ten. But when this one had rolled around, Crystal caught her in a weak moment and she'd said yes. Now she worried that everyone in Prescott would see through her glossy new exterior to the old Jamie beneath.

"Idiot," she told herself as she pulled into the quaint downtown historical district. "You've got nothing to prove. Nothing at all."

And honestly, if she did have something to prove, she was armed for the task. Last week she'd spent far too much money on a reunion wardrobe, and today she'd picked a sleek convertible import at the airport rental lot when she was usually an economy-model sort of girl. Her credit card limit should consider itself lucky that Crystal, who was the reunion treasurer, had sworn up and down that Matt O'Connell wasn't attending. Heaven knew how much money Jamie would have spent for sufficient ammo to deal with facing him.

Jamie's cell phone rang, so she wheeled into the first available spot and immediately regretted her choice of stopping places. She wrinkled her nose at the old sandstone storefront that lodged the O'Connell Insurance Agency's offices. There was no escaping the O'Connell family in Prescott, which was why she felt blessed to have escaped Prescott altogether.

She flipped open her persistently ringing phone. "Hello?"

"Hey, Jamie, it's Crystal. Are you here yet?"

She smiled at the excited tone of her friend's voice. Her welcoming committee might be small, but it was genuine.

"Just down the street from the Bluebonnet," Jamie said, referring to the Bluebonnet Inn, Prescott's only hotel with any measure of character.

"What? You're heading to the inn already? Don't you think you should stop to see your mom and dad first?"

"No." In fact, she'd been wondering if there was any diplomatic way to avoid seeing her father at all. She knew there wasn't, but "sweet and daughterly" during her parents' semiannual visits to Chicago was far easier to manage than "sweet and daughterly" smack in the middle of Prescott.

"You have to see him sooner or later."

"Later, thanks."

Crystal let loose one her drama-girl sighs. "You can hold a grudge tighter than my Corey can a dime, and that's saying a lot, Jamie Lee Delisle. You should go over to their place right now. It's the right thing to do, and…"

Jamie blocked the sound of Crystal's lecture and absently noted the hot-looking early-twentysomething guy who'd slowed to stroll by her car. She would have figured he was just checking out her exotic wheels, except for the "hey, babe" smile he was giving her. Maybe she should spend a stupid amount of money on a cut and highlights from Chicago's stylist to the stars (such as there were in Chicago) more often….

"Jamie? Are you listening to me? *Jamie?*"

Jamie grinned at the jailbait as he passed, then turned her attention back to her friend. "I'm listening now, and you're not fooling me, Crystal. The only reason you're all over my case is because you're running late. You're not at the inn yet, are you?"

"Late? I'm not late!"

That would be a first.

"Good, because I'm pulling into the parking lot," Jamie lied. "Meet me at the front door."

"Okay, so you caught me," Crystal said after a brief pause. "I'm still at the Cut Hut waiting for Ruby to blow-dry me. Can't have bad hair for reunion week. It's bad enough that I've still got twenty pounds of baby weight, and the baby's out of diapers."

"You'll look gorgeous," Jamie reassured her. "You always do. Tell you what, I'll go check in, get settled and give you thirty minutes to meet me in the lobby, okay?"

"Thirty should do it."

Which meant more like sixty.

They said their 'byes, then Jamie really headed to the Bluebonnet, which like most of Prescott was a mix of the old and the new. When she pulled in the lot to the side of the original building, she gave herself a second to admire the place. The front portion of the Bluebonnet was the old Prescott mansion, built of hardy stone by Hiram Prescott, who'd founded the town back in the 1800s and had owned everything from the mercantile to the whorehouse. The mansion bore the stamp of a man with no lack of pride. It rose to three solid stories, and its rooflines were ornamented by Victorian filigreed ironwork that the current owners had painted an unfortunate shade of salmon.

Sometime back in the 1980s, those same owners had also built an annex that smacked more of chain hotel than historic original, but Jamie had grown as adept at ignoring that as she had her surroundings in the Pick 'n Trade. As a child, Jamie had loved to walk slowly by the inn and pretend that it was still a private home...*her* private home. She'd had few opportunities to get much past the threshold before leaving Prescott, which was why she'd stretched her credit card far enough to reserve a suite in the pricier mansion. It wasn't too often that a girl got to live out her dreams.

Purse slung over her shoulder, Jamie walked up the inn's tall front steps, then entered its air-conditioned interior. She was thankful for the cool air, as the jump from cold winds curling off Lake Michigan to Texas warmth had left her internal thermostat messed up. Or maybe it was just part of the jitters that had grown stronger as she'd approached town.

A middle-aged woman stood behind the hotel's reception desk, which Jamie knew from her Bluebonnet addiction was a cut-down piece of the bar from Hiram Prescott's long-gone and very fancy saloon. Jamie approached, and the woman greeted her.

"Hi, I'm Jamie Delisle," Jamie said in return. "I've reserved a room in the main house." She extracted her credit card from her purse and slid the plastic across the counter.

"Right. Let me check on that." The woman frowned as she looked at whatever her computer screen was telling her. "Your reservation is for today?" she asked after what seemed to Jamie like an aeons-long pause.

"Yes, arriving today and departing Sunday, the

twenty-seventh," she replied. She knew she hadn't screwed this up. Once she'd committed to coming to Prescott, she'd made sure that her trip was going to be as painless as possible.

"Delisle…" the woman murmured, still focused on the computer. "Any other name it could be under?"

"No, and I made the reservation over three months ago. I'm supposed to have the Arabelle Suite," she said, not that she really expected the information to help.

The clerk looked at the monitor a bit longer, then shook her head. "I'm so sorry, I don't know what happened, Ms. Delisle. I don't have your name in the system. Would you happen to have your confirmation number?"

Jamie dug through her brand-new and too-small purse, which was among her reunion purchases. It took only a moment to realize that while she'd intentionally left the bulkier stuff like her checkbook behind, she'd also failed to pack her PDA in the move from the old bag to the new.

"I thought I brought it along, but I don't seem to have it. Is this a problem?"

The clerk gave a quick tick of an apologetic smile. "It looks like I have some good news and some bad news for you. The good news is that I have a room available, which is nearly a miracle considering that we have Thanksgiving visitors and folks for a high school reunion in town."

"I know. I'm here for the reunion," she said, trying to quell both her impatience and a surge of disappointment.

"Well, isn't that nice?" the clerk said.

Jamie nodded as the heavy entry door behind her opened and then closed with a thud.

"The bad news?" she asked the clerk, who'd just finished telling the person behind Jamie that she'd be right with them.

"Oh, yes… The bad news is that the only available room is in the annex, not the mansion."

"But considering that I made my reservation months ago, surely you can do a little moving around? I've wanted to stay in the mansion for as long as I can remember."

"I'm sorry, but if you had your confirmation number…"

Jamie began rummaging for her cell phone. Maybe she could call her next-door neighbor, who kept a key for emergencies, and see if she could go into Jamie's apartment and find her PDA. It had to be resting in its charger next to her computer.

"Just give me a second," she said, unable to capture her phone. Swear to heaven, she was going to bell that thing like she would a cat.

"If you don't mind stepping aside, I'll help the gentleman while you're looking."

"No hurry," the male behind her said, and Jamie froze as the fine hairs on the back of her neck stood at attention.

Impossible.

Well, technically not impossible, since to the best of her knowledge Matt O'Connell wasn't in a Turkish prison or at the bottom of the sea—both of which the guy deserved—but Jamie had been promised that her personal ghost of humiliations past wouldn't be in Prescott. His presence equaled an insurmountable worst-case scenario. Matt and lust and sex and guilt and anger were knotted together in her mind in a way that would make a Freudian psychologist pant and drool.

Survival instinct kicked in. Jamie didn't turn and didn't acknowledge her nemesis's presence. Instead she tried for the calm she summoned when dealing with rich but totally pain-in-the-butt clients. People just like O'Connell. Unfortunately she seemed to have left her calm in Chicago, along with that confirmation number.

Jamie knew she needed to focus on the crisis she faced, rather than the one standing close enough behind her that she fancied she could catch a whiff of subtle aftershave. But as she'd accepted when passing the site of her former home, old memories died damn hard.

Obviously, Matt would still be tall, unless one of the numerous ill wishes she'd cast on him fifteen years ago had come true. Perhaps fate had brought him a beer belly and male-pattern baldness to balance against those years when he'd been Prescott's favored son and star quarterback...and ironically enough, also the town's biggest piece of grief. She could hope, but she would *not* turn and look.

She maintained a congenial tone of voice for the clerk. "I'll have the confirmation number for you in no time, I promise. I just need to have a friend back home look it up for me. Now, can't you just book me into the mansion, and we can all get on with our day?"

"As I said, the best I can do, ma'am, is to give you a room in the annex. If we have some cancellations, then maybe——"

"Am I booked in the mansion?" asked the voice of humiliations past. "O'Connell. Matt O'Connell."

Right. Like Bond, James Bond. Or Ego, Huge Ego.

The clerk fiddled with the computer for a moment, then said that he was, indeed.

"Then why don't you give the lady my room?"

"Are you sure, Mr. O'Connell? Your father's secretary was here earlier and said—"

"I'm sure," he replied in a way that cut short the clerk's fawning.

"Then it looks as though we have a room available," the clerk said to Jamie.

Pride dictated that she should decline the offer. The idea of getting her lodging dreams fulfilled by the classmate she'd most despised sat no lighter than her mother's leaden chicken-fried steak. But Jamie was nothing if not practical, so she readied herself to face Matt O'Connell and get yet another dose of his near pity.

She eased her tense mouth into a polite smile and tried to cloak some of the anger that she was sure had worked its way up her spine and straight into her eyes. Then she turned.

Damn. He wasn't bald. Or fat. If anything, Matt was more gorgeous than ever, which just went to prove that Mother Nature could be an evil old crone. He still had the same thick brown hair with just enough wave to make it interesting. He wore it shorter now, though. More businessman than hotshot quarterback. His skin was still a golden tan, as though he spent time in the sun. Jamie was Chicago-pale, and feeling almost resentful for it. Well, for that and the fact that she still found him attractive, dammit.

"Thank you for offering your room," she said. "But you really don't have to do this."

Matt looked at her with some curiosity, plus the same frank appreciation that a lot of guys had shown since she'd emerged from her invisible phase. No big deal.

What shocked her was that she could detect zero spark of recognition in his blue eyes. Nada.

Jamie knew she wasn't the ridiculously skinny thing she used to be, and that she'd quit slouching years ago and learned to love her height, but just as she could see the younger iteration of Matt under the sun-creased lines at the corners of his eyes, couldn't he see *her?* Or maybe she'd been so invisible to him that she'd never existed at all.

"It's no problem. Really," he said as though sharing a secret, "I don't like all the fuss and ornate stuff in the old rooms."

Count yourself lucky you've seen them, hotshot.

"Well, thank you," she said again while trying to dial down on her resentment level. "It was very kind of you." And then she turned away before her false smile froze permanently in place.

The clerk took her credit card information, had her sign some paperwork, then set an old-fashioned brass skeleton key on the counter. "As you can see, the locks to the mansion rooms are vintage, too, so I'd suggest you keep your valuables in the office safe."

Jamie could feel Matt moving to her side. His continued attention made her supremely angry…mostly at herself. Considering the way he'd treated her just before graduation, she should be sobbing for joy that he couldn't recall her. She'd suffered enough O'Connell damage in her life, thank you very much.

"It's okay. I've got nothing worth stealing," Jamie said to the clerk.

The clerk nodded. "You have the Lonestar Suite, Ms. Delisle. Second floor, last door at the end of the hallway.

There's an elevator in the back parlor, along with the stairs just over there," she said, gesturing at the sweeping mahogany staircase with its rich Persian runner that dominated the entry. "Do you have any bags that you'd like help with?"

"No." She'd grab her suitcase from her car later... once she was certain that the lobby was free of Matt O'Connell. "Thank you," she added, then slung her purse back over her shoulder.

She turned away from the desk and was ready to make her break when Matt settled his hand on her arm, then stepped in front of her.

"Jamie? It *is* you, then, isn't it? Jamie Delisle?"

She supposed she could deny her identity, but it was bound to be plastered on her in the form of a big, fat name tag, come Friday night.

"Yes, I'm Jamie."

She got that O'Connell-patented slow grin, the one that had fueled her teen-girl fantasies, right up until the week before graduation, when he'd shredded what little pride she'd ever had.

"It's great to see you," he said, and, to Jamie's ears, he sounded sincere.

He reached out his hand, and she took it. He had a firm, warm grip, but not soft. She found herself ever so briefly wondering what he'd been doing since they'd both left Prescott. She always cut off Crystal's gossip when it strayed to Matt O'Connell.

"You look incredible," he was saying. "Amazing. Life's been treating you well, I take it?"

"Well enough," she replied, noting that not only had he *not* released her hand, he appeared to have forgotten that he held it. Weird, she thought. Very, very weird. But also entertaining.

"So you're here for the reunion, right?" he asked.

"I am." She tried to draw back her hand, but he just kept looking at her as though she were the most surprising thing he'd ever seen. She had to admit that her ego was happily preening under the attention.

"Maybe we can get together for a drink or something before then," he offered.

She thought back to those days when he'd treated her like a stray puppy. One with fleas. She knew she should turn him down cold, but some little gremlin in her mind wouldn't let her.

"That would be…interesting," she replied.

"Are you doing anything for dinner tonight?" he asked, still not giving up her hand.

"I haven't made any plans."

"Then have it with me. Please."

She was no fool. After a long, drab youth, she knew firsthand about the dynamics of power, and now it seemed she finally had some over Matt O'Connell. If she were going to be mature Jamie, the one who'd forged her own successful path away from Prescott, she should shrug off the thought. But she wasn't feeling especially mature at the moment. She was feeling more… giddy.

Jamie drew in a surprised breath. *Giddy?*

Yes, as giddy as a cheerleader surfing a sugar buzz, heaven help her. She had power! The question was, should she use it for good or evil? Evil, unfortunately, sounded very appealing.

She suspected that the growing sense of excitement

making her heart beat faster and her skin tingle was likely to get her in a whole lot of trouble, and didn't say much about the petty state of her soul. But this was fantasy land…a handful of days out of her real life back in Chicago. She could do what she wanted and then move on.

And right now, to the bottom of her hungry—okay, and petty—soul, Jamie Delisle wanted to prove to Matt O'Connell that revenge was a dish best served very, *very* hot.

CHAPTER TWO

MATT HARDLY HAD A CHANCE to dump his travel bag onto the middle of his bed before his cell phone rang. Before answering, he checked the caller ID to see if this was work or pleasure. Turned out it was neither.

"Hi, Dad."

"I heard you were in town," Jack O'Connell said.

"Your spies are everywhere, aren't they?"

His father laughed. "In Prescott, you'd better believe it. So how's the room?"

"Fine," Matt said as he looked around. It was like every other hotel room he'd been in, and over the years he'd been in his share.

"Fine? You *are* in the Lonestar Suite, aren't you?"

"I gave up the suite to Jamie Delisle," he said, knowing he was smiling like a fool at the thought of her. "We're having dinner tonight, too."

"Jamie *who?*"

"Delisle. She was in my graduating class.... Delisle... The Pick 'n Trade? Remember?" Or maybe his father had paid or talked Matt's way out of so many stunts that he'd forgotten that last one. Matt never would.

"Never mind about Jamie-whoever. It's your room

I'm thinking of. I sent my secretary over there this morning to perk it up some."

"What do you mean, perk it up?" It wasn't as though his dad cared about interior decor any more than Matt did.

"Just some welcome-home reminders since you refused to stay under your family's roof."

"I didn't refuse. It's just with the hours I'll probably be keeping—"

His father's sly chuckle sent Matt back a decade and a half. "Got something planned with the boys, son? A little prank brewing?"

"Hardly. The *boys* are in their thirties now, just like me. And most of them have wives and kids." Unlike him. And then it struck him that he'd never even asked Jamie if she was married. And immediately after that, he wondered why the thought had struck him in the first place. All he had in mind was a laid-back night of barbecue at Hanson's and some good company. Not getting laid.

"Come on, y'all have to be planning some sort of get-together. The team...or maybe that Kirk McKenzie? Word is he's back in these parts."

"I don't know." Matt sat on the foot of the bed and shook his head at the glut of bluebonnet pictures on the wall in front of him. Maybe he did care a little about decorating. "I've been busting my rear at work and haven't talked much to anyone. I'm just going to kick back, okay?"

"Well, whatever you do, keep Thanksgiving morning open. Your brother has the game films from Jett's first season as quarterback, and—"

"Deuce has *all* of the game films?" That could eat up the rest of the week.

"Of course, all of 'em. And he wants you to run through 'em with the kid. The scouts are thicker than flies on manure at the boy's games, and we can't afford to screw this up."

Matt hoped that Jett was holding up under the pressure of being the latest NFL hope of the O'Connell clan. And he hoped that if Jett didn't make it, the elder O'Connells wouldn't be as flat-out unforgiving as they'd been with Matt.

Football wasn't just a Texas-size thing with Matt's dad. It was his lifeblood. He'd been destined to be an NFL Hall of Famer until a back injury had cut his career short. When, first, Deuce hadn't played up to O'Connell snuff, and then Matt's career had ended, his dad had become more rabid in his need to see another O'Connell in the NFL.

"I haven't played a down of football in eleven years," Matt said to his father. "What am I going to be able to tell Jett?" And whatever it was, he was sure his nephew would have already heard it—and heard it and heard it—from both his dad and granddad.

His dad gave a hoarse laugh. "It's been more than thirty-five years since I stepped into the pocket, and I can guaran-damn-tee you never forget."

At least his dad hadn't. All these years later, Matt could recite most of his dad's—and older brother Deuce's—tales of football glory right along with them. Putting aside his family's bizarre expectations, he'd enjoyed his own time playing, but his life hadn't ended when after a bold—and in retrospect, stupid—play he'd called had totally blown out his left knee during his senior year of college. In fact, Matt pegged that event as the thing that had allowed him to really live.

"So, Thursday morning?" his dad asked.

"Yeah…Thursday morning for sure." With luck, anticipating his mother's fried turkey and apple-cornbread stuffing would coast him past the worst of the pain.

"And stop by the house today and say hello to your mother, or I'll never hear the end of it, come tonight."

"I was figuring on lunch there."

"Then watch out. Your mama's on a no-carbohydrate, no-fat binge. She'll be feeding you dried kelp or some other such garbage."

Matt laughed. "And for her I'll eat it, so long as she still does Thanksgiving up right. Talk to you later, Dad."

Gritty from his three-plus-hour drive from Houston, Matt took a quick shower and had just pulled on fresh jeans and a shirt when someone knocked at his door.

He took a look through the peephole, and Jamie, who had what appeared to be picture frames in her hands, laughed as though she could see his exercise of caution.

"I come bearing gifts," she called through the wood. "Your gifts."

Matt swung open the door, and she strolled inside.

"Just out of the shower?" she asked, letting her gaze travel from his bare feet to his still-wet hair.

"Yup."

Matt was more subtle in checking her out. First, he noted the lack of a wedding ring and his own rush of relief. Then he moved on. He didn't recall her legs being as long as they were in the short blue skirt she'd changed into. And he definitely didn't remember her smile being so confident. The legs were nice, but the smile was a heart-stopper. It made him linger on her eyes, an amber-brown that he'd always remembered, even though those eyes had usually looked on him with a sort of blunt and skeptical expression that had let him know his so-called status hadn't meant squat to her.

"I thought you might have more use for these than I do," she said, then handed him two framed eight-by-ten photos. "They were arranged on the dresser in my room."

Matt looked at the high school pictures and tried not to wince. Matt as quarterback. Matt as homecoming king. Dad seemed to be a little short on the Matt-behind-bars and Matt-acting-like-a-horse's-ass shots.

"My dad's idea of a welcome," he said, feeling damn embarrassed. He put the pictures facedown on the nightstand.

"Then I'd guess that the huge flower arrangement is from your dad, too?"

He didn't like the sound of this. "Flower arrangement?"

She nodded. "Horseshoe-shaped with the word *touchdown* printed on a big ribbon. It's standing right next to the bed, too. Overkill, don't you think?"

"You're kidding, right?" he asked, though he'd had stranger things arrive. The dominatrix-clad stripper in his dorm room his freshman year of college—just after his dad had complained that Matt was becoming pussy-whipped by a new girlfriend—wasn't easily forgotten. All in all, Matt preferred to believe that Deuce, a witness to the argument, had been behind that one.

"Yes, I'm kidding!" Jamie said. She shook her head in a bemused sort of way. "If you bought into that one, I'll bet you've got some interesting stories in your Big Man on Campus repertoire."

"One or two," he allowed.

Now that Jamie wasn't holding anything, he noticed that her top was one of those gauzy things just thin enough to make any red-blooded guy's eyes work overtime to pick up a few details, even if that guy generally did his best to act socially correct. And since Matt was in that league, after a brief glimpse he tried to keep his gaze north of the forbidden.

"There was also a six-pack of Shiner beer on ice, but I'm keeping that," Jamie said. "I've never tried it."

"Now it's my turn…. You're kidding, right? You made it all the way through high school without even stealing a sip of someone's Shiner?"

"I was a good girl," she said, after giving him a quick smile. "But by now, I've gotten over it."

She had been a good girl, too. Nice to everyone, quiet, and pretty in that same quiet way. She'd been too nice to play things on the surface, which was why he'd run like hell when she'd politely requested that he relieve her of her virginity.

Had she been any one of a number of other girls— the ones just out for some good, sweaty, no-commit-ment-required sex—he'd have done the deed with pleasure. But even back then, he'd known that Jamie was off limits. And the knowledge that as much as he had wanted her, he couldn't have her, was maybe a little of what had sparked the Pick 'n Trade fiasco.

In retrospect, he'd give himself credit for at least having known he was a horse's ass while busy acting like one. She'd deserved better for her first time with a guy, and he hoped she'd gotten it.

Jamie tilted her head and looped her honey-colored hair behind one ear. He wondered if her hair would feel sleek under his fingers. Not that he deserved to touch, but damn, he wanted to.

"Why are you looking at me that way?" she asked.

"What way?"

"Like I'd just practiced one of my *tang soo do* moves on you. Karate," she added when he couldn't get words past the old memories and to his mouth quickly enough. "You've got to be equipped if you live alone in the big city."

"I'm sure no one would mess with you twice."

She grinned. "I'm hoping not, but in some cases, once would be nice."

Once would be nice? Matt read a certain amount of suggestiveness into those words. Or maybe it was just wishful thinking.

"So what time do you want to meet for dinner?" she asked.

He yanked his mind off a little mattress mambo. "Six-thirty?"

"Good. That should give me some time to take care of a couple of things. Casual, I'm guessing?"

"How does barbecue at Hanson's sound?"

"Like heaven. There's a shortage of real Texas-style barbecue in Chicago."

"That's where you live now?"

"It's home," she said. "But I'll tell you more about that at dinner. Pick me up in my room and maybe you can share my first Shiner with me." She moved closer. He could see the gold flecks in her eyes and imagine the sweet taste of her mouth against his.

"You owe me a first *something,* after all," she said. And with that, she straightened his shirt collar, then left.

Hot someplace other than under the collar, Matt focused on that closed door while he tried to get his body under control. He was a believer in instinct, and his gut was telling him that Jamie Delisle was dealing him in some way he hadn't quite figured out. But one thing Jamie probably hadn't counted on…Matt was primed to play.

CHAPTER THREE

AFTER STARTING A LITTLE something simmering with Matt, Jamie made her way over to the mansion's front parlor and waited for ever-late Crystal to arrive. When she did, it was on a burst of sweet floral perfume and rapid-fire conversation. After teary-eyed hugs and a little dabbing of smeared mascara, they settled in plump armchairs in front of the fireplace, where behind glass doors, gas flames danced around ersatz logs.

She and Crystal talked about a lot of the same things they spoke about in their frequent calls to each other, but it was different now, as though they were reforging the connection that distance had a way of weakening. It wasn't long until Jamie felt as though she'd never been separated from her friend.

They were about halfway through gossiping about who would be at the reunion, with Jamie avoiding the subject of Matt O'Connell—and her accompanying conflicted emotional weirdness—when the man himself came into the room. Though she fought to be immune to his charm, Jamie couldn't help the small smile curving the corners of her mouth. Crystal appeared a little less pleased with his arrival.

"Well, Matt, I didn't know that you were coming to the reunion," she said in a nervous voice.

"Sure you did, Crystal. I sent you the check."

Crystal fanned her hand below her face as though the fire's heat had somehow escaped its prison and was cooking her. "Well, I got so many checks, you know…. But it's great to be seeing you in town again. I hear you have your own construction company in Houston?"

He smiled. "After seven years in business, I almost feel like I can ride out the bad times."

"Well, that's great! Just great!" her friend said with faux-hearty enthusiasm.

Matt smiled his thanks and came nearer. Jamie watched as he approached and felt a start of alarm at the mischief dancing in those blue eyes. He moved behind her, so that she was forced to look up at him. She was seldom at a height disadvantage, and she wasn't crazy about the vulnerability it brought. Matt settled his hands on her shoulders, then bent until his lips were close to her ear.

"Don't forget…six-thirty, your room," he said with just enough volume for avid Crystal to pick up the words.

"I'll be there," Jamie said as calmly as possible. Matt smiled and then settled a kiss against her cheek. Before pulling away, he brought his fingertips to her hair and rubbed a lock of it, his thumb softly brushing the corner of her jaw. A thrill chased through her, one she couldn't quite hide.

"Just as I'd imagined," he said, these words for her ears alone. Then he stood. "Have a nice afternoon, ladies."

Crystal's eyes had grown wide.

"What's up with you two?" she asked soon after Matt had left.

"He was teasing me a little," she said over the drumming of her heart. "I'm having dinner with him...that's all."

"Sounded more to me like you were heading straight for cookies in bed."

Actually, a big, fat slice of humble pie, Jamie thought, though she had no intention of sharing her plans for Mr. Smooth with her friend.

"Just a little friendly banter," she said aloud.

Crystal snorted. "Huh. Friendly. With the way you acted on the phone last month, I was all worried that you'd be mad when you found out Matt was coming to the reunion, after all. But don't tell *me* what's going on. Just because I've been one of your closest friends since sixth grade..."

"It's nothing. I swear."

"Well, I was going to invite you over for dinner so you can see how big Cassie's getting, but I guess I'll wait. Don't want to stand in the way of true love."

It was Jamie's turn to snort. "Huh. Love. I've got no time for love." Nor had she the inclination.

"More the fool you, then. But one day, ready or not, love's going to sneak up and bite you on that scrawny butt of yours."

"It wouldn't dare," Jamie told her.

"You're tough, but you're not immune." Crystal checked her watch, then popped to her feet. "Where did the time go? Corey's mom's been watching Cassie, and if I don't get back soon, she'll have my hide."

"I'll walk you out," Jamie said as she stood. "I need to drop in on my parents, anyway."

Crystal wrapped her in a hug. "That's my Jamie. Not immune at all, are you? I knew you'd do what's right."

And that was the problem…in the end, Jamie always did.

Less than a quarter hour later, she stood at the front door of her parents' condominium on the edge of town. The family's troubles had made their mark on her mom's tastes almost the same way they had Jamie's. The nearly austere dwelling was the dead opposite of the chaos in which she'd been raised. She was happy that her mom had this comfort. Still, even though Jamie now understood that her dad couldn't have helped himself, she hadn't been able to completely accept that he wasn't responsible for what he'd put their family through.

Jamie had just touched her finger to the bell when her mother swung open the door and folded her into a hug. She savored it. Lord knew she didn't get this much affection in Chicago.

"Come on in," her mom said. "I've got grilled cheese and tomato soup waiting for you."

"Just like I'm nine, all over again," Jamie said.

"Your daddy's in the kitchen finishing off the sandwiches. We've both missed you so much!"

"And I've missed you," Jamie said to her mother, who took her hand and led her to the condo's tidy kitchen. Her father had his back to them as he transferred a grilled cheese to a plate.

"Hey, Daddy," Jamie said, trying to keep that small, stubborn bit of resentment from bubbling up in her voice.

"Hey, darlin'!" Her father came around the counter and kissed her soundly on the cheek. "You're looking beautiful, but maybe a little underfed. Sit down and get ready for some of your mother's homemade soup. You want something to drink?"

"Water would be fine."

Though still tall and energetic, this Bob Delisle wasn't the same man with whom she'd spent her adolescent years. He was more focused and seemed content with his life, as did her mother. All of which was proof to Jamie that miracles could happen.

While they ate, they talked about Jamie's mom's promotion at the First Prescott Bank & Trust, where she'd worked since Jamie was five, and about the town's growth. After Jamie had been quizzed on her current social life—or consistent lack thereof—she turned the conversation's focus back to her parents.

"So what's new with you, Daddy?"

"Nothing much," he said. "Mostly just golfing and watching the investments I made with the money from the land sale. Who'd have ever thought that old junkyard would actually fund my retirement?"

Not Jamie. Her father's growing obsession with the place had colored every moment of her adolescent life. He'd always been a packrat, and thus well suited to own the Pick 'n Trade, but his packrat tendencies had become something scarier. Her dad could no longer part with any of his junk. Metal oil drums began to fill the front yard, arranged according to color and markings. Golf clubs were arrayed on a certain table, under a certain tarp that had to be angled just so. Any suggestion to pare down brought a panicked sort of rage from her father.

Her parents had fought almost nightly. She'd hidden her head under her pillow, blocking the sound of her mother's tears and wishing for morning to come. Life had fallen into the same state of ruin as the Pick 'n Trade. Jamie had retreated into herself, with only Crystal as a truly close friend.

But life had rolled on. Her father was better now. Her mother had managed to survive his illness with her marriage and sanity intact. And Jamie was no fool; she knew she needed to get the rest of the way over her past. She'd done well professionally, but except for short intervals, she'd never managed to sustain more than an impersonal personal life. It could be this was why she'd let Crystal persuade her into a Prescott trip. Maybe the time had come to exorcise the last of her ghosts.

To this day, the memory of the aftermath of the Pick 'n Trade's hijacking to the school lawn brought out her inner five-year-old. Her mind would skitter from the topic while her psyche hid in the corner, eyes closed and fingers in her ears, repeating "not gonna think about it…not gonna think about it…" Healthy? No. Effective? Sadly, yes, until lately. She was getting sick of that whiny kid in her brain.

"So, Jamie, any special reunion plans?" her mother asked in a bright voice that cut through the silence that had settled over them.

Jamie hesitated before answering. Bringing up Matt's name seemed risky, but they'd already spent fifteen years dancing around the events of that May of her senior year.

"I don't have a whole lot planned, though I'm going to Hanson's with Matt O'Connell tonight."

"Hanson's?" Her father nodded approvingly. "Couldn't do any better, darlin'."

Okay, maybe she'd been the only one with lingering O'Connell issues. Fifteen years of dancing by herself. Somehow, it figured. And tonight she'd take the next step in moving on.

BY THE TIME MATT AND JAMIE arrived at Hanson's, he was one hundred percent sure that she was up to something, and also one hundred percent sure that he didn't care what it was, so long as he had the pleasure of this evening. Despite an almost distracted undercurrent to her conversation, she was bright and witty and incredibly sexy.

She wore the same clothes she'd had on earlier, but she'd added some skinny gold bracelets around one wrist and changed to a pair of heels that brought her nearly to his height. Matt got a serious charge out of considering exactly how their bodies would align.

Mrs. Hanson, who'd seated them a minute or so earlier at one of the white-paper-topped tables, stopped back by, putting an end to his mental wanderings.

"Can I bring you two anything to drink while we wait for Merry to catch up?" she asked with a nod toward the long-time waitress, who was no doubt accustomed to Hanson's crowds.

"Iced tea for me," Jamie said.

"Make it two," Matt added.

Mrs. Hanson nodded. "Be right back."

"Is it just me, or does Mrs. Hanson look virtually no different than she did fifteen years ago?" Jamie asked after the older woman had departed.

Matt glanced over to the kitchen door, where the restaurant's co-owner was now chatting with her husband.

Jamie had a point. Other than maybe a little softening around the eyes, Mrs. H hadn't changed from those days when the football team would try to eat the kitchen bare after every home game.

"Yup. She's just about the same," he said.

"You don't find that a little…strange?"

He smiled. "Guess I never thought about it. Maybe we have an android in our midst."

"Or a plastic surgery junkie," Jamie suggested. "I once had this client who—" She came to an abrupt halt.

"Who wha—" The air escaped from Matt's chest as someone smacked him heartily on the back at the same time that a broad and gnarled hand settled on his shoulder. Matt looked up to see Clint Parnell, who'd been the local sheriff when the Dead Rebels were in their heyday. Needless to say, the sheriff hadn't exactly been a member of Matt's fan club.

"Sheriff Parnell, good to see you," Matt said after he'd sucked in some new wind. He expected that there'd been a measure of long-overdue punishment in the retired sheriff's back-pounding.

"Welcome home, Matt. Good to have you back in the area…for a visit."

Matt bit back a laugh at Parnell's provisional welcome. "Thanks. It's good to be here. And the lady across the table from me is none other than Jamie Delisle, though I doubt you saw as much of her as you did of me, back in the day."

The older man gave a courtly nod. "Hello again, Jamie. Your daddy and I are golfing in the same duffers' league these days. He's got one smooth backswing."

She smiled. "I'll pass along the compliment."

"Better not. He's full enough of himself, the old

rooster. Now I'll let you get on with your suppers," he said just as their waitress arrived with their drinks.

They placed their orders and then fielded greetings from other classmates who'd been drawn by the irresistible lure of Hanson's barbecue. And while Matt was happy enough to greet old friends, he wished he'd chosen a more intimate setting so maybe he could speak more privately to Jamie, too. Not that she seemed inclined to do so. He'd just asked how her father was doing when the food arrived, and her relief at a distraction was unmistakable.

Jamie had ordered the pulled pork, which she immediately doctored up with more of Hanson's secret sauce from the tall bottle on the table.

"Want your dill pickle?" she asked as she worked.

"Take it," Matt said. He'd no sooner spoken than it was off his plate.

"Thanks," she said, after the fact.

He liked her enthusiastic approach to eating. Most of the women he dated seemed to pretend that they got along just fine without food. He'd also caught more than one of those non-eaters scarfing down double-fudge-brownie ice cream in the middle of the night. Not that there was anything wrong with that. It was the honesty factor that bothered him.

Before reassembling her sandwich, Jamie put a fingertip to the sauce she'd added, then brought it to her mouth and slowly sucked on it. Okay, so she was toying with him, and this was every guy's trite fantasy, but every guy gravitated to the fantasy for a very good reason. Matt drew in a steadying breath as the fit of his jeans grew tighter.

"Good as you remembered?" he asked, then took a

swallow of iced tea, as though his hoarseness had been from a dry throat.

Jamie exhaled on a long, replete sigh, much as a lover would once she'd come apart in his arms. She gave him a tease of a smile, then said, "Better."

He shifted uncomfortably on the hard wooden bench. One thing hadn't changed since high school: he was still his own worst enemy. No point in getting ready to rock in the middle of a barbecue joint. No way to avoid getting ready to rock, either. Matt steeled himself for what might be the hardest meal of his life. Literally.

CHAPTER FOUR

JAMIE WISHED SHE'D KNOWN that revenge could be such hard work. Nerves in a knot, she forced herself to relax against the cool upholstery of Matt's car. Dinner had been a success, both in terms of ratcheting up his attraction to her, and unfortunately, hers to him. In fact, she was discovering that she might genuinely like the grown-up version of Matt O'Connell as much as she detested the way adolescent Matt had jerked with her pride.

Jamie's inner peace was in short supply. It didn't help that thong underwear and no panty hose beneath a relatively short skirt had proved to be an unnerving tactical combo. But she would not back down. She had embraced her inner tart and would use her to seize victory, even if she wasn't quite as comfortable as she'd been earlier today with the way she hungered for it. No doubt about it…a shrink could fund a posh retirement trying to untangle her feelings about Matt O'Connell.

She glanced over at Matt, so calm behind the wheel. She was glad she'd ceded to his wish to pamper a bad knee and not had them slip into her convertible when they'd left the Bluebonnet earlier in the evening. Heaven knew that his luxury sedan had more wiggle room…so to speak.

"Just for fun, why don't we take a cruise by some of the old high school haunts?" she suggested.

"Anything but the football stadium," he said. "I've got a feeling that my dad and brother are going to find some way to corral me there along with my nephew, Jett."

"Why would they want to do that?"

"Jett's the varsity quarterback, and the O'Connell motto seems to be 'train until you hate the game.'"

His dark tone surprised her. "You hated football?"

He hesitated before answering. "No. No, really…that was just a poor stab at humor, I guess."

And it seemed to Jamie that almost to spite himself, he headed toward the stadium. They were quiet as they drove past it and then the school nearby, both dim figures in the November starlight.

Jamie recalled cool October nights when the lights above the stadium would glow in the night sky, and it seemed that life itself centered on those boys on the field. She'd gone to most of the football games with Crystal and their odd-lot group of friends. She'd never been part of the popular set, and certainly not one of the cheerleaders in their vaunted location inside the playing field's fence.

And she had always dreamed of being Matt's girlfriend, even back in their freshman year, before he'd been moved up to the varsity team and become one of the stars. He'd been unfailingly polite to her, but when it had come to female attention, like most of the athletes he'd chosen to be seen with big-haired and big-breasted Kayleigh Hughes and her anatomically impossible friends. Still, Jamie had clung to the hope that he'd really notice her.

By spring of her senior year, Jamie had realized that time was running short. Matt had been offered a full scholarship to Oklahoma State, and without money or scholarship hopes of her own, Jamie was going to be trapped in drab Prescott for the rest of her natural life. And probably in death, too. She'd known with adolescent certainty that she had to grab fast, or she'd have no decent memories to cling to.

And so she'd set aside years of her mother's prudent advice and her own qualms, too. She'd offered herself to him. No mincing around the issue. No carelessness, either. She'd even had a pack of condoms she'd driven the next town over to buy. Those condoms had ended up in a garbage bin behind the library, because while Matt O'Connell had considered her decent to talk to, he'd made it excruciatingly clear that she wasn't getting so much as a kiss. Totally humiliated, Jamie had slunk off. Though Matt had never said the words, she'd been convinced that he'd rejected her for who she was: the weird junkman's nerd of a daughter. And a few nights later, Matt had packed up and moved the Pick 'n Trade's tables and barrels and horrendous trash, and reassembled the mess with amazing accuracy on the high school lawn.

Her father's rigid world had shattered, and he'd been hospitalized for the summer. Jamie had tried to tell herself that it was for the best…that things had to reach a peak before they improved. But nothing had felt better. In fact, she'd spent the summer sick with remorse because try as she might, she couldn't feel anything other than anger toward her dad. Ashamed, Jamie had refused to visit him or to even leave the house unless prodded by her mother.

And then, at least for Jamie, a miracle had happened. She'd been given an anonymous scholarship to the design school she'd always dreamed of attending. While she'd felt like a horrible daughter for leaving her mother, she'd have been crazy to have turned down such an opportunity. After that, it seemed that everything had changed...except deep inside, where Jamie still felt vestiges of that awful guilt.

And now here she was with Matt. She was older and wiser in the way of men, and tonight satisfaction would be hers...though not in the way she'd wanted it that long-gone May night.

"Let's head up to Trehan Point," she said to Matt.

He glanced over at her. "You're kidding, right?"

Channeling Uma Thurman, she gave a sexy laugh. "No, but you might want to move your mind out of the backseat, O'Connell. It just so happens that's the highest point around and I'd like to see how far out the town lights have grown."

"The town lights," he echoed, still sounding a tad skeptical, which, Jamie admitted, he had a right to be, considering her mixed motives.

"Yes, the town lights." She hesitated, but then decided the best way to handle a former football player was by the use of an old football adage: *The best defense is a good offense.* She dug into their common past and laid it right out there. "And you might recall that I'm the direct type. There will be no room for misinterpretation if I happen to ask for sex."

Matt laughed, though it wasn't a comfortable sound. "Good point."

Jamie forged on. "Now, let's go take a look at those lights before we head back to the Bluebonnet."

"Guess it sounds like a plan," he replied.

Jamie relaxed marginally as he looped the car around to take the road to the rougher and higher countryside.

The point, a secluded place, had been better known as Trojan Point during her high school years. It had been the premier make-out spot—not that she had known from personal experience. She'd ventured there once in daylight, only because she was the curious sort and had wanted to see what she was missing. But to-night, between the town's burgeoning development and her limited memory, she doubted she'd have been able to find the turnoff on her own. Matt sure seemed to know where he was heading, though.

"You've done this a few times, I take it," she said to him as he headed up the narrow road that dead-ended on a bluff above the town.

"One or two." He glanced at her. "And not always with a girl, either."

She worked in the decorating business and probably had more gay friends than straight. But Matt, gay? Nah. The vibes were wrong.

"Are you saying what I think you're saying, Matt O'Connell?" she asked, anyway.

He laughed. "It's interesting, the way your mind works. Not at all what I'd expected."

"In my case, still waters run a little murky. So who were you coming up here with?"

"If you'd asked me that question in high school, I'd have given you the old 'if I told you, I'd have to kill you' answer. But now, I guess there's no harm in sharing a little teenage stupidity."

"Heaven knows I had my share," Jamie said.

"Maybe, but you weren't a Dead Rebel."

She blinked. "A what?"

"You heard me…a Dead Rebel. We were the last of the breed, as you'd kind of figure given the club's name. Me, Kirk McKenzie and Caleb Tanner were the full membership by senior year."

"And what was the purpose of this, ah, club?"

"To live hard and die young like all good, dead rebels…James Dean…Jim Morrison…"

"Ick."

He laughed. "Well, it seemed kind of wild and tragic when we were kids."

"I'll have to take your word on that one. So what did you do up at the point?"

"We used to meet at the end of a side trail and plot our next piece of trouble."

"Such as?"

"The day all the toilet paper went missing in grade school."

"We were in—what?—fifth grade?"

"Kirk and I started young. By the time Caleb came to town, though, we were big-time."

"Men," Jamie said. "Too weird to survive on their own."

"No doubt about it," Matt agreed.

They'd reached the cul-de-sac at the tip of the point, and Matt pulled off so they were overlooking Prescott, then switched off the car. Tuesday seemed to be a rather low-attendance night at the point. No other car was there.

Jamie unbuckled her seat belt, wriggled her feet out of her silly stiletto pumps, then moved closer to him. He released his seat belt and then hooked his arm over her shoulders. She briefly wished for bench seats, but she figured she could work with the material available. Together they looked at the net of lights that made up Prescott.

"It's changed," Jamie said, taking in the expansion of what had once been a very small town.

"We all have," Matt replied.

"I'll assume in your case, it's for the better, unless you're still a toilet paper thief…or worse."

"Better," he said. "More who I want to be. How about you?"

Jamie didn't like that question turned back on her. Didn't like the way it made her think. There was no room for thought tonight. Not if she planned to retrieve her pride…or whatever it was she was seeking through this exercise in craziness.

"I like myself just fine," she said, though it wasn't quite true at the moment.

"The feeling's mutual."

She smiled, indisputably charmed by his comment. "Thank you."

Then they fell into one of those moments that she'd seen countless times in her favorite sappy romantic movies, but seldom experienced. It was as though they were being drawn toward each other, and even if her life itself were at risk, she doubted she could pull away. He came closer and cupped the back of her head with one strong hand. He was going to kiss her, and though that had been part of her general plan, her heart still jumped at the thought.

"I haven't asked you for sex, Matt O'Connell," she pointed out in a sex-kitten voice she hadn't known herself capable of.

"And all I'm asking for is a kiss," he replied. "One harmless kiss, and then we'll leave."

She hesitated, seeking a way to regain the upper hand. "If it's just one, you'd better make it good."

His chuckle told her that she'd succeeded. Jamie eased into the moment for which she'd waited a lifetime. Matt's mouth was hot and sure, leaving her little reason to worry about that inevitable first-kiss awkwardness.

"Okay, maybe more than one kiss," he said, his lips still close to hers.

After he'd suckled on her lower lip and she'd kissed the cleft in his chin that had always tempted her so, and after the car had grown warm and humid with their shared breath and desire, Matt said, "Hang on."

For reasons that had nothing to do with her ultimate goal—which was getting kind of fuzzy around the edges, along with her ability to hold a thought—Jamie prayed he wasn't putting a stop to the evening. Luckily, he just fiddled with the car's controls so that his seat reclined, then slid all the way back. Then he leaned across her and reached between her seat and the passenger door and moved hers back, then reclined it, too.

He took his time sitting upright, first stopping to kiss the skin at the base of her throat, then just beneath her ear. The man had a way about him that she wouldn't soon forget.

"We've got a little more room, at least," he said once he'd moved away and fully reclined his seat. "Come on over here."

Invitation warmed his voice, but Jamie was already hot. She took hold of the initiative and managed to get herself straddled over his thighs. It was no easy task with her height, and her skirt hiked up in the process.

After getting Matt to lower the car's front passenger window, both in furtherance of her plans and to ease the steamy heat coursing through her, Jamie kissed him in all the ways she'd once fantasized about. A totally sixteen-year-old part of her mind kept squealing, *Matt O'Connell is kissing me!* Then there was the adult portion of her brain saying, *Yeah, and he's also sliding his hand up the back of my thigh, which means that any second now...*

Matt groaned as his fingers feathered up the naked skin of her bottom. Jamie shivered with pleasure at his touch. She'd never considered that she'd be tempted to allow this encounter to reach its natural end. But she was...incredibly so. And because there was no rule against enjoying herself up to the very end, she let her tongue tangle with his for a while, then she leaned back just enough to unbutton his shirt.

"I've been meaning to do this...for about fifteen years," she said.

He dropped his arms in surrender. "You're killing me."

"Now, that wouldn't be good timing." She kept working on those buttons, pulling the shirttail from his jeans.

He helped her work the shirt free, and she tossed it into the backseat. Jamie ran her hands over his chest, going as much by feel as by the faint light available. Matt was muscled, not in a steroidal way, but with a firm definition that she hungered to see in full light. His skin was warm beneath her palms, and his heart beat a quick rhythm. She brought her mouth to the top of his shoulder and gently nipped.

"Careful," he said good-naturedly.

But caution wasn't part of her plan, so she settled her mouth over his and kissed him some more. His hands roamed everywhere they could reach. When he softly touched between her legs, she realized she was close to a precipice that would send her spiraling past reason. She needed to distract him.

Jamie made a sliver of space between them.

"Fair's fair," she said as she undid the ribbon tie that ran through the neckline of her top, then brought the garment over her head and off her body, taking care to keep her beloved gold bangle bracelets in place. She moved forward to let the blouse drop in the back, and Matt groaned again.

Good thing her recent wardrobe purchases included a definitely tarty push-up bra to match her thong underwear. Distraction—and just maybe victory—seemed to be hers. He ran his fingertips over the flesh of her breasts, where it sat plump above the bra's lace.

When he shifted his weight forward, obviously intent on bringing his mouth to follow the same path, Jamie's back hit the steering wheel, and she couldn't hold in a little yelp.

"Sorry," he said.

"It's okay," she murmured, then took his hand and settled it over her right breast. Matt was fast enough on the uptake, sliding his thumb back and forth across her sensitive nipple. She ruffled her fingers through the thick hair just behind his temples, and with utter honesty told him how good it felt to have him touching her.

"I'd like to touch you some more. And have you touch me," he said, then gave her a slow smile. "But we need some room. I don't know how I managed making-out like this as a teen."

"Limber joints and lack of other venues?" she suggested.

"Can't argue the knee thing, but I think it had more to do with the '81 Continental I drove. Could have lived in the backseat."

"Let's try this." Jamie settled her bottom in the middle of the console, but that didn't quite work, so she edged toward the passenger's side and braced her head against the door's armrest. Matt rid himself of his shoes and belt, then pulled an equal contortionist's move and managed to settle above her.

"Better than a sharp stick in the eye," he said before kissing her.

Jamie had never laughed and kissed quite like this before, and it seemed almost a shame that soon she would have to make her final move. But neither of them had the short build or long patience required to survive these cramped quarters.

She fused her mouth with his, savoring his taste, the feel of being skin to skin and the real hunger that was making her a little crazy. Plan and desire had become as muddled as all of her feelings about Matt. What she did next required no acting skills at all.

She reached for the closure to his jeans. "I want you to make love to me…. I want to feel you inside me. Don't say no this time."

He briefly rested his forehead against hers. "I was thinking more in terms of yes."

Then he kissed her again, levering his weight to the outside so she could touch him. She traced the shape of his erection and hungrily wished that this moment was for real.

As they both grew more desperate, she unzipped his jeans and then did her best to work them down his hips. He halted her while he extracted his wallet, which probably carried what he believed was a crucial condom.

Jamie had reached the point of no return. Much as she just wanted the release of making love with this man, she'd committed herself to revenge for the tanking of her teenage pride and the pain he'd brought her. And honestly, she thought while scrambling for the moral high ground, any man who'd jump for sex this quickly after paying her no mind at all before today deserved what he got.

Matt reached out and stuck his wallet on the dashboard. He was about to return to her when she said, "Could you take your jeans all the way off? I want to feel all of you. Please?" She arched her hips and worked out of her skirt as incentive.

Soon he was down to white briefs, and blue denim had been discarded into the back. He touched her again, slipping his fingers beneath the skimpy lace of her undies. He stroked her until her toes curled and she was holding on to her plan with a tenuous grip.

"Soon, sweetheart, or I'm not going to make it," Matt said between kisses.

Jamie worked up a nod, which was all she was capable of. But when he briefly moved away and cool air cascaded over her skin, her determination returned. If she didn't do this, she'd be letting hormones conquer self-esteem, and she'd never be able to live with herself.

While Matt groped for his wallet, Jamie unhooked

the front closure to her bra, then stretched her arms above her head and sighed.

"This feels positively decadent," she said, dangling her forearms out the open window.

Thank heaven for moonlight and the male fixation with breasts, because Matt was paying attention to exactly what she'd hoped.

Since she was running on pure adrenaline, the next part was easy. She dragged her right hand over her left wrist. Each of her pretty gold bracelets hit the rocky ground with an almost imperceptible *ping!*

"Oh, no!" she cried.

"What?"

She waggled her left hand in front of her breasts. "My bracelets! I just dropped my bracelets out the window!"

"Your bracelets?" he echoed.

"You know… The gold ones I had on. They're the first pieces of real jewelry I ever bought for myself." She wriggled a bit. "Guess I'd better go out there and get them."

"Jamie, we're the only ones up here. I swear those bracelets will be there later."

She'd have to give him points for sheer grit in the face of adversity. "But they're my *favorite* bracelets, and I don't want to be distracted while we make love."

Matt hesitated an instant, but Jamie knew the outcome wasn't in doubt. His sense of duty as a gentleman would inevitably kick in.

"All right. Don't move," he said. "I'll get 'em."

"You'd do that?" she asked, pushing along that chivalry imperative.

"Of course I would. Would you mind getting the flashlight out of the glove compartment?"

"Sure," Jamie said, then sat upright so she could get to the danged thing. "Here you go."

He took the light and was opening his door when she purred, "Hurry, now."

He smiled at her. Ignoring the fact that she was nothing short of naked at Trojan Point and about to commit a most heinous act, Jamie smiled back. He exited and closed the door. She sat as still as she could until he was to the very front of the car, then frantically threw herself into the driver's seat, locked the door, and then reached for the passenger-window switch and simultaneously started the engine.

When she turned on the headlights, she could see Matt frozen in place with a "what the *hell?*" look of shock on his features. Jamie bit her lower lip between her teeth and prepared to escape.

"Jamie!"

Apparently she hadn't gotten the passenger window quite all the way up.

He let loose a string of curse words that might have scared her, except she was in the car, and he wasn't. Hands shaking, she wheeled onto the road, whispering a few bad words of her own.

Was she crazy?

She must be, since she was pretty sure she'd just committed grand-theft auto. And that didn't even address the insanity of having managed to get a furious, near-naked man on her tail. Jamie took off. In a matter of heartbeats, all she could catch was the white of his briefs. As he receded in her—actually his—rearview mirror, laughter—some nervous and some of the belly-laugh variety—bubbled up.

She should have brought a camera. Crystal would never believe this. Of course she would never actually tell Crystal, either. Jamie knew what it felt like to have one's dignity publicly stripped, and she'd never do that to another soul. Not even Matt.

When she reached the bottom of the hill, she pulled to the side of the road, threw the car in Park and turned to rummage in the backseat. After a couple of grabs, she came up with Matt's jeans. It took only a moment's debate before she neatly dropped them on the roadside. After all, it wouldn't do to be cruel. Another half mile down the road—just before the edge of civilization— she pulled over again and got dressed. Her pulse finally slowed as she accepted that Matt wasn't going to loom up behind her like a crazed zombie from a campfire tale.

"Dead Rebel, huh? See what happens when you meet up with a ticked-off nerd," she said to the man she'd left behind. With that, Jamie cranked up the tunes and sped back to the Bluebonnet Inn.

CHAPTER FIVE

FIVE GOLD BRACELETS. Wednesday midmorning, Matt lined them up one by one on the small desk in his hotel room. It had been worth five gold bracelets for Jamie to get even with him last night. She'd probably found the deal a bargain, considering the sight he'd made, pissed-off and near naked in the glare of his car's headlights. And while he didn't exactly applaud her ingenuity, on some level he knew he'd deserved to get as good as he'd once given her...and her parents.

That was the killer of having crossed the same woman twice. He didn't know where the revenge might end. If Trehan Point was tit for tat—so to speak—over not having taken her there fifteen years ago, he didn't want to think what she might to do even the score on the Pick 'n Trade. That fell into another league entirely.

In his defense, he'd had no clue that her dad would take it so hard to see his junk collection moved. Sure, the guy had been attached to his junkyard, but there had been no way to know that he'd fall apart the way he did. It wasn't until years later, when Matt read an article on obsessive-compulsive disorder, that he fully understood what had happened. The behaviors listed in the article had exactly matched Mr. Delisle's.

Bad stunt...worse consequences. Matt should be over it, but he still felt like hell when he thought about that night. He couldn't begin to imagine how Jamie felt. And he couldn't quite remember why he'd thought that this Thanksgiving in Prescott might be a fine idea, either.

Damn good thing the deputy who'd happened upon him walking the road to town last night had shown a sense of humor...definitely more than Matt had been able to find at that moment. After finding his clothes and being dropped at the Bluebonnet, Matt had ignored the clerk's raised brows and collected a room key, plus the car keys Jamie had very wisely left at the front desk. He'd considered going straight to her room, but had decided he liked the idea of making her sweat his next move...whatever that might be.

Acknowledging he was too wired for sleep, he'd gotten dressed and headed out to CB's Roadhouse, the closest thing Prescott had to a dive joint, for a beer. The place was rougher around the edges than Matt had recalled when he'd snuck drinks there, long ago, but after the night he'd had, he'd felt pretty damn rough, too. He'd run into a couple of guys from the football team, and they'd sat at the bar and traded tales straight until last call.

This morning, an hour-and-a-half-long workout at the gym with Deuce had killed enough of Matt's residual anger that he was willing to admit he cared about what Jamie thought of him...even if he probably wouldn't see her for another fifteen years. And so he would go make peace.

He slid the bracelets over the waxy green paper covering the stem ends of the flowers he'd bought her after leaving the gym. The gesture would go a long way toward negotiating a truce, and if not far enough, the tropical birds of paradise—or whatever the florist had said they were—looked sharp enough to be of use in self-defense.

Matt made the trek into the main part of the inn and up to Jamie's suite. Only after he'd knocked on the door did he realize that he had no damn idea what he was going to say to her. He half hoped she'd already left for the day. No such luck, though. He heard a stirring, then a distant "be right there."

Since he didn't want to give away his trump card first thing, he tucked the flowers behind his back. He also tried to keep his expression blank of the emotions kicking around in his gut: annoyance, hesitance, hunger and, yeah, a bizarre dose of tenderness, too.

He heard her right at the door and caught her softly spoken "damn" as she likely looked through the peephole.

"What do you want?" she asked, and he was pleased that she sounded as emotionally ambivalent as he felt.

"Just to talk."

"About what?"

Some questions didn't deserve answers, and it seemed she quickly figured out that hers fell in that category because he could hear her muttering "swift one" to herself on the other side of the door.

"I'm not going to go crazy on you…I swear," he said.

"Really? Then step back and show me your hands."

He brought the flowers around front.

"Those are for me?" she asked.

"Only if you let me in."

A moment later, the rattling of a security chain preceded the opening of the door.

Matt stepped in and was again struck by how damned incredible-looking Jamie had become...or maybe had always been. There was nothing overdone about her, just a clean, sleek beauty that made him feel strangely tight about the chest.

"I've got to be leaving in a couple of minutes," she said.

"I won't take much of your time." He poked the flowers in the direction of the suite's front room. "But maybe we could sit?"

"Okay." She left the door open, which struck Matt as funny, considering how easily she'd handled him last night. And how willing he was finding himself to follow her lead again today. This, from a guy who'd had more than one woman end a relationship because of his bone-deep independent streak. He handed her the flowers, and she took them as gingerly as though they might detonate.

"Thanks," she said, then sat pinned to the arm of a fancy-looking blue brocade sofa. Instead of settling next to her and risking a stab wound from the orange birds' beaks, Matt opted for the armchair to her right.

"I was wondering if we could call it even?" he asked.

A tinge of pink climbed her cheeks, and she wouldn't meet his eyes. And again, he couldn't quite peg what was going on in her admirably devious mind. She could be ticked...or embarrassed. Either way, he was going to do what all smart guys did in the face of cluelessness and keep his mouth shut.

"I probably should apologize for last night," she said. "But it's the oddest thing...I just don't want to."

Matt laughed. "That's honest enough, but I hope you don't mind if *I* make a few apologies. About the Pick 'n Trade..."

She shook her head. "Ancient history. I'd like to leave it in the past."

She'd spoken too quickly for him to actually buy in on that ancient-history stuff, but because it wasn't one of his favorite topics, he'd let the matter slide.

"Okay, then, about last night." She looked ready to cut him off again, and this time, he wouldn't have it. "We're talking about this, Jamie, because I think we need to get something straight."

"What?"

"I wanted you that night back in high school.... I wanted you more than anything."

"Bull."

"No lie."

She hesitated, but then said, "Really?"

Matt relaxed and felt a smile spread across his face. Until she'd shown her belief in his word, he hadn't known how important it was to him. "Scout's honor."

"Don't you mean Dead Rebel's honor?"

"I'll have to think on it. That might be an oxymoron."

She laughed, but the sound was short-lived. "Well, thank you for telling me how you felt. I'd had no idea.... Not that it changes the outcome."

"But it was the reason I pushed you away. I knew what you wanted would only make you upset, later. And I was as messed-up as any eighteen-year-old guy could be when it came to turning down a night with a girl as sweet and pretty as you."

"Sweet? Even when offering myself up?"

He chuckled. "Even then. Despite the condom box, it was no 'do me' speech. And trust me, I'd heard plenty of those."

"I don't want to know from whom," she said primly, which was one hell of a feat coming from a woman who'd sounded like sex incarnate last night.

"Good thing, since I don't talk."

She fiddled with the paper covering the bouquet, clearly understanding that he referred to last night, as well. "Neither do I."

He nodded. "I knew that, but the jury's still out on the desk clerk and the deputy who picked me up last night."

She winced. "A *deputy?*" For a second he thought she might apologize, but she just started laughing. "Perfect."

"Depends on your point of view."

She resettled her right hand on the flowers, her fingers brushing against the bracelets he'd stuck there. Jamie looked down, and her eyes widened. The room grew warmer as she gave him a smile that nearly made him forget last night's outcome.

"You found these for me even after I'd left you up there like that?" she asked.

"I didn't want to think what you might do to me if I'd left them."

She slid the jewelry off the flowers and back onto her wrist.

"To show you how bad I am at this revenge game, it wasn't even until this morning that I thought about my poor bracelets. I drove back up to the point and looked everywhere."

"And came up empty, huh? I don't think I feel sorry for you." But he did…a little. "So what do you say, can we start over, for real this time?"

"What do you mean?"

"Hang on." He stood and made his way to the suite's

open door, with Jamie trailing after him. Once he was in the hallway, he closed himself out. Then he knocked.

"Yes?" she called from the other side of the door.

"It's Matt O'Connell. I heard you were in town and wondered if I could have a word?"

The door opened, and she stood there, a slight smile playing on her mouth.

"Hi, Jamie," he said, extending his hand. "It's been a long time."

She shook his hand. "Hi, Matt. It has."

"A group of us are getting together at CB's Roadhouse tonight...a bunch of my old football buddies and their wives and whoever...and I was wondering if maybe you'd come with me?"

"CB's?"

He nodded. "I know it's not exactly the Ritz."

"Well, it just so happens that my friend Crystal eloped with your old center, Corey Wayland, a few years back, and this morning I agreed to tag along to the bar with them."

"How about if I give you a ride, instead?"

He felt like a teenager all over again, waiting for her to answer.

"I'd like that," she said. "Very much."

Matt smiled. Maybe coming back to Prescott for a visit wasn't so bad, after all.

CB's ROADHOUSE MADE THE worst of Chicago's Rush Street bars look like paradise. Jamie's shoes stuck to the floor, which was sticky with spilled beer, her nose itched from the cigarette smoke, and yet she was having the most wonderful time of her life. The group that had taken over the bar probably covered a thirty-year span of Prescott football. In fact, the good-looking younger guy she'd seen when she first came to town was here. It seemed his name was Ty and he'd been a tailback a few years ago. While Matt had been briefly occupied catching up with new arrivals, Ty had bought Jamie a drink. The gesture had earned him a frown from Crystal, who was staying next to Jamie, like a mama duck.

"Where'd you meet Ty?" Crystal asked.

"We didn't exactly meet. He was admiring my rental car yesterday, when I first got to town."

"He's admiring more than that now," Crystal said over the music and loud conversation enveloping them. "Watch out for him. He's a slick one."

Jamie smiled, thinking of last night. "I've got a few moves of my own."

"I don't want to know," Crystal said. "Unless they involve Matt O'Connell. Are you going to tell me what's going on with you and Mr. Wonderful?"

"Nothing that will last a minute beyond this weekend." Jamie knew that was the truth, but she didn't like the way she began to feel all lonely once she'd admitted it. Even though loneliness had been her companion for too long, it was something she didn't allow herself to think about.

Just then, Corey came and took his wife by the hand. "Come on, sweetness, let's see if we can steal a corner of the dance floor."

Crystal hesitated, glancing toward Matt, who seemed to be trying to pry himself away from an older couple who were talking relentlessly.

"I'll be fine," Jamie said. "Go on and dance with your guy."

She smiled as Corey and Crystal made their way off. It had taken several years after college for those two to see that they were made for each other, but they appeared to have grabbed happiness for all it was worth. Wanting to temporarily seize a little of her own, Jamie set her empty glass on the bar, then worked her way through the shifting crowd toward Matt. As she neared, he smiled at her over his conversation partners' heads.

A hand closed over Jamie's waist. She looked over her shoulder. Ty seemed to be staking a claim. He also appeared to be a little unsteady on his feet, likely a direct result of the upside-down margaritas that the sexy, blond and fake-boobed bartender had been pouring into some of the guys' mouths. Jamie peeled his hand from her.

"Wanna dance?" he asked, swaying in place.

"Maybe later," she replied, then gave him a sunny smile. *Not that later's on your schedule, friend.*

"I was thinkin' more of now. How old are you, anyway? Doesn't really matter. Older women are hot."

Somehow, Jamie felt less than flattered.

Matt arrived. "This a friend of yours, Jamie?"

"A brief acquaintance," Jamie replied. "Ty…Matt. Matt…Ty."

"Well, if you don't mind, Ty, Jamie's promised me this dance."

Ty looked like he did mind, but apparently still possessed enough wits to realize that Matt had a few inches of height on him—and a lot more sobriety.

"Sure," he said with a broad wave of his arm. "I'll find you later, Jamie."

"Hope not," Jamie said under her breath as Matt led her toward the postage stamp of a dance floor. Corey and Crystal nudged over a bit, and by the time Matt and Jamie found enough space, the up-tempo music changed to a ballad.

Matt's brows raised in the classic "will you?" question, and he held his arms open to her. Jamie stepped into his embrace, then rested her cheek against his broad shoulder, closed her eyes and sighed as the noise and the smoke and the bodies pressing around them faded into the background. This one dance in this absurdly ratty bar with its beer signs glowing brightly from every wall suited her better than anything she could recall from her real life back in Chicago. Not that she could recall a whole lot with Matt's body close to hers.

She was more recalling how she'd felt last night, with his mouth hot on her and his hands touching her intimately. It occurred to her that she was quite possibly as loose as that legion of girls who'd once sweet-talked their way up to Trojan Point with him.

"So, what's your family going to do for Thanksgiving tomorrow?" he asked.

Family…Thanksgiving…

She'd discussed plans with her mom this morning, she knew she had. "Um, we're…" She tried to get her mind off sex and onto food—neither of which were bad topics, except sex seemed to have taken over her brain. "Mom's cooking an early turkey, then we're supposed to go to Boerne to see my aunt Shirley."

"Fried or roasted?"

Jamie blinked. "Aunt Shirley?"

He laughed. "Your mom's turkey."

"Roasted," she said.

"Deep fried at my house. Thanksgiving is my

mother's annual flirtation with the dark side…mainlined cholesterol and a damn good chance of burning the house down, all in one meal."

She smiled at the image.

"Got any plans for dessert, tomorrow?" he asked, then slid one hand lower…not quite far enough to settle across her bottom, but close enough that she could almost imagine the feel, and it was sending her beyond warm and all the way to red hot.

The song ended too darned soon, and Jamie hesitantly drew away.

He took her hands in his and leaned close to her ear. "What do you say we get out of here in a little bit? Maybe find someplace quieter where we can talk?"

"Sounds good."

"Jamie." Crystal tapped her on the shoulder. "I have to use the ladies' room."

"Uh-huh" was about all Jamie could work up, as she was too busy basking in Matt's gaze.

"Now."

Jamie, who knew there was no escaping the go-to-the-bathroom-in-pairs ritual, told Matt she'd be right back. He gave her hands a brief squeeze, then released her to Crystal's insistent prodding.

"Let's go." The shorter woman opened a lane in the crowd straight to the ladies' room, which proved to be just about like the rest of CB's—minus a few neon beer signs. Replacing the signs was a piece of graffiti saying, "Make Love, Not War." Another commentator had added "Hell, do both—get married!"

"You're not actually going to use the facilities in here, are you?" Jamie asked her friend.

"Heck no," Crystal said as the occupant of one stall called to the other looking for toilet paper and got a drunken snore in return. "I wouldn't get within five feet of those seats. If you've gotta pee...squat."

"Thanks, but no thanks," Jamie said. "So why are we here?"

"Reality check. I just wanted to be sure you're positive about what you're doing."

Jamie didn't mistake her friend's meaning. She was less clear on her own motivation, but wanting Matt seemed to override all the messy emotional stuff that came with wanting him. And maybe—just maybe—when she was free of the fog of desire, she'd really understand herself. But for now, she'd give Crystal a tidier answer.

"Oh, I know what I'm doing. Really, I do. It's like the good fairy came down and gave me my secret wish. Well...not this bathroom. But *him*." She was careful not to use Matt's name, since there was no telling who might be in the bathroom's two stalls, and the conscious occupant, at least, concerned her.

"I know you were sweet on him back in high school, but I also know how you need to reason your way through stuff. You're not the kind to have a fling," Crystal said.

There, she was right and wrong. A fling fifteen years in the planning was within Jamie's realm of reason.

Crystal frowned at their reflections in the mirror above the sinks. "And how well do you really know him? How well do any of us? It's been fifteen years and—"

"He's grown up fine," Jamie replied, and at least on this she was clear. "He's a gentleman, I promise. I'm not going to tell you what I did, but I wasn't very nice last night, and he's been nothing but wonderful back. So much as I love you for taking on the morning-after worry for me, I'm going to grab tonight and whatever other time he and I can find this weekend and—"

Crystal smiled. "I know what you'll be doing. And I promise, I'll try to keep my mother hen urges to myself. Not another word from me on the subject."

Jamie gave her friend an impulsive hug. "I love you for worrying, okay?"

The pair left the bathroom and worked their way toward Matt and Corey, who'd moved to the near corner of the bar, where some other former players were huddled. Just before they reached their destination, Crystal slowed.

"You swear you'll call me tomorrow?" she asked. "We're having Thanksgiving around one at our house. I want to hear from you in the morning and be sure you're okay."

"Mother hen break must be up," Jamie replied, earning a laugh from her friend.

Then another body bumped against her.

"Hey, ready for that dance?" Ty flung his arm around her shoulder, sending her staggering into Crystal.

"Oh, sweet heaven," Crystal said as Jamie regained her balance. "Let me go get Corey and have him scrape that thing right off you."

"I can handle it," Jamie replied, trying to duck from beneath the guy's heavy arm. "Ty…"

"Yeah, tie me up, baby."

She was sure he'd regret that awful line once cold-sober morning arrived.

"Doesn't matter whether you want help…. Cavalry's

approaching," Crystal said in a chipper voice as Matt and Corey neared.

"Got a little Ty in the ointment?" Corey asked.

"That was horrible," Crystal said, but laughed at her husband's pun, anyway.

Jamie wiggled free of her drunken admirer and moved to Matt's side.

"Ready to leave?" he asked, his brows drawn closer in a concerned frown.

"Sure," she said, but Ty wasn't done.

"The lady's not leavin'. She was getting ready to dance…" He swayed a hokey little step. "With…me!"

"Uh, I don't think so," Jamie said.

Ty staggered, and Matt placed a hand on his shoulder to steady him.

"You trying to start something?" the tequila-laced man asked.

"Just trying to get on my way," Matt replied.

Jamie yelped as Ty drew back his fist to swing. Balance and consciousness weren't working in the guy's favor. He fell forward, and Matt reached to catch him. It wasn't exactly a clean move, and Ty's skull bounced against Matt's jaw. She winced at Matt's well-deserved curse word.

Matt and Corey dragged the drunken man to the bar, frisked him for car keys and tossed those to the bartender. What amazed Jamie was how the small commotion made hardly a ripple in the bar's activity. Matt was settling their bill when she noticed that the lower left corner of his mouth was already puffy, and that a small drop of blood was forming. She grabbed a cocktail napkin and was going to dab at it, but he folded her hand in his and told her in mock seriousness not to mess with his rescuer image. And since she'd never before been rescued, she humored him.

They said goodbye to Corey and Crystal, who intended to party on since they had a babysitter for a few more hours.

"What is it with you, Jamie Delisle?" Matt asked as they neared the door. "Two nights together, and I've been dumped near-naked on the roadside and gotten a fat lip."

The warm light in his eyes made her feel positively loopy.

"I've always been an overachiever," she replied.

Matt laughed, and the sound rang wonderfully as they stepped into the clear night. She shivered a little at the cold breeze chasing over her skin. It seemed a change of weather was in store for Prescott.

As they returned to the Bluebonnet, she considered a dozen dumb ways to flirt Matt into her bed, including the kiss-and-make-it-better gambit, but decided that both of them deserved some dignity this time around. Except that when being normal Jamie, and not tart Jamie, she'd never done very well at taking the initiative with a man. She wanted tonight to be so different from last night. Memorable in a *real* sort of way.

Matt parked, then ushered her from the car and closed her door after her. In the quiet of the night, they clasped hands and walked toward the inn's front entry. Her heart seemed to slow and her world to narrow down to this one moment as she struggled for words that wouldn't come.

She needn't have worried.

Matt stopped. "Will you let me make love to you, Jamie?"

Such a simple question, and she'd known the answer forever.

"Yes," she said, and her heart began to beat again.

CHAPTER SIX

MATT VIEWED LIFE AS A wild mix of bad and good. While he wasn't crazy about having a dumb-ass drunk pass out and whop him one in the jaw, he also felt some level of appreciation that the dumb-ass had given him an excuse to leave CB's without further explanation. Crowds held no appeal for him tonight. Only Jamie did.

And now that they were back in her suite and she was busy corralling him through the sitting room and toward the bedroom while her quick fingers took care of his shirt buttons, he could safely say there was no place on earth he'd rather be. Except in her bed, of course.

He was about to help Jamie lose her top when her hands closed over his. "First, we need some game rules."

"Game rules?" he asked, then kissed a sweet spot on her throat that he was pretty sure he hadn't gotten to yet.

"Yes. Like this is a fling, and only a fling. We don't have to pretend it's more than that, or say things we don't mean."

He slid his hands from beneath hers and down the sleek line of her waist to her hips. "But I'm allowed to say the things I *do* mean? Say, like, you amaze me, Jamie Delisle?"

She briefly frowned, then asked, "I do?"

Matt found her hesitation very un-Jamie-like and very interesting. "You do."

"Then feel free to say it."

"Good to know," he replied. "And since you said rules, plural, I'm assuming there're more?"

She nodded. "The second rule is that neither of us is allowed to wake up in the morning and act all squirrelly. We should just accept that we did what we did…. We had some fun, and—"

"*Some?* Trust me, honey, we're going to have a lot of fun." He waltzed them around so that he was now backing her toward the bedroom.

"You know what I mean," she said while unbuckling his belt. Then she let her hands fall to her sides. "I just don't want to mess this up."

If he were going to give her the flat-out honesty she wanted, he'd have to admit that he was nervous and didn't want to mess this up, either. But he figured that more action and less talk would help them both get past this beginning awkwardness. Honesty could wait its turn.

"I'm not much for rules," he said. "But if you want mine, I can give 'em to you in two words…. *Naked* and *happy*." And then he scooped her up, walked the rest of the way to the bed and dropped her in the middle of it.

She lay against the dark green comforter, her silky hair appearing almost gold in contrast. She was the most perfect temptation Matt could ever imagine. He wasn't a gimme-now kind of guy, but he wanted to dive onto that mattress and get his hands on her before she could even draw a breath.

"That's it? Those are all of your rules?" she asked.

He shrugged out of his shirt. "Once we've got *naked*

and *happy* down, I figure everything else will take care of itself."

Her gaze was almost greedy as she took him in. "It just might, at that."

He smiled, damn glad that she liked what she saw as much as he had last night...just before she'd ditched him. He stuck his wallet on the nightstand before pushing aside the corner of the comforter, where it had been turned down, then sat and pulled off his boots.

Jamie rolled onto her side and propped her head up with her hand. "Think you might hurry along?"

Matt laughed at her Queen of the Universe tone. "Just maybe."

By the time he was down to his briefs, he caught her eyeing the lone chocolate the staff must have left on the pillow when they'd turned down the bed. For the fun of it, he reached for the candy.

"No, you don't," she said, then dove for it. She rested stomach down as she peeled back the foil and ate the morsel. "I can take a lot of grief from a guy, but chocolate-poaching is pushing, it, my friend," she said when she'd finished.

Matt knew she was joking around, but her words struck a chord. He thought about all the pain he'd caused her and her family, and how he'd wished since then that he could take it all back.

"No more grief," he said solemnly. "Ever. I promise."

She stilled for an instant, her eyes wide.

"Damn," she whispered, then turned her head away from him.

Okay, so he'd screwed up big-time. He was no

stranger to that event. Matt swung his legs onto the mattress and moved closer.

"You okay over there?" he asked.

She nodded her head with that rapid, jerky movement he knew to the bottom of his male gut went with a woman's tears. But just to be sure, he gently brought her face back to his.

"Aw, Jamie, don't cry. I'm not worth it." He kissed her temple, then feathered a caress against her jaw.

She sighed.

"I'm sorry," he said. "I didn't mean to upset you."

She reached up and cupped the back of his head with her hand. "You didn't."

Matt knew by her tentative smile that she was lying, and he was grateful that she'd chosen to do so. When she drew him down to her, he went with the flow. He tasted her mouth and nipped on her full lower lip. He moved on and pressed his tongue against the strong pulse beating just beneath the delicate skin of her throat—tough and yet somehow fragile, just like Jamie.

Sweet Jamie. Good thing he'd turned her down when they were eighteen because she'd have been wasted on his arrogance. But now he was older and, he hoped, one hell of a lot more attuned to a woman like her. He could savor her wit and her inherent sexiness, adult to adult. And he could kiss and touch her all he wanted. Problem was, he didn't see an end to all this wanting.

She didn't object when he began to work her free from her clothes. When he paused to admire what he'd uncovered, he noticed that she wore a bra as sexy as the one she'd had on last night. Her breasts were full and beautiful, and he was pretty sure that if he couldn't hold them in his hands, and *now,* he was going to lose his mind.

Matt reached behind her, and she drew upward enough that he could unhook her bra and slip it from her. He sat back on his heels and looked at her, then touched his fingertip—which he noticed was trembling, dammit—to one pebbled, rosy nipple.

"I don't think I can hold back," he said, knowing that this first time was going to be over way too fast to keep him happy for long.

She took his hand and settled it fully over her breast. "Thanks for the info, but no one's asking you to."

Matt felt a smile split his face. "If I die of pleasure tonight, let my family know I went a happy man."

Some time later, sweaty and seriously aroused, Jamie gave a quick thought to Matt's set of game rules.

Naked?

Check. They'd been buck-naked for a while now, and she could say with absolute authority that his body was every bit as gorgeous as she'd suspected last night.

Happy?

Double-check. In fact, once she'd let go of those messy emotions that Matt had sent bubbling to the surface with his sweet promise to her, she'd begun to work her way toward delirious.

The man made love with the same thoroughness that she expected he applied to every part of his life. He'd paid exquisite attention to every bit of her, and said the sort of hot, sweet and flirting-with-dirty things that she'd always fantasized hearing from a guy. For the first time ever—well, second, counting last night—Jamie felt like a sex goddess instead of a mild and tidy lover.

Matt's hand slid between her legs. He began to ready her with his fingers deep inside her, moving in the same easy rhythm that he was using to feed on her mouth. She felt herself nearing her peak, and didn't want to go alone. Without taking her mouth from his, she reached blindly for the nightstand and the condom packet he'd earlier pulled from his wallet. Her hand did a vague dance across the wooden surface.

Nothing...nothing...nothing...wallet...nothing. Damn.

She tried to wriggle closer to the bed's edge, but that was an impossibility with two-hundred-odd pounds of insistent and very talented male above her.

Matt broke off their kiss. "Going somewhere, sweetheart?"

Jamie wasted no time on subtleties. "Condom. Now."

His slow smile made her heart slam.

"High school flashback," he said, all the while still driving her mad with his touch. "Jamie bossing me around with a box of condoms."

"Maybe you could listen this time?"

He kissed her again. "My pleasure."

Matt reached over and got the condom, then began to sheathe himself. While he did, Jamie kept contact with him...touching here and kissing there.

When he was ready, he settled her beneath him. It seemed the most natural thing in the world to tilt her pelvis up and wrap one leg high over his hips as he began to enter her.

"This is right," she said. They were simple words— silly, in some ways—but once they escaped, she was floored by their accuracy. This *was* right. So right that it was scary.

He whispered her name, then surged the rest of the way inside her. They lay there for a moment, gazes locked. Jamie was rattled by the fact that he looked as emotionally shell-shocked as she felt. She needed to get back to sass and pure physical thrill. That, she could handle.

She rocked her hips just a little, and his eyes grew darker. He dipped down his head and kissed her once, hard.

"Move it along, O'Connell," she ordered, though it would have worked better if her voice hadn't quavered.

As they moved together, Jamie told herself to focus on the skin-to-skin stuff. To fix in her mind the way their breathing sounded harsh and hungry in the cocoon of this bed. The way they fit together so perfectly. But the closer she drew to coming apart in his embrace, the more some little part of her mind shut down. It wasn't so much an out-of-body experience as a not-quite-*in*-her-body moment.

Matt stilled. "Where are you off to now?"

"Nowhere," she lied, breaking her first rule of honesty.

He shook his head. "Stop thinking. Just let go, sweetheart."

But if she let go, she'd be open to him, body and soul. She closed her eyes, trying to will away the hesitance.

"Jamie, look at me."

She did, and was knocked for a loop by the intensity—and oddly, vulnerability, too—in his eyes.

"Let this matter," he said. "Let *us* matter."

She nodded.

"Give me your hands."

She held her palms up and he locked his hands with hers, pinning them just far enough above her head that she knew he held her there, but not so far as to make her uncomfortable.

"Now, don't leave me," he said, then began to move faster and harder, each stroke pushing her closer to release.

"Now," he commanded, and Jamie could no more have stopped herself from coming than she could her heart from beating. She arched and cried out, and Matt tipped back his head and gasped and shuddered as he came, too.

A few minutes passed, after which Jamie could almost hear her thoughts above the beating of her heart. Matt, who'd collapsed with the bulk of his weight levered to one side of her, made a male sound of satisfaction.

"That," he murmured into the mattress as much as he did to her, "was beyond right."

Jamie's pulse zipped again, but this time it was with a weak, unnamed anxiety. "You might have earned yourself that touchdown ribbon to go on your flower arrangement," she said, taking refuge in lame humor.

He chuckled, then after resettling them so that she was resting against his chest, he said, "I'd say we pretty much earned ourselves the game ball."

She smiled. "That's what I get for bringing up sports analogies, huh?"

"Always a risk."

"I think I can bear a weekend of them, so long as you're included in the deal," she said, feeling just a bit of that natural sass begin to return.

"A whole weekend?" he asked in a sleepy-sounding voice.

She smiled. "I'll scrape by."

As Matt nodded off, Jamie settled in and sought peace and perspective. This had been about sex…there was no kidding herself on that count. No matter, though, because she knew her life would never be the same. The lingering hurt...the worry that with this man, in particular, she would never be quite enough...her embarrassment over having flung herself at him years ago—all of it was gone. She had battled her self-doubt, and it would no longer own her.

Jamie reached out and stroked Matt's thick hair. Maybe old memories didn't have to die. Maybe they just had to be viewed a new way....

MATT WAITED UNTIL HE WAS sure Jamie was asleep before opening his eyes and letting his thoughts ride wild. And these thoughts were damn wild.

He didn't often think about love. He thought a lot about business—the construction bids he'd won, those he'd lost, and how miserably hard it was to get the trades on site and working during hunting season.

Oh, and lust. He thought about lust—and acted on it—with decent frequency. What shook him tonight was that though he'd just experienced some of the best sex of his life, it hadn't been about lust. At least, not purely lust. Jamie had worked her way under his skin in an amazingly short amount of time.

Matt smoothed the hair back from her temple, and she sighed and snuggled in closer. Or maybe, he thought, it hadn't been that short a time, after all. He'd known her since...hell, he couldn't even recall a time when he hadn't known Jamie. Or a time when he hadn't courted her favor...when he hadn't looked for her in the cafeteria, even if he hadn't had the balls to go to her table in the far corner of the room and sit with her small group of friends.

And now he had to say that even though he'd gone stretches without thinking of Jamie, he had never forgotten her.

And never would.

Damn. He'd been blindsided by something—not love, because he was convinced that love was beyond his ken. But something fundamental had shifted inside him. Even her joking about just a weekend together hadn't set well. He wanted more. And what he wanted, he generally found a way to get. He had the money to fly to Chicago when his schedule permitted. And he was sure he could sweet-talk Jamie into sneaking down to Houston, now and again.

Jamie shifted and murmured something in her sleep. He decided to take the sound as one of agreement. Matt smiled. This wasn't love, but whatever it was, it felt damn good to him.

CHAPTER SEVEN

"GAME FILMS!"

Jamie stretched and looked at Matt, who'd bolted awake next to her.

"Is this a new game?" she asked. Heaven knew they'd played a whole lot of those last night, but most hadn't been talk-based.

"A game?"

"You know...now we're speaking in code?"

He ran a hand through his rumpled hair. "No. I was supposed to go watch Jett's game films with my brother and him first thing this morning, which was like..." He trailed off and checked the bedside clock. "Over two hours ago."

"You should get going, then," she said in what she hoped was a gracious and cheery end-of-fling tone.

He rolled closer and kissed her. "Should... But I don't want to. Not yet, at least."

Even though she knew she was delaying the inevitable chill of reality, Jamie's mood was buoyed.

"Do you have any other plan in mind?" she asked, thinking an hour or so spent in bed and in the suite's oversize steam shower might be the way to greet the day.

"Maybe that we spend the whole day together... turkey two ways?"

Clearly, she hadn't thought through this yen for to-getherness. Turkey two ways was really more like three: roasted, fried and tortured, which was her take on a meal with Matt and her dad seated at the same table. Maybe that made her a big, clucking chicken, but just now, she was okay with that. Some skeletons needed to stay the heck at the back of the closet, and the long-ago disappearance of the Pick 'n Trade was one of them.

"Any other plan?" she asked brightly over the knot that had formed in her throat.

Matt took her hand, wove his fingers between hers and kissed the top of her hand before asking, "Is this about me with your family?"

She nodded. "More or less."

"It's inevitable, Jamie."

Those were not fling words. "Last I'd heard, only death and taxes fell into that category."

"Funny," he said, but Jamie caught the implicit *not* in his tone. He let go of her hand. "And as tempted as I am to argue this one until I win, I'm not going to mess up the time we're guaranteed to have together. I'll go watch some game films and eat some bird. You can call me when you're back from Boerne with your folks, and maybe you can have dessert at my parents' house."

Now, that she could handle.

"Right," she said. "And before then…" She set her mouth against his, and her mind—and body—to starting the morning right.

BY LATE AFTERNOON, MATT WAS pretty sure his eyeballs were going to crumble to dust and pour from their sockets if he had to watch one more series of downs. His dad had segued straight from Jett's games to the NFL's Thanksgiving offerings. Deuce and Jett had been allowed to flee the den and its cluster of overstuffed leather recliners, while Matt had received the royal command to stay. Parental-bonding time with Big Jack could be a real pain in the rear.

As they watched Detroit's quarterback eat artificial sod after his offensive line folded like cardboard, Matt's dad said, "That could have been you, son."

Matt grinned. "I'm damn glad it's not."

His dad waved off the joke. "You know what I mean. You'd have gone high in the draft. You'd have been set for life—"

"I'm not exactly starving, you know." He'd never even been able to get his father to drop by a job site. If he'd see the size of projects Matt had begun to take on, he just might drop the football litany.

"All that could have been yours, and you had to hot-dog that damn play," his dad said.

Or maybe not.

Even before his senior year of college, he'd had a couple of knee-repair surgeries. "If it wasn't that play, another bad hit wouldn't have been long in coming. And who knows, I might have inherited my knees from you, Dad."

Bright red crept up his father's neck, and he popped his recliner out of launch position. Matt considered that it wasn't good policy to goad someone who should be on high blood pressure medication.

"And of course they could have come from Mom's side of the family, too," he added.

"As they likely did," his dad replied, and then reclined his chair again.

Matt, however, eased his chair upright, then checked his watch for at least the tenth time in the past fifteen minutes. He'd given Jamie his cell phone number and told her to call when she was ready to come out to his folks' place. As far as timing went, *now* would be a good time, and for the sake of his sanity, hours ago would have been even better.

"Have someplace else you need to be?" his dad asked.

"No, but I have someone I'll be bringing here. I'm hoping she can make it before the pecan pie."

"Who?" his dad asked, though he didn't really sound all that curious.

"Jamie Delisle."

Jack snorted. "That name again. Went years without hearing it, and now I get it twice from you in a couple of days. Didn't know she was a friend of yours."

"She wasn't, exactly," Matt said. "But we crossed paths in town and have been spending some time together. Tomorrow we'll probably go to the reunion together, too."

"Hope she's nothing like her father."

Since his dad seemed to grow crankier with each passing year, and had become so set in his opinions that he was pretty much concrete-encased, Matt had half expected this response. Still, the possibility remained that if he called him on it, his dad would back down.

"What do you mean?" he asked.

"Come on, son. We all know he's the town crazy. Mind you, every town needs a crazy or two for a little character, but we generally don't invite 'em to sit down at Thanksgiving supper."

A better man would have lectured his dad about his friggin' medieval views on mental health, but Matt didn't want a battle just before Jamie walked in the door. "Mom says that Jamie's dad is doing just fine."

His dad waved off the comment. "No point in arguing about this. You'll be back to work in a few days, and she'll be back in Chicago."

Something stunk, and it wasn't just the cigar stumps in his dad's ashtray. "You know where Jamie lives?"

Jack shrugged. "I've been in this town my whole life. I know everything I need to."

And the stink grew, but as his dad had just pointed out, this wasn't Matt's issue. He had grown up, had moved far from home, and he could pick up with Jamie once Prescott was again behind him. Still, that didn't feel quite right to him, and Matt didn't know why.

"In fact," his dad was saying, "I even have a good guess on why you were late this morning."

"Not that the specifics concern you. I apologized to Deuce and Jett, and we got through the films, anyway. No harm…no foul."

"Wrong. Those aren't the rules, and you know it. You can have a foul without harm on the field and off. The fact that it's a foul is enough. This family has a football mission. You can either get with the program or get out of the way."

Obsessions sure came in a variety of forms.

"This might be treatable," Matt said mostly to himself.

"What did you say?" His father's face was set in the same intractable lines Matt recalled seeing every time he'd tried to back off the "mission."

"I just pointed out that it's your goal and not mine,"

Matt said. "And this morning, if I'd seen any hesitance in Jett over this latest plan, I'd be all over both you and Deuce. But Jett wants it, so I'll keep my mouth shut."

"That's a start," his father said. "Now, what time is this Jamie person coming over?"

Matt shook his head. "I don't know."

And he also didn't know how the hell he'd insulate Jamie from his father's particular brand of tunnel vision, once she was here. It struck him that her visit might not be the best approach. Maybe small doses, if ever required, made more sense than a Thanksgiving trial by fire. Or maybe he had a yellow streak, but he'd figure that out later.

Feeling better for having made a decision, Matt rose. "I need to go make a call."

It was time to punt.

CHAPTER EIGHT

FRIDAY MIDMORNING, JAMIE walked down Main Street, a couple of fat shopping bags in her right hand. There were many things she adored about her line of work, but topping her list just now was the fact that retail therapy was not only mandatory, it was conducted on her clients' budgets.

It was going to take her a whole lot of buying to get past the sense that today held great potential to be awful. It wasn't simply tonight's reunion, though she remained hesitant on that front. And it wasn't Crystal calling earlier and reading her the riot act over how little time Jamie had spent with her. It was this danged cloud of confusion over her feelings for Matt.

She was nearly sure she loved him—an insane act, no matter how she viewed it. She didn't even want him at the same table as her father, and after last night, she suspected that he felt the same way about her mixing with his family.

Yesterday, when he'd called and said that there had been unexpected visitors at his family's house, and that maybe stopping in wouldn't be a good idea, she'd been pathetically relieved. And later in the night when he'd made love to her, it had felt like apology sex…and not totally in a good way. This did not bode well for a future, or even a present. So here she was, giving her business credit card a high-stress workout, feeling as cross and edgy as though she'd been smacked with a double dose of PMS.

Jamie adjusted her handbag's strap over her shoulder, and then strolled to check out a couple of stores she'd glimpsed when she'd parked in front of the O'Connell family's insurance agency on Tuesday. She'd just come out of the vintage print shop and back onto the walk when she bumped into a large, older man.

"Sorry," she said immediately. "I lost you in the glare of the sun."

Then she realized she was speaking to Jack O'Connell, who'd changed little since she'd last seen him... maybe added a few pounds and some more wrinkles sloping down from his mouth. Encountering him should be no big deal, but with her jitters of doom in full swing, she wanted the heck out of there.

"No problem," Jack said. "No problem at all."

She backed another step, praying he wouldn't recognize her. "Well...thanks."

He appeared ready to move on, and Jamie willed him to do so. But then recognition struck. "You're Jamie Delisle, aren't you?"

Once again she was faced with the debate over lying to an O'Connell male about her identity, and once again she realized only the truth would do. "Yes, I am."

His smile seemed a little fake around the edges, but Jamie was in no position to comment.

"Well, you're looking fine, Jamie," he said with a hearty sincerity that also seemed to ring a little false. "Matt mentioned yesterday that he's been spending time with you."

"We've bumped into each other," she replied. How much and how well, Jack needn't know.

"Really? Matt made it sound far more than that."

For which Matt would pay. Jamie could feel a blush working its way up her face. She *so* didn't need this.

"I've enjoyed your son's company," she replied.

"And I think he's enjoyed yours. I think he mentioned that you're attending the reunion together tonight?"

She nodded. "Yes."

"And so how are you keeping yourself busy until the big event?"

No point in mentioning that she was soon meeting Matt for lunch at the inn. "I thought I'd shop for a few clients. I'm an interior decorator in Chicago."

"So Matt told me," he replied. "And we're all pleased that you put our gift to good use."

In a childhood filled with hated hand-me-downs, at least she could say she'd never received a thing from the O'Connells.

"What gift?" she asked.

Jack shifted from one foot to the other like an aged schoolboy.

"Why, nothing," he finally said. "My mouth just got ahead of my brain."

She doubted that Jack O'Connell had more than a handful of unscripted moments each day, and she knew for sure that this wasn't one of them. There was a spark of something purposeful and maybe a little petty in the man's eyes, and at this moment she lacked the diplomacy to let it drop.

"Mr. O'Connell, why don't you just say what you intended to? What gift?"

"Well, I was thinking of the scholarship." He hesitated a moment. "I assume Matt did tell you, didn't he? With all that you've been together the past few days, the topic had to have come up."

"The scholarship?"

"Your scholarship. The one to that Georgia design school."

Jamie raised her hand, palm out. "Slowly, please. You're telling me that your family paid for my education?"

"It wasn't my idea," he said. "I've got to give my son the credit. Matt said it was only right. For all the trouble the boy made, he had a good heart.... And luckily a father with deep pockets."

"I'm not buying in, Mr. O'Connell. He would have told me this by now," she said, sounding one heck of a lot more certain than she felt.

"He's a little sweet on you, Jamie...always has been, his mama told me last night. He might not want you to feel you're beholden to us. Not that you are, of course," he hastily added.

Had the man slammed Jamie to the sidewalk, she could have felt no more attacked. Four years in Savannah at art and design school had been expensive, and until this moment she'd known nothing but gratitude for the benefactor who'd made it possible. Now, in a way that she couldn't even quite understand, she felt betrayed. And guilty. And truly shattered at the thought that she might be in the least beholden to this man.

The front door of O'Connell Insurance Agency opened and an overdone redhead stuck her head out. "Mr. O'Connell? That call you've been waiting for just came in."

"I'll be right there, Rhonda," he said to the woman, then gave another glance Jamie's way.

"Well, Jamie, duty calls. I'm sorry if I've said more than I should have." He gave her a clumsy pat on the shoulder with one broad hand, then walked off.

Furious and nearly physically ill, Jamie watched as Jack O'Connell strolled up the middle of the walk as though he owned the town. And then a horrible thought struck her.

Forget the town...he owned *her.* All these years she'd thought herself free of Prescott and the O'Connells, and they'd paid for her freedom. The whole family owned her...*including Matt.*

She thought of the past two nights, of the growing feeling that Matt truly cared for her, and realized that she'd been fooled by the town prankster one last time. He'd known all along that he'd shaped her success...yet more handouts to the junkman's daughter. He'd known, and even as they had grown closer, he hadn't shared this.

Jamie tried to push back the lump tightening her throat. She would not be owned. She would not be pitied. Never again. And she would begin to repay the O'Connells today. Just up the street was the bank where her mother worked.

Heedless of the passers-by with their bags of Christmas gifts, Jamie marched up to the ATM machine and dug through her purse until she'd found her card. She jammed it into the slot and tapped in her security code.

"Withdraw...savings..." she said as she selected her options.

Could this machine go no faster?

She tried for five hundred dollars, a good, solid number for a down payment on regaining her pride. The machine would have none of it, telling her that she'd be over her daily limit, but would she like to make another transaction?

Damn straight she did, and the two people now waiting in line for the machine could just wait. Again, she tapped in her personal identification number. Her requests for four and then three hundred were met with the same cold shoulder. She began to feel as though the world was conspiring against her. A crisp and perfect November day was crumbling to chilly gray ashes.

"Oh, for heaven's sake...two hundred, then," she said to the ATM.

Tears blurred her eyes as she entered her personal identification number, but the numbers were just part of the scrambled mental mishmash of embarrassment, anger and, as always, a big shot of self-recrimination. She obviously slipped with the ID because the machine asked her to reenter it.

"Right," she said, and tried to focus.

How could she have been so stupid as to involve herself with Matt O'Connell? He'd never meant anything but humiliation to her.

She typed in the numbers a second time.

Error: Invalid PIN. Please try again, announced the stupid machine.

She hit the buttons one last time, and the screen went ominously blank.

"Damn!" Jamie hit the cancel button, but it was too late. The ATM issued its final judgment.

Error: Invalid PIN. Card retained. Contact your financial institution for assistance.

She smacked the cancel button twice more. "Come on! Spit it out! I can't take any more!"

But the machine was as cold and insensitive as the world at large, and paid her no mind. Inside the First Prescott Bank & Trust, however, waited a mother's arms. Ignoring the bystanders' curious looks, Jamie pushed through the bank door and headed to the line for the tellers' windows, stopping only when she recalled that her mother had been promoted. Behind Jamie sat a maze of cubicles, guarded by a receptionist and several waiting customers. And somewhere in the maze was her mom.

Jamie approached.

"Hi," she said to the receptionist. "I'm Carleen Delisle's daughter, Jamie."

The receptionist smiled. "And don't you look just like her, too?"

Jamie managed a distracted nod. "I was wondering if I might see her for a second? Really, I promise it won't be any longer than that."

The receptionist gestured toward a clipboard on the counter. "I'd like to send you on back, Jamie, but as you can see, we've got people waiting. It's the day after Thanksgiving and everyone is lining up for those holiday loans."

If she were eighteen, Jamie could have, in good conscience, dissolved into a pool of tears. But she was thirty-three and had lost enough of her pride today.

"I'll just leave her a note," she said. "Do you have some paper?"

"Of course! Here you go, but if you want to wait, I'm sure we'll have an open chair, soon."

Jamie looked over to the small seating area, which

was thick with customers, most of whom were giving her a "don't you believe it" look. She jotted a quick note to her mom about the machine eating her card, her checkbook being in Chicago, and her need for some major cash today, then folded it over and was about to hand it to the receptionist when her mom emerged from her cubicle with an elderly client.

Her mom's happy smile when she saw her daughter knocked another hole in Jamie's composure.

"Hang on a second, honey," her mom said to Jamie, and then walked the client to the door.

"Cora Williams," the receptionist called, then crossed out a name on her clipboard.

The woman named Cora rose, and as she passed Jamie, slowed. Jamie was sure her face was a horror, complete with raccoon eyes from runny mascara.

"You go on," the woman said. "I can keep a little longer."

"You're sure?"

She nodded. "Of course. Go talk to your mother."

"Thank you," Jamie said, with a definite hitch between the two words. Like it or not, a real crying jag was going to work its way out.

"Come on back to my cubicle," Jamie's mom said, then anchored a hand under her elbow, not that Jamie was planning to run off.

Jamie took a quick glance at her mom's corporate-standard surroundings, grabbed the box of tissues from a low bookcase, and sat. She pulled out a tissue and held it at the ready.

"What's wrong, sweetheart?" Jamie's mom asked, and the dam was broken.

"That…that…miserable machine outside ate my ATM card, I left my checkbook in Chicago, and I need five hundred dollars right now, but other than that…nothing." She wiped at the tears streaming from her eyes.

"I see…. Well, at least I see a little of it," her mother said after a pause. "We'll get your card back, and I can lend you five hundred dollars, but none of that tells me what this is about."

"It's about Matt O'Connell," Jamie said after blowing her nose.

"Matt? You owe him money?"

"No. Yes. Sort of." Jamie tried to slow her words. "Mom, who paid for my time away at school?"

Her mother sighed. "Is this what the five hundred dollars is about?"

Jamie nodded, then dabbed at her eyes again.

"All these years later," her mother said. "Funny how here in Prescott nothing can be left to gather rust anymore."

"Just tell me," Jamie said.

"The money for your schooling came from the O'Connell family."

"Why didn't you tell me this fifteen years ago?" Jamie asked more sharply than she'd intended, but she was so damn tired of holding in her emotions.

"Inside voices, honey," her mom said, in a wry reminder that these low walls had many ears, and Prescott a gossip network that was unrivaled.

"And so, the reason?" Jamie prompted more quietly.

"Back when you left, I didn't tell you because you were in such a fragile state over your daddy's problems that I didn't want to add to the mix. Maybe I was wrong in saying nothing, but, Jamie, I had bigger issues on my mind. I didn't know if your father would ever be better enough to lead a normal life, and I didn't know how we could possibly afford the cost of the psychiatrists and the hospital to set him on the road back."

She paused for a moment, folding one hand over the other on the desk in front of her. "So if I decided not to tell you where your schooling was coming from, maybe it was because I had grief enough to handle. I figured if you knew it was O'Connell money, you'd turn it down."

Mom had her pegged.

"I would have, and I will now."

Her mom shook her head. "It's good to have enough success to afford pride, isn't it, sweetheart?"

"You think I'm *wrong* to want to pay them back?"

"Not wrong, but I also don't want you to feel as though you were somehow duped. I've known both Jack and Helen my entire life, and if I don't always like Jack's methods, I know that the family came to me with the best of intentions. At least Helen did. And I took the money in the same way…with only your future in mind."

"I understand." But even as she spoke, Jamie felt weary, weepy and still a lot confused. "But why didn't you tell me later?"

Her mother's shoulders rose in a slight shrug. "As time passed, it seemed less important. We'd all moved on. You have your career. Your father and I are back on track, and from all indications, Matt has grown into a fine man."

Jamie opened her palm and looked at her tissue, wadded into a crumpled white clump. "Fine enough," she replied. "Now, about that five hundred dollars…"

"There's no turning you back once you get an idea in

your head, is there?" Her mother pushed away from her desk. "Wait here. I'll be right back with your money."

Jamie let her eyes ease shut. If only she could tidy the rest of her life this easily.

CHAPTER NINE

MATT SAT IN THE PARLOR at the Bluebonnet, waiting for Jamie. In a way he was glad that she was late, because now he could take comfort in the fact that she wasn't perfect. She'd been gracious about the way he'd yanked back his dessert invitation last night. Too gracious, which had just made him feel like more of a yellow-livered bastard for having done it.

As five minutes late ticked its way toward ten, he tried her cell phone, but got no answer. By the time she was fifteen minutes overdue, he decided that their playing field was pretty much even again. He was about to go up to her room and see if she'd fallen back asleep when she came into the parlor.

Matt rose for his chair, thinking to kiss her.

"Here," she said, thrusting an envelope at him.

Matt took it, as he was being offered no choice. When he looked more closely, he saw that it was a bank envelope. Curious, he slid out the contents and found five crisp hundred dollar bills.

"What's this?" he asked, and then noticed that not only was this situation not right, Jamie didn't look right, either. Though her expression was neutral, he could see that she'd been crying. "Are you okay, sweetheart?"

"It's a down payment, and you might want to hold off on that 'sweetheart' stuff."

Matt crossed the room and closed the parlor door. When he returned, he gestured to Jamie with the envelope. "A down payment for what?"

"I ran into your dad a while ago."

Which fell into the category of a nonanswer.

"And you're paying me for the pleasure? I've got my doubts," he said.

Her mask of neutrality was gone, replaced by the kind of anger that most men fled from. "I'm paying you for my education. Granted, I'm about seventy thousand shy, but five hundred a month is the best I can do right now."

Matt dropped the envelope onto a low table next to a wing chair. "What?"

"Please don't play stupid," Jamie said. "This is awful enough already. And you want to know the worst of it?"

Really, he just wanted to know what the hell was going on, but maybe if she kept talking, he'd figure it out, so he nodded.

"The worst is that you paid me for nothing. I could have stopped the whole thing."

Stupid was definitely no act. "*What* whole thing?"

She walked to the fireplace and stood silently in front of it, her arms wrapped around her middle. Matt didn't know what had her so upset, suspected he was going to hate the answer, but no matter what she said, he needed to hold her. He went to her and compromised by settling his hands on her shoulders, which appeared to be about all she'd accept.

"Jamie, I need to know what we're talking about."

"The Pick 'n Trade," she said, one word tumbling over the next. "I *let* you do it, Matt."

"Let me? You mean you let me move that stuff?"

She nodded. "I saw the whole thing. My room was in the front of the house, and my mom and dad's in the back. I was up that night. I hadn't slept well since I'd embarrassed myself so horribly asking you for sex. Anyway, I saw you and the guys pull up in that pickup, and it didn't take long for me to know what you were there for."

The pieces still weren't falling together very well in his mind. "So you watched us and didn't stop us?"

"Yes."

He wasn't sure if he was supposed to be ticked off. It had been so long ago that if he was ticked off, it was in some weird, dispassionate way. "Just so I have this straight, mind telling me why?"

She wiped her fingertips below her eyes before she spoke, then shook her head at the traces of makeup that she'd caught. "I was pretty confused back then. My dad had developed OCD...obsessive—"

"Obsessive-compulsive disorder," Matt said. "I know what it is."

She nodded. "I suppose you must, by now. That May, everything had gone to pieces. We were broke because Dad had raided our savings to buy more stuff. My mom had tried to explain to me what was going on, but I didn't fully get it, and to the degree I did, I just didn't care. All I wanted was for him to *stop*. He was ruining my life. I was the town geek, and the only guy I had ever wanted had just turned me down flat. And could I blame him? After all, look how we lived!"

Matt took her hands, no longer caring if she fought back. "Jamie…sweetheart…"

"No. I need to finish this. I want to leave tonight with all of this *really* in my past."

"Tonight?"

"The sooner the better for both of us, I think. I don't want to spoil your reunion."

"The hell with the reunion!"

"Just listen. That night, when you guys showed up, I was going to go get my mom, but then I realized I could *use* you. You were going to do for me what I couldn't do for my family. You were going to make it all disappear. I kind of knew my father would break, if you did. And I'm such an awful human that I wanted him to."

This woman was going to break his heart.

"So not only did I get my way in blowing up my father's life, I got rewarded with a full scholarship to design school. And you want to know what makes me an even worse person? I feel guilty for that, but I'm downright furious that you knew your family did this, and in all the time we've been together, you haven't said a word."

Finally, he got the big picture, and he was beginning to feel pretty pissed off, himself. He left go of her hands. "So my family paid your way through school?"

"You know they did."

"Actually, Jamie, I didn't. But that part makes sense to me. A little restitution to keep my record clean before I left for college. You want to know what doesn't make sense?"

"What?" she asked in a tight voice.

"That you'd think I knew about the money. That hurts."

"Your father said it was your idea."

"Of course he would. He's not wild about your family, which is the real reason I backed out of last night. I didn't want you to hear the same garbage I'd heard. Bad call on my part, it seems. For that, I'm sorry. But to think that you'd believe—"

She shook her head. "I didn't, at first. But then he said how you'd been sweet on me and how you wouldn't say anything now because it might hurt my feelings…" She trailed off. "It sounds stupid, saying it now, looking at you and knowing what kind of man you are." She sighed and scrubbed her hands over her face. "I guess the bottom line is that this is all too messy for me. I can't handle it."

"Can't or just don't want to?"

"Can't."

He shook his head. "I don't believe you. I think you're just afraid. And I think that you're letting your fear make you lose."

"This isn't a football game," she said, and there couldn't have been worse words for his ears. "You can't apply some two-bit sports psychology to this."

He took her by the arms, wishing he could either kiss her awake to the Jamie he knew, or shake some sense into her. "You're damn right it's not football. That's a game…one that you play for a few years and put aside with other memories. This is *life* we're talking about. And unless it's some game—a fling or some stunt you're pulling on me—maybe you're too damn scared to grab it. And trust me, I know what I'm talking about."

"I don't know, Matt," she said. The way she was looking right through him let him know she'd already written them off. And he was so pissed that at that moment, he was willing to let her.

Matt dropped his hands and stepped away. "At least go to the reunion tonight."

She shook her head. "I've already changed my return ticket."

She offered her hand, and it took Matt an instant to realize that she wanted them to part as business associates or casual friends might. The hell with that.

He shoved his right hand in his pocket. "Yeah...well, I'll never forget you, Jamie Delisle. Never have and never will." And then he left before they could find some new way to hurt each other, because tough as he was, Matt had reached his limit.

JAMIE KNEW SHE WAS GOING to miss her flight. In fact, that was about the only thing she knew for sure. She'd left Matt six hours ago, called down to the desk and told them that she'd be checking out early, yet here she remained in her fussy and fancy cave of a suite, so frozen with self-doubt that she might as well be carved from a block of ice.

Matt had said she was being a coward. But was she? Wasn't there some point in a relationship where the people involved had to decide whether it was too damaged to survive? Maybe that was where she and Matt were.

Except, scared as she was of all the mess that would attend seeing Matt again, in her heart, she didn't want it to end. It seemed that in the battle of stubborn-mindedness versus six hours of stewing, the truth had finally risen. She loved Matt O'Connell.

She'd been a coward when she'd told him she didn't want to fight for them. She'd been so scared about having to admit to him—and to herself—how awful she'd been the night of the Pick 'n Trade's move that she hadn't been able to think straight. Life had made much more sense when she'd been able to maintain the personal fiction that she'd been the good girl...the wronged girl. Now that she'd had to look at the whole tangled picture, she felt lost. And until they got their pasts unraveled—however long that might take—she had some very, very messy days in front of her, too.

But was it worth it to give up a man she loved and wonderful games like Naked and Happy in exchange for some peace in life? Could she even imagine going back to Chicago and never hearing from Matt again?

Now, that *terrified* her.

"Idiot," Jamie told herself. She hurriedly called down to the front desk and told them she'd be staying after all, then flipped her suitcase up onto the bed. If she was going to undo the day's damage, she needed to move quickly.

Cocktail hour had just ended by the time she made it to Live Oaks Country Club and stuck on her name tag, complete with hideous senior photo. The ballroom's dance floor was packed with milling people, and it seemed that most of them were more than happy to talk over the reunion committee's organizer, who was handing out prizes for silly things like "Traveled the Farthest" and "Most Kids."

Jamie looked for Matt, but saw him nowhere. Nervous and worried that she'd totally blown it and Matt had left town, she stopped at the cash bar to get a drink. Crystal came up behind her. Her friend wrapped her in a hug and scolded her at the same time.

"Where have you been, and why weren't you answering your phone today? I even tried to corner Matt to ask what the heck was going on, but he kept slipping away from me."

Jamie moved back far enough to ask, "So Matt's here?"

"Somewhere," she said with a vague wave of her hand. "I'll have a white zinfandel," she said to the bartender. "Jamie, what do you want?"

"Vodka on the rocks," she replied. If she was going to go for Dutch courage, she might as well go the entire distance.

After they had their drinks, Crystal nudged her through the crowd toward the spot she'd saved at their table close to the front of the room.

Jamie exchanged greetings with people and became increasingly adept at picking identities off name tags and not making a fool of herself. They were almost to Crystal's table when a new speaker came up to the microphone. It was Crystal's Corey. Crystal, with the ease of a devoted wife and mom to a chatty child, shushed everyone around them. Amazingly, it worked.

"I'll make this quick," Corey announced, and was answered with applause.

"Thanks," he said dryly. "At our fifth reunion, our football coach gave me the special duty of presenting the game ball from the 1990 championship to our quarterback. Unfortunately, the recipient didn't show. Neither did he see fit to attend our tenth reunion. So now that he's here for our fifteenth, and because Crystal's been making noises about putting the ball in the give-away bag, I'd like to present this to Matt O'Connell." Corey hefted the football in the air. "Matt…come on up and take this off my hands."

The crowd cheered, and Jamie's heart pounded louder and louder as she waited to see him. He took the three steps on the right side of the stage. She clenched her drink tighter, had a sip and immediately started coughing. Because she simply was not a vodka girl, she abandoned the drink on the table.

"Honey, are you all right?" Crystal asked while patting her back.

"Fine," she managed to gasp.

Matt came to the microphone, accepted the ball and shook hands with Corey, then smiled at the crowd. Jamie ached to be able to get to him, to touch him, to tell him how sorry she was for turning chicken.

"I'll make this even shorter than Corey did," Matt said to the gathering, earning more cheers. "I just want to say—"

It was almost as though she'd willed him to look her way, because he spotted her. Shock and something else— *Lord, don't let it be anger*—were stamped on his face. Jamie was so intent on putting everything she wanted to say into one look that she nearly forgot to breathe.

Matt shook his head and turned his eyes away. "I just want to say…"

He trailed off, looking as scattered as Jamie felt. Why had she thought that a crowd of a couple of hundred was the appropriate place to seek him out?

Matt gave a low laugh. "I'm really screwing up, aren't I?"

He looked back at her. Thinking to simplify matters, Jamie turned to exit the room. She'd just wait outside and catch him when she wouldn't trip him up.

"Jamie!"

She swung around at the sound of her name echoing from the microphone.

Matt's expression held such confusion, but she didn't know what to do other than to mouth "it's okay" and shake her head to say that she wasn't really leaving.

"No!"

She drew in a sharp breath as he threw the football.

"Oh, no…" It came spiraling toward her in a perfect arc. She'd been no gym-class whiz, so she just stuck her hands in the air, shut her eyes and prayed. The ball smacked against her palms, and she drew it in.

The crowd went wild. Totally overdosed on emotion—and utterly confused over what throwing a ball at her was supposed to mean—Jamie said to Crystal, "I think I just broke a nail."

Onstage, Matt was looking a little less peaked. "You know you can't leave with that ball, right?" he asked her.

She nodded.

"I guess I'm not going to be short, after all," he said to the audience. "So bear with me a minute." He looked down to his feet, then back to the crowd. "The great thing about reunions, other than the chance to win a piece of luggage or a case of diapers, is that it gives all of us an opportunity to remember what we did right, and maybe to think a little on what we did wrong. It just so happens that I covered both categories pretty equally. Right now, though, I want to fix a wrong."

He hesitated an instant, and the warm look that he gave Jamie made tears start in her eyes.

"I want to publicly apologize to Jamie Delisle for moving her father's belongings. No matter who else rightly or wrongly feels they should take the blame for being a messed-up kid, I need to be responsible for myself. It was wrong, and it pretty much tops my list of bad things."

He blew out a breath. "Okay, that's done," he said, and got a few low laughs in response. "Now, I also want to share with you what currently tops my list of good things...and that's falling in love."

"Oh...my...stars!" Crystal gasped. Jamie shushed her, but didn't take her eyes from Matt.

"Sweetheart, if I'd had a measure of sense back then, I'd have known what I do now. I'm in love with you, Jamie, and I think if you'd just slow down a minute, you'd find that you might love me, too. At least I'm hoping so."

She nodded, and he laughed, a joyful sound she wouldn't forget if she lived to be one hundred.

"Well, then, if you stay right there, I think we can leave the rest of this crowd to carry on without us, don't you?"

Still clutching that football, Jamie nodded another yes, her laughter and tears a crazy mix.

Matt was in front of her before she'd even realized he'd left the stage. He took the football from her hands and casually tossed it back to Corey, who now stood next to Crystal.

He took Jamie in his arms.

"Jamie, will you let me make love to you tonight and every night for as long as we both might agree?"

She leaned close and kissed him. "I have a feeling that's going to be a very, very long time."

A wise man might have said that you can never go home again, but Jamie Delisle was thrilled she hadn't listened.

READY AND WILLING
Tanya Michaels

PROLOGUE

12:01 a.m., June 2, 1991

THOUGH FIFTEEN-YEAR-OLD Noah Tanner had never been up to Trojan Point at night before, he had entertained fantasies about making out with a pretty classmate there once he got his license next month. Instead, he was hiking through the dark underbrush of a side trail to pick his first real fight. His older brother, Caleb, would have the advantage of age, height and weight, but Noah didn't care. Every guy had his breaking point.

Especially guys who had worked so damned hard to stay out of trouble, as Noah had done for almost two years. He'd been trying to atone for the mistake he'd made shortly after their mother had dropped her three sons in this one-horse Texas town so she could recover from their father's death.

Noah had no idea if she'd recovered since the calls she made to his grandmother's farm were few and far between. *Maybe she's moved on and we're just painful reminders.* Caleb bitterly wrote off their mother as a selfish bitch who didn't care about her own children. At least he had the smarts not to say it in front of their younger brother, Josiah.

While Noah didn't know why his mother hadn't returned, he was grateful their grandmother, Annabelle, had taken them in. That's what he regretted most about his single brush with being bad—the disappointment in his grandmother's eyes. Noah had been in a department store, staring at a jacket he knew Caleb would like, remembering that his older brother's birthday was just around the corner. He'd also realized that their mother probably wouldn't even send a gift. Anger had welled up in him over the way they'd been dumped and forgotten, and the next thing he knew, he'd been in the fitting room, tearing out the tag so he could stroll out of the store wearing the jacket. When he'd been caught, he hadn't known just how long his impulsive action would haunt him.

His teachers and neighbors were quick to remind him of the incident, especially when Caleb's pranks only confirmed the town gossip that the Tanner boys were no good—so unwanted they'd been foisted off on their charitable grandmother. Caleb had been pissed off since their father's death, and being ditched in Prescott had done nothing to downsize the chip on his shoulder.

Their grandmother had hoped making friends would help Caleb; unfortunately, football player Matt O'Connell and hot-rodding daredevil Kirk McKenzie just fed Caleb's bad attitude. Noah considered it a minor miracle that all three of them had lived through their senior year, much less earned high school diplomas. While Noah had learned his lesson fast and hard, whenever Caleb got caught, it only seemed to fuel his rage. And their grandmother's heartache. Part of Noah thought he should just ignore Caleb and wish his older brother good riddance after the graduation ceremony tomorrow. Technically, later today. But the more furious part of Noah wanted his chance to get it all off his chest before Caleb high-tailed out of town abandoning his two younger brothers. Noah had gone to Caleb's room tonight, but—surprise, surprise—his brother had snuck out.

That had been enough to send Noah over the edge.

Knowing where his brother had most likely gone, he'd followed, his fury growing with each step. He was angry that his grandmother could barely look her friends in the eye at church on Sundays. Angry that just last week, she'd received a call from thirteen-year-old Josiah's principal about a dangerous stunt Josiah had performed, seeking to emulate his "cool" older brother. Angry that half the people in town still judged Noah every time they looked at him. Yes, his initial screwup was his own fault, but Caleb's constant run-ins with Officer Hardy and other town authorities kept gossip about the Tanner boys from dying down.

"Hardy has it in for me," Caleb had complained more than once. "He's trying to make a name for himself in a town with a nonexistent crime rate, so he keeps busting me and my friends. If he wants to be a real policeman, he should get the hell out Prescott. Anybody with half a brain would get out of here as soon as he got a chance."

Though Noah was only about eighty-percent sure where he was going in the dark, he caught the sound of a familiar voice and followed it, his irritation hotter than the muggy summer night. *Caleb.*

"…The Pick 'n Trade is unbeatable, O'Connell. Your best idea yet."

"Right up until I got caught," Matt O'Connell answered.

"Come on, man." Just hearing his brother's admiring tone made Noah clench his fists. "You're a freakin' *legend!* Did you see the look on people's faces when they saw all that crap on the high school lawn? Who cares if you ticked off that crazy Delisle guy? And thanks for not ratting us out."

I knew it. Though Caleb had smirkingly denied any involvement in the recent town prank, his protests were unconvincing. Caleb always took pride in his exploits and had probably only distanced himself from this final prank to make sure it didn't prevent his escape.

There was a pause, then Matt's voice again. "It was no big deal."

A breeze stirred, bringing with it the scent of the illegal campfire and making it harder for Noah to hear, but he caught Matt's explanation that his dad had once again covered for his son. *Must be nice to have a father who bails you out.* Noah's stomach churned. Missing his dad wasn't the raw pain it used to be, but it still sucked.

Kirk McKenzie echoed some of what Noah felt. "Wouldn't have worked that way if it had been me they'd caught. The last thing my old man would have done was save my ass with the sheriff."

Noah was close enough to see them now, through the pecan and oak trees. Matt shrugged, changing the subject. "So I heard that after what happened last night, Amanda broke up with you."

"It was just as well," Kirk answered. "I was going to break it off with her after graduation, anyway."

"When you taking off?" Matt asked.

Kirk had barely finished his explanation before Caleb started sharing his own plans for getting the hell out of Prescott. "I've already told my grandmother I've got a friend in Austin who can get me a job. She's just thrilled at the thought of my being employed. How about you, Matt? You gonna work at the golf club again this summer?"

The football player shook his head. "I'm moving up to Oklahoma to live with my uncle and get in shape before the season starts."

Caleb grinned, his expression eerily illuminated by the fire. "Are you gonna remember us when you make the NFL? Seriously, you know hanging out with you guys is the only thing that made this shit town bearable for the past two years."

The genuine emotion in Caleb's voice stopped Noah in his tracks. When was the last time he'd heard anything besides anger and cynicism from his brother? Something burned through Noah and it took him a moment to define it as…envy.

God, he'd felt so alone the past two years, constantly fighting with Caleb, trying to keep Joe from following in their older brother's footsteps, struggling to be a good-enough grandson for all three of them, so his grandmother wouldn't decide *she* didn't want them, either. He felt trapped between a rock and a hard place—shunned by some because he was one of the "Wild Tanner boys" and having to keep his distance from others itching for trouble who'd presumed he'd be as much "fun" as his brother.

Caleb's taste in friends might be questionable, but at least he *had* close friends.

Matt had raised his bottle of beer, and all three of them were speaking now. "To Jim Morrison, James

Dean and all the rebels who knew when to die. You went out big, and we salute you."

As they chugged the beer they'd probably charmed a pretty twenty-one-year-old into buying for them, a sudden burst of sadness replaced the anger Noah had been nursing. *Forget it.* Caleb was leaving tomorrow. No point in confronting him now. Noah wasn't much of a fighter, anyway.

Turning to go back down the way he came, Noah reminded himself that getting in trouble wasn't worth the grief it caused even though, for a moment, he wished he could be just like Caleb.

CHAPTER ONE

November 23, 2006

I'M A DUMB-ASS, NOAH TANNER thought to himself. A dumb-ass with a twenty-pound turkey.

It was the only logical explanation for why he had believed this Thanksgiving would be the first he and his brothers spent together in the past decade. Caleb and Joe had both said they would come to Dallas for the holiday, but that had been sentiment talking. All three of them had been rocked by their grandmother's death in August. Noah hadn't been able to track down his restless older brother until weeks after the service, and Josiah had been in Tokyo when she passed—so they both had legitimate excuses for missing the funeral. Unlike Gwendolyn Tanner, who had sent flowers but hadn't bothered to attend.

Big surprise. After all, the mother-child bond was apparently lost on good old Gwen. The last time Noah had seen his mom had been Joe's graduation from MIT.

Once Caleb had moved away from Prescott, taking his bad influence with him, Noah and his grandmother had been able to turn Josiah's aptitude with computers toward something useful. The kid now pulled down six figures a year designing video games on the West Coast. *Guess all those afternoons he spent at Archie's Arcade weren't a waste, after all.*

The ringing phone suddenly underscored how quiet the apartment was—football hadn't started yet, and Noah was in no mood to watch floats and musical acts parade down the streets of New York. Unfolding his six-two frame from a kitchen chair, he reached for the receiver that hung above the counter. "Hello?"

"Happy Thanksgiving," Joe said cheerfully. "I wish I was there with you guys, but figured calling was the next best thing. Don't hate me, okay, bro? We had a major deadline change because we just got news our toughest competitor is trying to release their version of a similar PC game a week before us. We've got to step up design if we want to hit the market first."

"Sure, I understand." What was a holiday with family compared to software that allowed players to be one of eight hunters tracking down alien invaders?

"I really am sorry to cancel. You and Caleb should go ahead to the house without me. No point in us delaying again because of my hectic schedule."

No point except the nauseous feeling Noah sometimes got when he thought about selling off their grandmother's place. Putting it on the market was the only logical thing to do, since she'd left it to three grandsons scattered across the States.

"Actually, Caleb didn't show, either," Noah said casually.

"Oh. Man, I'm sorry." Pity laced Joe's voice.

Great. Now I'm the thirty-one-year-old bachelor all alone with only overcooked poultry for company. Which was ridiculous. Routine favors for neighbors and friends had earned him numerous dinner invitations. Even Stefanie had asked him to join her family in San Antonio... then admitted she'd yet to tell them about the breakup and was hoping to continue stalling until after the holiday season. She was laboring under the misconception that her relatives liked Noah better than her and wouldn't understand why she'd ended their four-month relationship.

The short silence obviously made Joe feel worse. "You want me to see if I could still make it for the weekend? If I pull an all-nighter and manage to find a flight tomorrow evening..."

A sympathy visit? "No. Tickets would cost you a fortune at this point, and you'd be stressed about your deadline. We'll get together some other time."

"What about...her house?" Even if Joe hadn't made much time to visit Texas in the past few years, his love for their late grandmother was clear in his halting speech.

"I could go by myself," Noah said impulsively. Since he rarely made impulsive decisions, he assumed this one stemmed from wanting to lessen Joe's guilt. That, and a too-quiet holiday. "Why the hell not? I could use a change of scenery."

"Really? Great idea." His little brother's tone was equal parts enthusiasm and relief. "You know we trust you to accept an offer for all of us."

An offer? The place wasn't even on the market yet. "It will need some work before we can sell."

"Yeah, but I have no skills in that department. I'll send plenty of money to offset costs, but *you're* the carpenter. Last time I saw Caleb, he wasn't sober enough to operate sandpaper, much less tools."

Noah winced. "That was years ago. He's probably grown up since then, just like you and me."

"You didn't have much growing up to do, bro. I don't care what some of our idiot neighbors said about you, you were mature even as a kid."

Joe meant it as a compliment, but it had often felt to Noah like a curse. Did his brothers think he'd *enjoyed* knocking himself out with community service, trying to redeem not only himself but all three of them? Not that it had worked. When kids in his own graduating class had cooked up mean-spirited stunts, Noah had always been the first one the principal suspected. Sometimes he wondered why he even bothered maintaining his perfect GPA and cleaning out rain gutters for his grandmother's friends. Hadn't anyone realized he would have preferred spending his spare time necking with one of the Prescott Panther cheerleaders?

If I had it all to do again...

Stupid, useless thought. If he did have it to do again, he'd probably follow the same path he'd taken the first time, except for trying to steal that leather jacket. Too bad he couldn't fix that mistake.

Since then, Noah had fixed many things, especially with his restoration business. So it seemed disrespectful that he was letting his grandmother's place slide into disrepair. "All right, I'll go to Prescott. I'm holding you to the finance part, though." Noah could afford the time away from work, but not funding renovations on top of the lost revenue.

"I'll put a blank check in the mail first thing tomorrow," Joe promised. "And call me if you need anything else."

Why? Noah wondered as they disconnected. Despite being the only optimist in the family, eventually even he had learned not to rely on his brothers.

Still, the Tanners had turned out better than many had predicted. At least neither of Noah's brothers were in state penitentiaries—unless prison was what had detained Caleb. Noah wasn't sticking around to find out.

As soon as he could pack and find recipients for all of this food, he was out of here. Returning to the town that had been happy to say goodbye to the Tanner boys.

"Brianne McCormick? I'm Sheriff Rick Hardy." His introduction was unnecessary. Most people in Prescott knew the square-jawed lawman by sight, even those who'd only lived here a month. "I'd like to ask a moment of your time, ma'am."

Bree's mouth went as dry as a creek bed during a summer drought. *Oh God, oh God, oh God.* Her usual reaction to the police.

"S-sure. I have a client meeting me here in, um, half an hour, but until then…" Gripping the white paper bag she held, she willed her hands not to shake as she unlocked the office door. Maybe the sheriff would attribute any trembling to the forty-degree weather. *Calm down. You didn't* do *anything.*

But when had innocence ever protected her?

The sheriff removed his hat, revealing dark hair sprinkled liberally with authoritative silver. "Don't mean to interrupt. This should only take a few minutes."

"No problem. We're expecting it to be pretty quiet

today, with it being a holiday weekend." She was the only one scheduled to come in this Saturday. "I'd planned to eat an early lunch at my desk and get a jump on next week."

He slanted his hazel eyes toward her bag with a smile that could have made him handsome if he weren't a cop. "Hanson's barbecue?"

She nodded.

"Best in the state," he said as he followed her inside the chilly, dimly lit office. The heat had been turned down when everyone left Wednesday, before the cold front that had blown in on Thanksgiving. It had stayed in the thirties before going up a degree or two yesterday afternoon—practically arctic for this part of Texas.

Reaching a hand inside her tiny office, she flipped a switch. Fluorescent lights flickered on with a faint buzz. "Please, have a seat." She tensed up even more when she glanced at the photo atop her desk, she and her father outside Reliant Stadium before a football game on his birthday. "I, um, I'm just going to adjust the thermostat."

By the time she returned, she'd regained her composure. She rounded the desk and slid into her chair, ignoring her phone's flashing red message light while the sheriff explained the reason for his visit.

"I don't know if you've heard yet through the town's impressive rumor mill, but there was a residential break-in two nights ago." His expression hardened. "Some lowlife apparently thought the holiday would be an opportune time to steal."

"A break-in?" While it was true that gossiping was the town's major pastime, newcomers were never the first to hear anything. Besides, she'd been preoccupied—renovating her small house, taking care of her dad and trying to prove to those in charge at Prescott Realty that they'd made a good choice in hiring their first new employee in five years.

Sheriff Hardy leaned forward in his chair. "I'm here because the house in question is on sale, owned by one Frank Garcia. I understand he's recently canceled the contract with his original broker and is now listed through you?"

The personal connection startled her. "That's right. Mr. Garcia is in the middle of a move to New Mexico, and we've been showing the house in his absence and relaying any offers. He was robbed?"

"Not exactly. His cousin walked through with one of my officers and doesn't seem to think anything's missing. Maybe Frank doesn't have enough still here to have made it worth the burglar's while. Or maybe something spooked the intruder into leaving empty-handed. This is just a matter of routine investigation, Ms. McCormick. I'll be interviewing Frank's former real estate agent as well. You have access to the house, correct?"

You have access to the house. No matter how "routine" this was, the statement rang accusatory in her ears. "Of course, but so do all the other Realtors in town. We placed a lock box on his front door, with a key to the house, so agents can show the home to clients. Although most agents call first, the modernized lock box sends me, as Mr. Garcia's representative, an e-mail whenever anyone uses it. I checked e-mail from my laptop yesterday, but there wasn't any new activity."

"I wouldn't expect there to be, since it looks as if the intruder came in through the back. Have you noticed anything suspicious on walk-throughs? Maybe a strange car parked nearby, or a supposed interested buyer who wasn't asking the right questions?"

"You mean someone who looked more like they were casing the joint than evaluating closet space? No, not at all. Everyone's been so…nice." The idea of criminal activity in Prescott was surreal. Though she wasn't naive enough to think crime didn't exist here, it certainly wasn't evidenced in the town's relaxed pace and old-fashioned charm. Then again, recent growth and the resulting changes were why she herself had been able to find a job here.

"If you remember something or see anything in the area, call the police station," the sheriff advised her. "Although nothing appears to have been stolen, I take every investigation very seriously. Don't hesitate to let me know about any details, even if they seem silly. You might be surprised at the tips that turn out to be important."

"Okay." The police asking for her help—how ironic was that?

The sheriff stood. "This may turn out to simply be a case of a transient taking advantage of shelter because of the cold snap. Garcia's house is off the beaten path and clearly empty. Still, I wish more people in this town would lock their doors and windows."

Bree thought back to an apartment she'd had in Houston, where the windows had been painted shut and her neighbors had gone to the expense of adding bars over the panes. In comparison, Prescott had seemed a safe, sleepy town—the perfect fresh start for a widower ex-felon and his daughter.

"Can I get you anything else to eat, hon?"

"No, ma'am." Noah looked up sheepishly at Mrs. Hanson, who'd always had a kind smile for him. He swore the plump, blue-eyed woman hadn't aged a day in the past decade. "I already ate more than I should." He could travel the world as extensively as his jet-setting genius little brother and never find food as good as they served in this unassuming barbecue and steakhouse. Ducking into Hanson's for dinner had served the dual purposes of satisfying the craving he'd had ever since his last trip to Prescott and postponing his inevitable arrival at Annabelle James's farmhouse.

It just wouldn't be the same place without his grandmother's presence—her stern but affectionate reminders on everything from chores to hygiene, the smell of homemade sausage gravy cooking before church, the way she'd refused to ever say a negative word about her daughter but hadn't begrudged the boys their anger, either. As a teen, Noah had winced each time Caleb took a hostile tone or was caught in a new scrape, nervous that Annabelle would seize the opportunity to toss them out and reclaim her peace and quiet. Terrified after he himself had betrayed her trust when she'd allowed him to go into a department store by himself. Now he was shocked he'd ever had so little faith in her.

She had loved them unconditionally, even when they weren't particularly likable. Was that why Caleb hadn't been able to make himself return? Maybe he felt guilty over the stress he'd caused the bighearted woman. Or maybe he simply didn't give a damn. Hard to tell with Caleb.

Pushing his empty plate away, Noah vowed to worry less about Caleb. Joe, too. Their successes and mistakes were out of his hands. Perhaps selling the farmhouse, ridding himself of part of their shared past, would free him from his self-imposed burden. Free sounded like fun.

The first step would actually be walking the entire property, which at its southernmost end was only half a mile from the road leading to Trehan Point. He needed to decide what changes to make to the house and the two small outer buildings, what should be fixed to get the best price and what was minor enough to be left for new owners. It wasn't as if he hadn't set foot on the farm since his grandmother died—he'd been there in September, to give away the belongings she'd designated for friends and the rest to several charities she'd supported. He'd continued paying the electricity, water and phone service every month because he'd known he and his brothers would need to come back soon.

Only "soon" turned out to be several months later, and here he was alone.

At the thought of how long he'd already stalled, he pulled out his wallet and left a generous tip. As he climbed into his Chevy pickup, he had one final misgiving about driving to the farm tonight. He could stay in town and get an early start in the morning—after all, he'd always wanted to stay at the Bluebonnet Inn. As a carpenter who often restored antiques, he'd be interested in seeing what the owners had done with the historic building. *Then take a tour.* Throwing the truck into Reverse, he backed out of the parking lot.

Prescott's picturesque downtown area was small and relatively unchanged. Most of the growth was taking place on the outskirts. There were several new subdivisions and strip malls. Between the patches of encroaching civilization, however, stretches of no-man's land remained. Heading toward the farms and residential ranches that circled Prescott, he found himself on a two-lane road with only rain ditches and fenced pastureland running along the sides. There was no lighting here except for the stars crowding the sky. The stillness that seemed peaceful now could be awfully stifling to a teenage boy. Though he and Caleb seemed to have less in common with each passing year, Noah, too, had been eager to escape to a bigger city once he'd graduated. He'd wanted the anonymity.

Staring ahead, he almost missed the flash of headlights to his right, just below street level. A car had gone into the ditch, and a woman stood near the hood. He couldn't make out any of her features from here, but her curves were nicely silhouetted.

He veered toward the right, flipped on his hazards and parked. He'd forgotten his cell phone in Dallas so he couldn't call for assistance, but he was pretty good with cars. Caleb had been better, but at least Noah had never hot-wired a vehicle.

Noah shut his cab door and called out a greeting from several yards away. "Hello. Need a hand?"

At the truck's approach, the stranded woman had moved to the driver's seat, halfway inside with her hand on the open door. Her delicate features, short brown hair and full mouth were captured in the glow of the car's interior light.

"Hi," she returned, her voice neutral despite her I'm-prepared-to-jump-in-and-lock-all-the-doors posture. "I swerved to miss a deer and lost control for a minute, but I think the front-end damage is mostly cosmetic."

"I'm Noah. I'd be happy to take a look for you."

"That's not necessary. I'm just going to gun the accelerator and get her back up on the road. No offense, but I'd prefer you not come any closer. Also, my cell phone's right here and I have a can of pepper spray in my hand."

Noah stopped short, not sure whether he was amused or insulted by her warning. To think, he'd thought her delicate-looking!

So much for the myth of damsels in distress.

CHAPTER TWO

NICE, BREE.

Women all over the world complained that chivalry was dead, and here she was, driving nails into its coffin. Still, she was too aware of predators and con artists, especially given her father's history, and this morning's news of a robbery. The message Frank Garcia had left her had been even more upsetting than the sheriff's visit. According to Frank, his house had been ransacked and was temporarily off limits to prospective buyers. He'd sounded violated and jittery. So when a strange man parked behind her in the middle of the night and approached, Brianne worried more about safety than manners.

"I throw myself on your mercy, ma'am." Though she couldn't see it, she was certain she heard a smile in his voice. She practically detected dimples. "I'm unarmed, don't even have a cell."

Basic self-defense classes taught that physical strength was a weapon, but she found herself thinking that the way he drawled "ma'am" was dangerous in its own right. When the sheriff had called her that, it sure hadn't sounded like warm butterscotch syrup being drizzled over rapidly melting ice cream.

"Sorry if I seem ungrateful," she said, even as she

was surprised she felt the need to explain herself, "but a woman can't be too careful."

He was quiet for a moment, and she wished she could get a better look at him. She felt exposed down here in the glow of light.

"Fair enough," he finally said. "How about I go back to my truck, and you give it your best shot getting her up on the road? If that doesn't work, we'll renegotiate. And if it turns out you need my help, maybe there's someone you can call who would put in a description and good word for Noah Tanner. I'm harmless."

Yeah, right. His amused tone and deep voice sounded more wicked than virtuous.

"You're well known in Prescott? I don't recognize you." Pity, too. Everything from his attempt to help to his unmistakably broad shoulders told her she wouldn't mind knowing him.

Bree stifled a sigh at the thought. Just because she'd been too busy for a social life didn't mean she was desperate enough to get weak-kneed over a strange man on the side of the road.

"Went to high school here," Noah said. "I live in Dallas, but got back in town tonight, in time for dinner at Hanson's. You could ask Mrs. H. about me."

She nearly salivated at the mention of her favorite restaurant. "You're a fan of their barbecue?"

"More like devotee. Eating their food is definitely one of the more enjoyable things a man can do with his mouth."

Ignoring the spark of warmth in her blood, she refused to speculate on the other things. "I should be going, Mr. Tanner. But maybe I'll see you around town."

"Call me Noah. And your name is…?"

"Bree."

"Nice to meet you, Bree."

She waggled her fingers in a quick goodbye as she ducked into her car. Locking her doors, she watched as the man strode toward his truck.

Who said nothing exciting ever happened in small towns?

First there'd been her moment of panic when she'd glimpsed the deer, then more panic when her car had careened off the road, then a whoosh of attraction to the tall stranger who'd appeared out of nowhere to offer his services. *His help,* she amended. Anything else she'd detected might have been a reaction to the moonlight, her dating dry spell or her scenting Hanson's barbecue sauce on the breeze. In the regular old light of day, Noah Tanner might not even be good-looking.

Wondering if they'd meet again, she jammed her foot onto the accelerator, watching carefully for Noah and oncoming traffic as her car jerked backward. He stood by his truck, ready to lend aid. In a few minutes, she had the little four-door squared on the road and, though she doubted he could see it, offered one last wave. Then she drove off into the night—which would be far more mysterious and romantic if she weren't on her way home to feed the cat, microwave a frozen dinner and call her dad.

Maybe *mysterious* and *romantic* were overrated. Her gaze flicked to her rearview mirror and she grinned at the glimpse of Noah's truck in the growing distance. *Maybe not.*

WHEN BREE TOOK HER FATHER to lunch Monday at Hanson's barbecue, it wasn't just because her encounter with Noah Tanner lingered in her mind. She loved the food. A sentiment many others shared, judging by the noon crowd.

"Any chance I can get a double order of ribs with a side of onion rings?" Larry McCormick asked as they seated themselves at one of the few available tables.

Bree shot her father a stern look. "Right before your checkup? No. You can have a sandwich and a side salad."

"Great. It's not bad enough my daughter insists on dragging me to the doctor, now she's policing what I eat."

"If you weren't so stubborn, I wouldn't have to drag you." Her mom had died when Bree was only a year old, and since then Bree and her father had had a colorful and sometimes bumpy relationship. Despite past hiccups, Bree loved him and was committed to taking care of her only remaining family. "We both know you never would have gone if I hadn't taken the initiative and made your appointment with Dr. Stevens."

The clinic was close enough that he could have walked from work, but Bree's offer of lunch ensured he wouldn't conveniently "forget." Luckily her new job had a flexible schedule. She worked enough weekends and evenings to afford a few hours off in the afternoon.

"You worry too much," her father scoffed. "I'm perfectly healthy. And I still think it'll be weird, seeing a woman doctor."

"It will be fine, Dad. Believe it or not, I nagged you into going because I'd like to *keep* you perfectly healthy."

He lowered his gaze. "It's not right, you feeling like you have to look after me, helping me find an apartment, the job at the bookstore, even driving me to the doctor. I'm your father. I was planning to give you everything."

She sighed with frustration. His "wanting better" for her had been his excuse for getting talked into numerous crooked schemes, including the time he'd lost his honest job as a janitor because he'd let small-time art thieves into a building. All Bree had wanted was a parent, especially during her two stints as a foster child. Her father's first sentence had been relatively short, but the penalty had been more severe for his second strike, accessory to multiple counts of grand theft auto when he'd been the official lookout for a pair of brothers who stole luxury cars.

In every letter Larry had written from prison, he'd sworn he was going straight for real this time, was even learning computer skills in the joint. *Your old man's going to make something of himself, Bree.* She would have loved him more if he'd just stayed in custodial work.

"Good to see you two again," the waitress said in greeting. Debby Sue was forty, a blonde with a modern take on the beehive and a pretty face despite what looked like sun-related premature aging.

"Nowhere else in this town has such great service," Larry said with a wink.

Debby Sue rolled her eyes but widened her grin. "Flatterer. Can I get y'all started off with something to drink?"

They both ordered, and as the waitress turned to saunter away, Bree asked impulsively, "Hey, Debby Sue, do you happen to know a guy named Noah Tanner?"

"You're talking about one of those wild Tanner boys. I didn't know them that well because they were all younger than me and I'd moved away with my first husband. Thank the sweet heavens I divorced that loser *and* the one after him or I wouldn't be dating my Hank now. That man knows how to—"

Bree cleared her throat gently.

"But you didn't want to hear about Hank and what a dynamo he is, did you? None of the Tanners stayed in Prescott, but when I came back, people occasionally still told stories about them and their friends. There were three Tanner brothers. Noah, Caleb and another one. Town bad boys. The kind all the girls at Prescott High wanted to date and all the fathers wanted to run out with a shotgun, if you know what I mean."

Bree knew. She recalled his voice in the dark and imagined what Noah Tanner must have been like.

Debby Sue cocked her head to the side; it was a wonder she didn't topple over from the weight of her hair. "Why do you ask?"

"Oh. No reason," Bree said lamely. "I had a little car trouble, and Noah offered to help. I was just wondering about him since I'd never seen him in town. Guess he's visiting."

"Maybe he was in town for the recent reunion? I don't know when he graduated, but I sure hope he stays. Having a Tanner back would give the girls something new to talk about at the Cut Hut. When I went in this morning to get my roots touched up, it was all about Frank Garcia's break-in and Rosalie Thwarp's latest affair. But nothing was stolen at Frank's and the whole town has known for years that poor Rosalie's husband is not interested in women."

Bree, who'd never heard of Rosalie Thwarp, simply blinked at the information.

"Prescott was more exciting when that movie was being filmed here," the waitress said with a sigh.

Once Debby Sue had bustled off, a brief silence

reigned. Bree liked her, but the waitress always left her feeling as if she needed a brief recovery period.

"When you told me how you dented your car," Larry finally said, "you didn't mention a man stopping to help."

"He stopped to ask if I needed assistance. I told him I didn't, and he stayed just long enough to make sure I got back on the road. End of story."

Her father waited a moment, then added in a low voice, "You also didn't mention that break-in at Frank's. I'm surprised you haven't asked me about it."

"Why would I? You fell asleep on my couch on Thanksgiving and stayed the night. Besides, the car keys were in my nightstand drawer, and I'm a light sleeper," she blurted before she'd thought better of it. Oh, hell. "I mean…I know you've retired from that kind of work."

"So it *did* cross your mind that with my daughter being his agent, I not only knew the house was empty but had a way to get in," he teased.

"Dad, I didn't—"

"It's fine. Robberies around here are rare, and I have a track record. You had to think about it at least long enough to rule me out."

She fiddled with her silverware. If she who knew and loved him worried about his track record, what would others think if they found out? He'd been arrested four or five times, though given some of the minor charges and his cooperation with the police, he'd only done time twice. Still, it was the type of background that inspired a town lynch mob more than the welcome wagon, and she knew all Sheriff Hardy had to do was run a background check to get Larry's information. Assuming the officer wasn't already aware. So far, the only person

who definitely knew was Larry's employer, an elderly
man who ran a bookstore and seemed less inclined than
some of his fellow citizens to gossip. Still…

"You look awfully worried," her father remarked.

"Not about you being retired," she hastened to assure
him. "I trust you."

His eyes crinkled at the corners when he grinned.
"Just not enough to tell me about this mystery man you
met on the road. Noah, right?"

"That was no big deal."

She barely cared if she saw Noah again. As far back
as she could remember, Bree had yearned for the
straight and narrow, the chance to get her father away
from some of his cronies. Finally, here in Prescott, she
had a shot at achieving her goal. The last thing she
needed in her life was a bad boy.

IT WASN'T MUCH, BUT IT was a start. Noah had spent all
day Sunday cataloging what needed to be done on the
property and making a list of supplies. Then he'd
worked outside Monday morning, cutting the grass in
the yard and making repairs to the fence. Any further
work required a trip to the hardware store in town to
supplement the tools he'd brought with him.

Heading into the house for a quick shower to steam
out the worst of his body's aches, he reflected that the
past day and a half had been therapeutic. The physical
labor had done a lot to melt away tension. Even without
his grandmother here, the farm was a refuge.

Though he was self-employed and didn't work in a
busy office with tons of colleagues, he regularly dealt
with clients, contractors and others. Then there were

calls from people like elderly Mrs. Tompkins downstairs, who sought him out to change air-conditioning filters, fix the garbage disposal and have dinner with her unmarried granddaughter. Since leaving Hanson's two nights ago, the only human interaction he'd had was a quick call to Joe to make sure a check was on its way to Prescott and stopping to help that sassy brunette with her car.

Not that Bree needed his help, which had put him at a loss. Noah was used to people depending on him. Since she hadn't, he'd ended up half flirting with her instead, wishing there'd been an opportunity to give her a lift and talk longer. Now that he thought about it, too many of his conversations were about what he could do for other people, whether it was work or Stef asking him to act out a loving charade for her family. Why not have more exchanges that were simply *fun?*

He finished dressing in the room that had become his when he was thirteen—staying in the master suite seemed too awkward—then headed for his truck. He'd immediately fallen back into the habit of leaving his keys in the unlocked cab. On this somewhat isolated piece of property, it seemed unnecessary to lock the door, much less activate the antitheft alarm he would have used in Dallas.

Forty minutes later, he'd parallel parked at the curb and was stepping through a door with Hardware & Home Supply stenciled on the glass. A cowbell signaled his entry. Noah nodded greetings to a couple of people whose faces were vaguely familiar. He glanced at the lengthy list he'd compiled on a yellow sheet of legal paper. *Definitely gonna need a cart.*

His only choice was a squeaky basket with a severely

misaligned front wheel, but he grabbed it and began systematically combing the aisles. He was wrestling the half-full cart around a corner and into the paint section when he noticed a woman bent over a selection of greens. Glancing from her bobbed brown hair to the curve of her butt in a pair of khaki slacks, he felt himself grin. The hair was a match, and while he hadn't glimpsed her from this particular angle, he thought the curves were the same.

"Bree?"

The woman straightened, her gaze arrowing toward him. Her brown eyes were soft and deep and, currently, wide with surprise. "Mr. Tanner?"

"Noah. Don't worry, I'm not stalking you. Just needed a few materials." He indicated the plumbing equipment, plaster and wallpaper he'd gathered.

"A *few?* And here I thought they'd name me shopper of the year for all the money I've been spending. I recently bought a house," she explained. "Great price, great potential, but I may have been overly optimistic about the renovations. Or my aptitude for them."

"Any particular project you're having trouble with? I'll be in town for at least a week or two if you need help." It hit him belatedly that no matter how accustomed he was to volunteering assistance, Bree might find the offer bizarre. But instead of backtracking and sounding as nervous as when he'd asked Mary Seaton to the '93 Panthers senior prom, he simply smiled. "I enjoy working with my hands. I'm a carpenter. Not half bad with minor plumbing and wiring, either."

"Oh." Bree's gaze, which had flicked to his fingers

on the handle of the cart, lifted to his face. "So, you're in town on business, then?"

"Not exactly. I'm getting my late grandmother's farm ready to put on the market."

"You're kidding! That's—Lord, I hope she didn't just pass away and that you aren't selling because you have to. I was going to be incredibly tacky and take the opportunity to ask if you had a real estate agent yet." She shot him a sheepish smile. "That's what I do."

"You're not being tacky. Seizing opportunity is my motto." As of right now. "What if we had dinner at Hanson's and discussed this further?" After thinking that what he needed in his life was more spontaneous fun, he'd once again crossed paths with this very attractive woman. Even Noah wasn't enough of a Boy Scout not to take advantage of the situation.

CHAPTER THREE

BEFORE BREE LEFT THE hardware store to pick up her dad at the clinic, she'd whittled Noah's offer down to lunch tomorrow. Even with the possibility that he needed a real estate agent—or perhaps, *especially* with that possibility—dinner had seemed too much like a date. Besides, as she'd told him, she had plans tonight after work. Not that her father would object if she canceled on pizza and the football game at his apartment, but she'd convinced him to move to Prescott with her. Part of her reasoning had been so that they could make up for lost time.

And so you can keep an eye on him? she asked herself as she drove to an afternoon consultation with a prospective new client.

No, she genuinely enjoyed spending time with her old man, and she believed him when he said he'd gone straight. She couldn't picture him planning to stay after hours and steal hardcovers from the bookstore or casing the First Prescott Bank & Trust on Main Street. Still, she knew how susceptible he was to bad influences—it seemed there was at least one other thief in or around Prescott, and it would be the McCormick luck that, left idle, her dad would become fast friends with him. Or her.

Interesting that Noah Tanner, a reputed troublemaker according to Debby Sue, had returned to Prescott the same day Bree had heard of her first crime here. But that was exactly the sort of coincidence that had always tagged Bree in foster care and at school. If someone's lunch money was missing, people made assumptions about the felon's daughter. She prided herself on not leaping to those kind of snap judgments. Besides, even with the picture Debby Sue had painted, Bree couldn't quite see Noah doing anything really *wrong*.

Oh, he was definitely sexy enough to be a bad boy— her first look at him in broad daylight had confirmed a rangy, rugged man who filled out his jeans well, and then there were those penetrating light blue eyes of his. Noah was bold, too. Some men might invite a woman they've just met to dinner, but offer to help with her house? Though he hadn't stressed the words with over-the-top emphasis, when he'd said he liked to use his hands, her entire body had melted into a breathy sigh.

Despite his reputation, there was something about him that seemed innately good. And not just in bed. *You barely know him, you have no idea what sort of person he is.* Maybe a month of small-town living had turned her naive.

She made it to her office and was just opening her e-mail when she heard a woman's voice asking for her at the reception desk in the outer lobby. Her three-thirty appointment—Bree glanced at her day planner to make sure she had the name right, then stood when a pretty, dark-haired woman in jeans and a black leather coat appeared.

"Hi, you must be Wanda Baker."

The woman nodded. "That's me. Ms. Baker, Prescott High's soon-to-be-newest history teacher. My goal is to find a place and close before the second semester starts in January. Is that impossible?"

"Obviously our timetable will depend on your specifications and what's available," Bree said as the woman shrugged out of her jacket and settled into a chair. "But I'll work as hard as I can to help you reach your goal. Can I get you anything to drink? Coffee, water or a soda?"

Wanda shook her head. "Thanks, but I'm good."

"All right, then let's talk about what you want me to look for."

After Wanda left, Bree had just enough time to catch up on e-mails and phone messages before showing a newlywed couple the small O'Brien farm. Most of the original homestead had been sold off in parcels, leaving just the patch of land where the house sat. It was in need of some repair, but the happy couple looked as if they were already imagining repainting the dining room side by side. Bree felt a little pang as she thought about the recent repairs she'd been shouldering alone on her own fixer-upper. Her dad occasionally pitched in to the extent of his abilities, but it wasn't quite the same.

Because the newlyweds decided to make an offer, Bree was busy later into the evening than she'd planned and called her father to let him know she was en route.

"I'll order the food now," Larry said. "You should still be here by kickoff. And if the pizza arrives before you do, I'll try to save you a slice."

"With your cholesterol count, you're lucky I'm letting *you* have a slice," Bree countered.

"Hey, Dr. Stevens said it wasn't half bad for a man my age. She turned out to be a pretty smart lady, a real cutie, too. Just my luck she's seeing someone."

Bree laughed. "Don't tell me you asked her out."

"Nah, we were just making conversation. There are worse things, though, than dating, Bree. You might want to try it sometime."

"I think this is where I inform you my cell connection is getting weak and hang up."

He was chuckling as she disconnected. Truthfully, Bree didn't miss dating that much. As it turned out, she had some trust issues that made relationships difficult for her. Only a few had seemed worth the effort, but even her last good relationship hadn't been compelling enough to transform into a long-distance affair. She'd ended it as soon as she knew she wanted to move to Prescott. *I do miss sex, though.* Oh, well. No one said you could have everything.

Actually, a few of her dad's cronies *had* said that, but they were in prison for trying, so she tended to ignore their advice.

Thinking back to the phone call with her father, she wondered if *he* would ever date. A real relationship would require honesty about his past, but revealing a criminal record wasn't exactly the easiest thing to do when wooing the ladies. Though Bree couldn't really remember her mom beyond pictures Larry had saved, he'd assured her the woman was an angel. "Had to have been to put up with me, but when she was alive, I stayed honest. I wanted her to be proud." Since then, he'd kept the details of any of his romances well away from his daughter. His rap sheet notwithstanding, he could be charmingly old-fashioned and gallant.

The Towne Landing apartment building was located near the center of downtown, convenient since her father had replaced his expired driver's license but lacked a car. He could walk almost anywhere he needed to be, and Bree helped with the rest. The building had been a low-rent hotel decades ago, unlike the much newer, much larger complex a few miles away, which boasted modern conveniences and private exterior entrances to each apartment. Unless one counted fire escapes, the only entrances to Towne Landing units were found inside. The lobby housed vending machines, the tenant Laundromat, a small sitting area and elevators that took residents and visitors to the four apartments on each floor. Worn around the edges but clean, Towne Landing had been within her dad's price range.

The open parking lot didn't require any security codes, but spaces were numbered and signs warned that improperly parked guests would be towed. Larry had given her his permit to display through the windshield. Tightening her coat around her, she hurried into the building. The temperature had reached fifty today, but had been dropping rapidly since the sun set.

Her dad smiled as he opened the door to his third-floor apartment. "The pizza beat you by five minutes, so I actually got to buy us a meal for a change."

Bree had once asked Mrs. Hanson if they'd ever considered delivery. "But then all the folks that work nearby wouldn't stop what they were doing for a much-deserved lunch break," the woman had responded. "And Mr. Hanson and I would fall behind on Prescott news."

Over dinner, Bree and her father compared their work days and speculated on who would win tonight's football game. It wasn't until halftime that Bree realized she'd left her cell phone in the car and was supposed to call two homeowners to confirm showings in the morning.

"I need to run down before it gets any later," she told her dad. "I'll be right back."

"I could go for you," he offered.

Instead of remarking that he didn't need to be out in the cold or that she could be back in less time than it would take him, she joked. "Are you kidding? I figure this way you're stuck washing the plates."

She considered the elevator but decided to take the stairs. It was only three stories and the very least she could do to compensate for the pepperoni pie with olives and extra cheese. She pushed open the heavy door, blinking at the lights that were much brighter, but also harsher, than in the hallway. When the door clanged shut behind her, she jumped, then told herself she was a grown woman who didn't freak out at every sound. Of course, hearing footsteps a moment later didn't exactly soothe her jitters.

Scooting to the inside to let the other person pass, Bree glanced toward what first appeared to be a man not much taller than her. After a moment, however, she realized there was a woman beneath the baggy clothes. While not rushing, the other female wasn't exactly taking her time. *Maybe she gets freaked out in stairwells, too.* Pizza or not, Bree was taking the elevator back to her dad's floor.

"Hi," Bree said. Seemed odd to be the only two people here and not acknowledge each other.

The woman flashed a quick smile before lowering her gaze and the glasses covering it. While the navy-blue hooded sweatshirt was completely appropriate to the weather, the oversize white-framed sunglasses were a little less timely. For all Bree knew, the woman had had her pupils dilated today, but it seemed more likely—and far more interesting—that she didn't want to be recognized. Was she leaving a lover? First Debby Sue and Hank, then Rosalie Thwarp and her numerous affairs, now an attractive woman sneaking out the stairwell, having obviously come from someone's apartment...

Is everyone in this town getting some but me?

NOAH TANNER KNOCKED AGAINST the doorjamb at precisely noon. The digital clock in the corner of Bree's computer screen had just changed from 11:59, not that she'd been glancing at it every few minutes.

"You're certainly punctual," she observed.

"I was known for it in high school," he teased. "Well, that and perfect attendance."

I'll bet. Her gaze slid from the long-sleeved blue shirt that matched his eyes to the flattering cut of his casual black pants. Even if Debby Sue hadn't told her about the Tanner reputation, Bree never would have believed his teen legacy hinged on something as mundane as the zero-tardiness award.

She rolled her eyes. "Do I look gullible to you?"

He completed an appreciative once-over of his own, enough to bring a warm flush to her skin without making her squirm. "Wasn't the first adjective that came to mind, no."

Standing, she reached for her purse and jacket. "We should go. I don't want to rush through lunch, but I do have another appointment later."

"Ready when you are. I don't like to rush, either. I much prefer savoring."

Can't argue with that.

Pausing outside on the sidewalk, he glanced from a red pickup truck to Bree. "Are you the type of woman who prefers to be in the driver's seat?"

"As a matter of fact—" she pointed her keyless remote pad at the car parked several spaces away "—some have even called me controlling."

Noah chuckled as he followed her. "Been called that a time or two myself."

"Really?" He'd appeared fairly laid-back when she'd seen him, and while she was certain there was more than what people saw on the surface, he seemed like a man who could subtly maneuver people into doing what he wanted.

"When my little brother was fourteen, he thought I was every historical tyrant brought to life in one, with the sole purpose of ruining his fun."

"Ah. I didn't have a brother."

"Sisters?" he asked as he opened the passenger door.

"Nope, only child." She buckled her seat belt. "According to my dad, I can be an unholy nag. It's been just me and my father since I was a toddler," she added.

A shadow passed over Noah's face before he said casually, "For me and my brothers, it was the grandmother I mentioned. She didn't completely raise us, but she finished the job best she could."

So he'd grown up in the house he was now selling? She experienced another frisson of guilt over being so delighted to learn he might need a real estate agent. "When did the farmhouse pass to you?" It seemed like a less painful question than, "When did she die?"

"A few months ago. I really meant to take care of

the property sooner, but life doesn't always go according to plan."

"Tell me about it. Ten years ago, I was a college freshman majoring in biology and…" In the throes of her first successful relationship. Also, after being left parentless at her high school graduation, she'd been so angry with her father she hadn't even been answering his letters. Now she was a single real estate agent who had dinner with her dad twice a week. "Anyway, a lot's changed."

Noah leaned back in his seat, glancing out the window. "It's funny how much some things change while others don't at all."

"What about Prescott?" she asked. "I know it's been growing over the past few years, but is it pretty much the way you remember it?"

"Mostly. I noticed Archie's Arcade is a cell phone store now, but a lot of other things are the same. Mr. and Mrs. Hanson are so similar it's eerie. I swear they just picked one age and stuck with it."

"My dad had a similar observation after looking at all the community pictures on their wall." She grinned sheepishly. "We've been spending a lot of time at Hanson's."

Noah's expression turned wistful. "Are you and your father pretty close?"

"Getting there, now that we both live in Prescott. But before, well, we went through some tough times. Do you still have family here?"

"Not since we lost my grandmother. My youngest brother is in California now, cashing in on a misspent youth by designing video games. My older brother… you could say we're still going through a few of those tough times."

She'd been so intent on hearing more about Noah's life that she'd missed the turn onto Main Street. "Oops." The next light was a one-way, so they'd need to go an extra intersection to double back. "You didn't say anything about my missing the left."

He shrugged. "I'm not a backseat driver. You caught it immediately. It's not like I would have let you go as far as Laredo."

"Well, no. Like you said, I realized my mistake as soon as I passed the turn. I've just known a lot of guys who either want to drive or give tips and suggestions the entire time."

"Then you've known a lot of idiots," Noah said lightly. "What's wrong with just enjoying the ride?"

That depended on where the ride took you.

"So, is it just you and your dad doing the renovations on your house, or do you have other help, like a boyfriend? That's my suave, clever attempt at finding out if you're seeing anyone."

She laughed, though she probably shouldn't encourage him. "I'm single."

"Well, that works out nicely for me, then. Or could."

Oh, boy. Pulling into a full parking lot that attested to Hanson's popularity, she forced herself to sound politely distant. "I don't see how. You're not staying in town long, and I don't get involved with clients."

"Fair enough." He opened his door, then grinned back at her. "But we both agreed life doesn't always go as planned, so who knows how long I'll be in Prescott? And I'm not a client yet."

CHAPTER FOUR

As Bree climbed out of the car, she had the sneaking suspicion that lunch with Noah Tanner had been a very bad idea. The man was irresistible, but she was serious about the no-dating-clients policy. As the newest real estate agent in town, she was struggling to establish a reputation—and not the kind that included sleeping with men she represented.

She might even have found a delicate way to reiterate this if Noah hadn't turned away from her, a preoccupied expression on his handsome face. Just as quickly, he looked back. "Why don't you go inside and find us a table, if there's not already a waiting list? I'll be right with you."

Surprised, she watched as he crossed the parking lot to help an older woman with three large paper bags. Probably some office secretary who'd been sent out to bring back lunch.

Bemused by the way Noah flirted with her one moment and seemed a hot Good Samaritan the next, Bree stepped inside the restaurant. She didn't know what to make of the man, but it shouldn't matter, since he'd most likely be gone in a couple of days. He could say what he wanted about life changing direction, but that seemed like exactly the kind of classic line used to seduce a woman into a temporary fling.

"Hey there, girlfriend, you're makin' a right habit of this." Debby Sue paused, shifting the tray of iced teas she carried.

"Hi. Are there any free tables left, or should I give someone my name?"

"I think there's one or two in the back corner. By the way, I wanted to tell you, you were right about Noah Tanner being in town. I don't know how long he's staying, but he definitely didn't just come for the reunion. I wouldn't know him if he stopped to help me with *my* car, but Ruby at the Cut Hut saw him buying groceries and said he's hunkier than ever. My Hank is already more than I can handle, but we've got lots of ladies in town who would welcome some new prospects in the dating pool.

"I heard that sexy devil Kirk McKenzie moved back, too," Debby Sue added, "but he's already involved with someone. You don't happen to know if Noah's single?"

"I'm ninety-nine percent sure." The other percent maintained that even guys who *seemed* noble could forget to reveal certain pertinent details when it suited them. "But I don't think he's settling here permanently."

Debby Sue was too pleased to have the scoop on his love life to worry about the disclaimer. "Wait until I tell Ruby! By the way, she asked when we're going to see you in there for your first appointment? Queenie—that's the gal who runs the place—is willing to knock off fifty percent as a welcome-to-Prescott special."

Bree really should make time for a haircut, and she assumed that since Debby Sue was the only one in town sporting a tower of blond hair, it was a personal choice, not a stylist error. "Is that a discount she offers everyone, or just people with gossip on good-looking men who are visiting?"

Debby Sue grinned. "I—" But the rest of her words were lost as she sucked in a breath. "Well, hello, there. I don't believe we've met. I'm Debby Sue, and welcome to the best barbecue place in all of Texas."

Bree looked over her shoulder in time to see Noah smile.

"It certainly is that. I'm Noah Tanner."

Debby Sue's mouth fell open.

Noah turned to Bree. "So, how long's the wait?"

"According to Debby Sue, we might luck into a table in the back."

The waitress's mouth snapped closed again as her gaze locked with Bree's. Dozens of questions were clear in her expression, but all she said was "So I'll tell Ruby we'll be seeing you soon at the Cut Hut, right?" The unspoken implication being that if Bree didn't show up voluntarily, the women from the salon would drag her there bodily in order to get the latest news on Noah. And how Bree came to be lunching with him.

Muttering vague promises, Bree followed Noah as he scouted for the vacant tables. She was more focused on navigating the room and claiming a seat before someone beat them to it than the people she was passing. But she and Noah both paused when a commanding voice said, "Ms. McCormick?"

Sheriff Hardy. The man rose from his chair, the deputy seated across from him turning in Bree's direction.

"Hello, Sheriff." Had he hailed her because of news on the Garcia break-in?

Hardy's gaze had darted beyond her, however. "Tanner. I heard this morning you were back in town."

"Only temporarily." And for the first time that Bree had seen, Noah's laid-back demeanor was replaced with understated hostility. These two men didn't like each other. Because Noah had been such a rabble-rouser in his youth? "I'll be gone soon enough."

So much for that you-never-know-what-life-will-bring nonsense. Bree was a little depressed to have been right.

"I see. And what business brings you to town?"

"My grandmother's farm. Ms. McCormick and I are meeting for lunch to discuss putting it up for sale."

The sheriff nodded, then glanced back at Bree. "It's still breaking news, but have you heard about the attempted theft at Towne Landing last night?"

Her *dad's* building? Maybe it wasn't really that shocking a coincidence, considering there were only two apartment complexes in town. Still, it was enough to make her heart pound uncomfortably in her chest. "N-no, I hadn't."

"I'm surprised," Hardy said lightly. "We interviewed a couple of residents this morning and I understand your father, Larry McCormick, lives in the building. So far I haven't managed to track him down for questioning, but I thought perhaps he'd told you what was going on."

Damn, damn, damn. She didn't like the way Hardy had drawled her dad's name or the veiled threat to "track him down." Whether the sheriff had been aware of Larry's past before or had just uncovered it during routine investigation of this latest burglary, she hoped it didn't become common knowledge. Her dad had reformed and deserved a second chance.

Not to mention, her own job could suffer. People might be loathe to turn over their house keys to the ex-con's kid.

Noah's hand dropped to her arm, unexpectedly anchoring her and providing rescue from the rising swell of alarm. "Well, Sheriff, thank you for updating Ms. McCormick. I'm sure she'll want to call her father and double-check that he's not too distressed. I imagine a theft in his building could be very upsetting."

"Yes, I believe you have some experience with how much theft can distress others," the sheriff said.

His gaze narrowing to slits, Noah didn't respond, merely steered her away.

"Thank you," she said to Noah. "For ending the conversation. Policemen make me nervous." She was glad he didn't ask why, but based on the short exchange with Hardy, perhaps he had his own secrets he wanted to keep.

"Would you like to call your father?" he asked, pulling out a chair for her.

"Yes, but not here. I'll call him from my car or my office. I really am surprised I didn't hear this from him first."

"Maybe he didn't want to worry you."

Maybe he was afraid I would suspect him. "You're probably right."

He handed her a laminated menu. "Think some food will take your mind off it?"

"I'm afraid I'm not really hungry anymore."

Noah glanced over his shoulder, in the direction they'd come, then nodded. "Yeah, everything still smells good, but I have to say the ambience is less than appetizing today. We could get out of here if you'd like."

"Just leave? Won't that look strange?"

"We haven't ordered yet. When's your appointment later? We could skip lunch and go see the farm, instead. You'd probably have to do a walk-through before we could discuss terms, anyway, right?"

Despite the tension now knotting inside her, Bree laughed. "So you initially invite me to dinner, and now I'm going back to your place without even getting fed first. Are you always such a fast worker?"

He smiled enigmatically.

NOAH WAS SURPRISED WHEN Bree handed him the keys to her car once they were outside. "You want me to drive?"

"You're the one who knows where we're going," she said, even though her job must require her following directions to new places all the time. "I already made a wrong turn coming here."

Just the geographic one, or was she regretting her decision to join him for lunch? She seemed drained and…spooked. Either the attempted break-in had left her worried for her dad's safety, or she'd been understating the fact when she said police made her nervous. Too bad they couldn't have run into Hardy on the way *out*— at least then Bree wouldn't have to skip a great meal.

Noah glanced past her, watching a middle-aged couple approach their battered station wagon. "Give me just a minute."

"What, you think they're about to have car trouble? Because they seem capable of carrying their two take-out bags."

Though he didn't make a practice of walking away from a lady while she was speaking to him, Noah hurried toward the couple. Three minutes and forty dollars later, he returned to the car, pleased with himself.

Bree, however, was incredulous. "You took their food?"

"They made a decent profit, trust me." Thank goodness Joe's check had arrived. "This was quicker than waiting around for a to-go order, and now if you change your mind later, you won't be left hungry all afternoon."

Bree's chocolatey gaze softened, her expression one of admiration. "That was incredibly thoughtful."

"It wasn't that big a deal," he insisted, turning the key in the ignition. "They weren't in a huge hurry, and *I* might get hungry later, too."

"Still, it's sweet."

"I just don't want you thinking I'm something I'm not." He hadn't exactly been thinking noble thoughts when she'd explained she didn't date clients. Drawn to her on such an elemental level, he was debating the odds of changing her mind.

"Noah?"

"Yeah?" He slid her a guilty sideways glance.

"About not wanting me to see you for something you aren't… I have a little confession to make. I've actually heard bits and pieces of your history."

"Which bits and pieces were those?"

Though he wasn't looking at her, he wondered if there was a blush on her face to match her bashful tone. "Well, you know, that you and your brothers were the town bad boys."

He didn't think his one indiscretion qualified him for the same status as Caleb and his friends. "Whoever you heard that from was probably thinking of my brother, Caleb. He definitely ran with a wild crowd."

"What about you and your other brother?"

"Joe did go through a phase where he wanted to emulate Caleb, but once Caleb graduated and left town, my grandmother and I helped Joe get on the right path."

"And Joe would be the brother who called you a tyrant?"

"Yup." He grinned at the memory. "He was quite a handful, but I turned out to be more stubborn than he was."

"And what about you? Never had the urge to be bad?"

Hell, yes. But she meant fifteen years ago, not every time he'd glanced at her. "Well, I wasn't perfect, but of the three of us I was the most conservative. I knew our grandmother didn't have to take us in. She deserved some gratitude."

"You were scared." Bree's blunt assessment was tempered by the empathy in her voice. "It's tough when you're in a home you don't really feel is yours."

"You sound as if you're speaking from experience."

"What I said about my dad raising me was true, but... there were times I stayed with other people, too. And I was always aware that I didn't quite fit into the family."

"That sucks. You deserve to be loved. Deserved, I mean. All kids should be loved, don't you think?" He caught her smile out of the corner of his eye.

But then she sobered. "I'm not sure what to think. I assumed Prescott would be this simple, slow-paced place, but the last few days have been confusing."

Was she including him in part of that? Or merely reflecting on whatever it was that had put such fear in her eyes when Sheriff Hardy confronted her?

Thinking of the sheriff, Noah clenched his jaw. "I can believe you heard stories about me. I would just question whether or not they were true. Hardy hinted at my being a thief because when I was an idiot teenager, I once tried to steal a jacket. And no matter how much I tried to make up for it later, when Caleb Tanner is your older brother, everyone's just waiting for *you* to spike the homecoming punch or cause car accidents. It didn't help that a few troublemakers in my graduating class tried to revive the Dead Rebels Club, sort of."

"Dead Rebels?"

"Live fast, die young." He rolled his eyes. "Something like that. Caleb and a couple of his friends used it as an excuse to sneak out and plan pranks that would make high school girls giggle on Monday mornings." Then again, Caleb had spent more nights parked up at Trojan Point than Noah ever had. Caleb had liked the notoriety. Maybe it was his way of getting attention. "There were a couple pranks during my senior year, and I'm sure Sheriff Hardy is just one of many who believed I had a hand in them. It's so flippin' frustrating to work that hard to get people to respect you, only to be judged on one stupid mistake and who you're related to."

"God, do I know that feeling."

The stark bitterness in her short sentence surprised him. "You do?"

"I—I...I didn't mean to say that. It just slipped out. Is it okay with you if we talk about something else?"

"Sure." They weren't far from the farm now, so he started telling her about the property, trying to keep the conversation as light as possible.

Today certainly hadn't gone the way he planned. Then again, when he'd come to town to replace the weak steps in Annabelle's front porch and repair leaks in the roof, he hadn't planned on meeting Bree, either. But for reasons he didn't bother examining, he was really glad he had.

THEY JUST BARELY MADE IT back to her office on time. Bree let him drive on the way back, too, since he claimed to know a few back-road shortcuts.

"Actually, I know more than a few, but some of the ones we could take in my truck would be a lot tougher on your car. Thanks for making the time to come see the place."

"No problem. It's my job." Except that her job didn't usually include a quickly eaten barbecue sandwich while sitting on a wraparound front porch and imagining what a client's childhood had been like. He hadn't discussed it in specifics, but she had learned that his father had died from a blood clot in Noah's early teens. He spoke lovingly of his grandmother, but his mother was conspicuously absent from conversation. *She must have dumped them here,* Bree surmised. Had he and his brothers known it was for good, or had he waited for her to come back?

It seemed as if too much of Bree's adolescence had been spent waiting for her father to return, whether it was because of jail time or because she knew just enough to be nervous about the "jobs" he went to at night that she could never sleep until he got home. She'd never come close to telling anyone in Prescott about her family history until today, when she'd empathized with Noah.

Since he wouldn't be a permanent fixture in her life…it would be like telling your secrets to a stranger on a plane, unburdening yourself to someone who wouldn't be around to complicate matters in a month. Come to think of it, maybe that was the allure of a one-night stand, though it involved a different kind of "un-burdening" and much different secrets. But Bree, who had enough trouble trusting people she *did* know, had never wanted to have sex with a stranger. She'd only been on a plane twice. And she wasn't going to tell Noah Tanner information that could hurt her or her father's chances of starting over here.

He parked the car, then handed her the keys. "So I'll see you again soon?"

She swallowed. Not because of the perfectly inno-cent question, but the expression in his eyes. She would have called it eager, except that sounded too boyish. The way Noah was looking at her was *all* man.

Bree opened the passenger door. "Well, you'll defi-nitely see me again. When depends on how long you need for remodeling the interior. You just let me know when to bring by the paperwork we discussed and take the shots." Today, she'd taken several outdoor pictures on the digital camera she carried with her. She'd also want inside photos for the eventual Web listing.

"It's not a complete remodel," he said as he fell into step with her on the sidewalk. "I'll let the new owners redecorate according to their tastes. I just want to repair anything that's damaged or scuzzy with age."

"Scuzzy?"

"It's a technical term."

They parted ways a moment later, Noah turning to-ward his truck and Bree reaching for the front door. But she hadn't even opened it when a female voice called out her name.

Wanda Baker hurried across the parking lot. "Hey, Bree. I'm a few minutes early."

"No problem." Bree held the door for both of them. "I just got back from viewing a property we're about to put up for sale, so your timing is perfect."

Wanda brightened. "Think it's a property I might be interested in?"

"Sorry, I wish it was. Nice location, but a lot bigger than what you're looking for. Don't worry, I called ahead and set up plenty of appointments for us today. I think you'll like what I found."

Once they'd reached Bree's office, Wanda lowered her voice. "I know I liked what I saw when I was walking up. I thought maybe he was your boyfriend, but that was your last appointment?"

Bree nodded, fighting not to echo Wanda's appreciation of Noah's form.

"He is hot. Please tell me all the men in Prescott look like that."

"Not exactly." From what she could tell, Noah was one of a kind.

CHAPTER FIVE

BREE CALLED HER FATHER as soon as she got home that night, anxiously waiting for him to answer the phone as she stirred a quick sauce for some tortellini.

"I take it you've heard about the break-in?" Larry interrupted her breathless greeting.

"The sheriff himself told me. Dad, I'm sure he knows about your record."

"No question about that, especially since I walked down to the police station to tell him this afternoon."

"You *what?*" She gripped the kitchen counter for support.

"I wanted to be as up front as possible. I told him that I'd heard because all the tenants were talking about it in the laundry room this morning, that some guy on the fifth had been robbed. I told Sheriff Hardy that if it would save him any time with background checks, I wanted him to know that I had a rap sheet, and that you and I were watching the game and having a pizza. I then gave him a rundown of the game, which could've been won if the quarterback hadn't been an egomaniac who refused to pass the ball, and the approximate time I signed the check for the delivery boy. I also told him that I'd prefer people didn't know about my history, but that if it came to light in the course of his investigation, that I understood actions came with consequences."

His words tugged at her heart. "Oh, Dad. I'm proud of you. What did he say?"

There was a long silence before her father answered. "The good sheriff was less magnanimous than you. He found it interesting that I would toddle down to the station-house with such a thorough, detailed story. He also found it interesting that my main alibi for both of the recent crimes was my daughter. Honestly, I think he believes a clever crook would be deliberately frank about his past in order to deflect suspicion from himself in the present. It hadn't occurred to me that he'd take my visit that way."

That's because her father had never been a particularly clever crook. Unfortunately, Hardy, despite any good qualities he might have, seemed to be one of those unyielding men who believed that once a person broke the law, they were likely to do so again. If he was honestly still holding a moment of teen rebellion against Noah, wouldn't he assume a convicted thief like her father was beyond redemption?

"He suspects you, doesn't he?"

"It was implied. But try not to worry, honey. He can't prove me guilty of something I didn't do."

Right, because no innocent person had *ever* been convicted of a crime they didn't commit, she thought sarcastically. But her more immediate concern was being under the sheriff's eagle-eye scrutiny. If he began actively investigating her father—and worse, her, as an accessory through alibi—Hardy would ruin the fresh start she'd desperately wanted to make. Damn, she hoped the lawman soon found other leads to pursue.

It wasn't until much later, as she and her calico tabby, Mr. Darcy, were watching a *CSI* repeat that she recalled the woman in the stairwell last night. Bree had been so blindsided by the news today, preoccupied with Noah and her reaction to him, that it hadn't occurred to her to tell Sheriff Hardy she'd seen a potentially suspicious person.

Maybe *suspicious* was a stretch. After all, the woman hadn't been running, and she'd taken the time to smile in response to Bree's greeting. *For all you know, she was covering a bruise with those sunglasses. Or maybe she just listened to too much Corey Hart in the eighties.*

Even if there was more to it than that, would Sheriff Hardy even believe Bree's last-minute story about a strange woman leaving the building? It would seem awfully convenient for Bree to offer up a mysterious lady now that the sheriff had indicated he didn't trust Larry. She caught herself nibbling at her thumbnail, a girlhood habit she'd mostly conquered, except for the night before her real estate exam. Maybe she needed to do a little investigation of her own, see if she could find out more about the robbery and the woman in sunglasses. Then, if she pieced together anything substantial, she'd talk to Sheriff Hardy.

Somewhere in her schedule of a busy job, house renovations, spending time with her father and her always surprising run-ins with Noah Tanner, surely she had time for some extracurricular PI work, too. Mystery-solving *Veronica Mars* balanced a full plate, and *she* hadn't even reached her twenties. Bree refused to let the fact that Veronica was also a television character discourage her.

Pasting a wide smile on her face, Bree opened the glass door that led inside the pink-curtained Cut Hut. It had occurred to her as she brushed her teeth last night that if a woman wanted to do some digging in this town, there was no better place to get started than the salon. Luckily, when she'd called that morning, a woman named Lorna had informed her that they could absolutely squeeze in an afternoon appointment.

"Good afternoon." An attractive woman with a less-attractive wad of gum poked in the side of her mouth glanced up from a small desk at the front of the salon. Her eyes were a wide baby-blue and her violet hair was oddly flattering, even though clearly not a shade nature had intended. "I'm Delila, welcome to the Cut Hut. I keep saying if I ever run this place, we're calling it DeLovely's."

"You're never going to run this place," a woman said from where she was shampooing a patron's hair.

Delila nodded toward the woman who had spoken. "That's Ruby. And we shampoo up front so nobody misses out on anything important. The big dryers are in the back since any poor dear sitting under those can't hear any of the good stuff, anyway."

"Although old Mrs. Spiegel got awfully good at reading lips there for a while," a busty brunette added from where she was cutting hair.

"And that's Lorna. Quinn owns the place, but everyone calls her Queenie. She had to step out for a few minutes."

Ruby snorted. "What she had to do was find herself some bread and chips. Who does she think she's fooling with this no-carb diet?"

Ignoring the commentary, Delila glanced back at Bree. "You must be Brianne, right?"

"That's me."

Lorna whistled as she motioned for her customer to lean her head forward. "The same Brianne who caught wind of Noah Tanner coming back to town?"

"Being in town," Bree amended. "I never said he was staying. In fact, I'm a real estate agent, and I took a look at his property yesterday. He's getting it ready to put on the market."

"And would you consider it a hot property?" Ruby asked with a smirk. The woman whose hair she was shampooing laughed.

"You were in the actual house where Caleb Tanner used to sleep at night?" Lorna asked. "Be still, my beating heart."

Granted, Bree had never seen Caleb Tanner, but it was hard to imagine he was more appealing than Noah. "Caleb was the one who was really bad, right?"

"Oh, honey." Lorna actually stopped clipping to turn and look at Bree. "From the time I spent with him up at Trojan Point, I can say he was very, very good."

The others hooted.

"Trojan Point?" Bree asked, following Delila to an empty chair.

"Trehan Point, a bluff just outside town," Ruby supplied. "Reported to be a pretty little view, but I don't know anyone who's ever parked up there to admire the stars and the landscape."

"So what are we doing with your hair today?" Delila asked.

Actually, since that hadn't been Bree's primary

reason for booking an appointment, she hadn't given it much thought. "Oh, just a trim. I like the style I wear now, but it's already started to grow out."

"So this is just to keep the shape and lose any split ends. You want me to wash it first?"

Ruby, finished at the shampoo station, was wrapping a towel around her customer's head.

"Sure," Bree decided. "Why not?"

The simple luxury of the warm water and someone massaging her scalp felt fantastic. By the time the shampoo was done, Bree felt relaxed enough to sound completely casual when she asked, "So have you all heard about these break-ins? I'm fairly new to Prescott, and I was shocked. Is this kind of thing normal?"

Lorna handed change to the woman leaving, then returned to her station to sweep up. "Not in the past five years. Every once in a while we get some nut who comes through or someone down enough on their luck to feel desperate, or more often, rebellious teenagers looking for something more fun to do than cow-tipping. Mostly, though, people in Prescott take care of their own and no one wants to mess with Sheriff Hardy."

"That man would be hot if he weren't so intimidating," Ruby commented. "Damn shame he never settled down."

"It's just the two victims so far, right?" Bree asked.

"Frank Garcia and that guy over at the Landing," Delila confirmed. "Lorna, what was his name again?"

"Steve Blevins. My kid sister went out with him back in the day. Works over at the garage, I think. Can't imagine Stevie owning much that would be worth the trouble of stealing."

"But that's the weird thing about these so-called robberies," Ruby said. "If anything was actually taken, the police are keeping the details to themselves. I heard nothing was stolen."

So why go to the trouble of breaking and entering? Bree wondered. Maybe it *was* kids. She could easily imagine teens rationalizing it as a harmless prank or dare. Maybe even some kind of initiation to a club—like those Dead Rebels? But that had been years ago, when Noah was in high school.

If not teenagers, her only other guess was that someone was looking for something. Was there any common link between the two men?

The beauty shop door opened, and a redhead in a fancy pantsuit sauntered in, looking immaculate except for…cheese-curl dust sticking to her rose-colored lipstick. "Queenie's back, what did I miss?"

"Meet Brianne McCormick," Delila said. "One of the town's newer residents."

"Welcome, welcome. Debby Sue said she'd get you in here. So tell me, is it true you're dating Noah Tanner?"

"Um, no. I'm helping him sell his grandmother's house. That is, when he's ready."

"Is that all?" Quinn looked disappointed. "Oh, well. Hardly much time to get more gossip than that today, anyway. Jolie should be here for her standing Wednesday manicure pretty soon."

"That would be Jolie Wright," Delila said softly.

"The mayor's wife?" Bree had seen the couple at Hanson's, but didn't really know them except for what she'd heard or read in the paper.

People in Prescott spoke about Michael Wright as though he were a candidate for sainthood. Apparently, many of his ancestors had been mayors, but Michael hadn't rested on his family name. He'd gone away to college, then did a stint of charity work in Mexico, building orphanages, administering medical supplies…the kinds of unselfish, no-strings acts that often seemed too good to be true. Bree knew less about Jolie, but she remembered being surprised by how young the other woman seemed. Not that the couple's ages were inappropriately disproportional, just that the fair-haired woman with the almost-shy smile hadn't been who Bree expected to see on the arm of the town's leading citizen. *She can't be much older than I am.*

Unless she had a truly gifted plastic surgeon, always a possibility.

"I think Jolie comes in more to 'stay in touch' than she does to keep her nails in shape," Lorna opined, "but it makes her uncomfortable when we gossip about her husband's constituents."

"You'd think it would be useful for her to spy and let him know what everyone in town is up to," Ruby said. "But that's just not how the Wrights work. A more upstanding couple, I've never seen."

"Well, before Jolie arrives and we have to put an end to our girl-talk, will you gals tell me something?" Bree asked. "Debby Sue told me all about Rosalie Thwarp and her extramarital activities. I think I might have bumped into her the other day on the way from a rendezvous, but I don't actually know what she looks like."

"You can't miss Rosalie," Queenie said. "She's six feet tall and blind as a bat without her horn-rimmed glasses. Great skin, nice body, but if she doesn't stop frying her hair with those home perms, the girls and I are going to stage an intervention."

"Oh." Six feet was way too tall to have been the stranger in the stairwell.

"All done except for the blow-dry," Delila pronounced.

Relaxing into the white noise, Bree pondered what she'd learned so far: not a hell of a lot. Afterward, she dutifully admired her reflection and told Delila what a good job she'd done.

Queenie rang up Bree's total on the register. "You come back and see us."

A waft of cool air drifted inside as the door opened.

"Jolie, right on time."

"Afternoon, Quinn. Ladies."

Bree tucked her wallet away, turning to see a woman with honey-gold hair removing a pair of slim designer sunglasses.

Mrs. Wright froze, her eyes widening for a millisecond before the welcome expression returned to her face. "H-hello. I don't believe we've met. I'm Jolie Wright."

"Brianne McCormick." *Am I nuts or did we meet two nights ago?* The sunglasses, of course, were radically different, but the features they'd partially obscured seemed identical. Then there was the nervousness that had disappeared so quickly, probably no one else had even noticed it. But Bree was convinced it hadn't been a figment of her imagination.

Debby Sue had been right. There was no shortage of interesting discoveries at the Cut Hut.

BY THE TIME BREE DROVE toward home that night, her nerves were shot. Though her father had told her not to worry, how could she not? Especially when she'd returned from lunch to find the deputy she'd seen at Hanson's talking to her boss. Nobody had said anything to her about the man's visit, but when he saw her walk in, he'd stood a few minutes later and shut the blinds in his office. How could that be a good sign?

Maybe you're paranoid. Which didn't change the fact that Sheriff Hardy was investigating not only her father, but her, as well.

She needed answers, but had to be careful who she asked. Even Debby Sue, friendly neighborhood gossip, might not like it if Bree tried to dig up dirt on Jolie Wright. The Wrights were the town's golden couple. There was, however, one person Bree knew who'd grown up in Prescott but didn't seem emotionally invested in its present or future. How well did he know the town's citizens?

Was Jolie Wright stepping out on her husband? Difficult to believe, but not impossible. For all Bree knew, Jolie attended a Tuesday night AA meeting and didn't want anyone in town to know. These were the kinds of possibilities Bree needed to rule out before going to the sheriff with their stairwell encounter. She didn't want to antagonize the mayor and his wife unless she had good reason, but even more, she didn't want her father's standing in the community tarnished, not now when he was trying so hard to do the right thing.

She usually programmed current-client numbers into her phone and now, steering her car down an otherwise empty road, she punched the button for Noah Tanner.

"Hello?" His deep voice was as rich as it was soothing, like her first bite of chocolate when she was particularly stressed.

"Hi, it's Bree. Is this a bad time?"

"Not at all. Any chance you're calling because you miss me like crazy and can't stop thinking about me?"

"No." She almost grinned. "I need some help."

"Really? Then you've come to the right guy. What can I do?"

How much should she tell him? If she just started asking random questions about Jolie, would he want to know why? Could they discuss the break-ins without her mentioning what her personal stake was?

"Bree?"

"Sorry, I'm in the car. The connection was fuzzy for a moment."

"Uh-huh. You're not in any kind of trouble, are you?"

"Of course not." Not yet, anyway. What had that deputy told her boss? Maybe her paycheck was already in danger.

"I was just about to throw a couple of steaks on the broiler," Noah said coaxingly. "How far away are you? Maybe you could join me for dinner, have a glass of wine and tell me what's wrong."

God, that sounded tempting. She didn't confide in people often, and the thought of sharing her worries with someone else was a luxury. Sharing it with a man who looked like Noah, over a bottle of wine… "I don't know if that's such a good idea."

"I'm ready and willing to help, Bree. But you have to let me."

Logically, she saw his point. Emotionally, she wondered if turning to him now would just become one more reason to miss him when he was gone.

CHAPTER SIX

THE SCENT OF LIGHTLY marinated and expertly seared sirloin met Bree as soon as Noah opened the door for her. "Oh, man." She took a deep breath. "That is heaven."

"I do like a girl who isn't hard to please." He helped her out of her jacket.

"How do people stay in this town and not immediately become overweight? I've never had such an appetite in all my life."

"It's the fresh air. And the locals have all kinds of clever suggestions for working off the calories. I don't suppose you've heard of Trehan Point?"

Her eyes narrowed. "What about it?"

"Some great hiking trails leading up to the bluff, if you're into outdoor exercise."

"Hiking, right. I'll make a note."

"You should. People moving here ask you all about the town, don't they?"

She nodded, following him into a warm, cozy kitchen. "Sometimes I use my being relatively new here as a bond, sharing their perspective, letting them know it's a great place for newcomers. Other people seem to want a more 'expert' opinion, though, and I avoid mentioning that I'm not from here if I can help it. Not that I'd lie."

"You just omit unnecessary facts?" Noah asked as he handed her the promised glass of white wine.

"I've learned to be careful about handing over pieces of information to anyone who asks."

"Are we talking about Prescott, or you?"

She bit her lip. Now seemed like a good time to take her first sip of wine.

Noah moved toward the stove, giving her space. "Hope you don't mind your steak a little pink in the center."

"Perfect."

"That's a relief. I cooked them the way I like them, then remembered as you were pulling up that Stef always preferred hers well done. Might as well eat leather, in my opinion."

"Who's Stef?"

He grinned over his shoulder. "So you don't like giving out information but have no problem asking the questions? She's someone I dated for a while in Dallas. Didn't work out."

She leaned back in the kitchen chair she'd selected. "Irreconcilable steak preferences?"

"That, and she developed this weird philosophy about me."

Bree frowned, thinking about how she was out in the middle of nowhere with a guy she'd only known a few days. "How weird?"

It wasn't until he started putting baked potatoes on the plates that she realized she hadn't offered to do anything to help, and was letting herself be waited on. Foreign, but decadently pleasant.

"When I first met her, parts of her life were kind of screwed up. We started dating and she made a lot of improvements, went back to get a degree, got out of an unhealthy co-dependent situation with a former roommate…really got her act together. A few months after we'd known each other, she'd changed. In positive ways, but she wasn't the same person."

"So you helped her out, and she dumped you when she didn't need you anymore? Typical."

Noah carried the plates over to the table. "Anyone ever tell you that you have a cynical streak a mile wide?"

"There are worse things to be than a cynic," Bree argued.

"Fair enough. But Stefanie didn't exactly leave for the reason you're suggesting. She thought I 'need to be needed.' Those were her words. She was afraid that with her life more or less in order…well, I'm not entirely sure what she thought. But she said I was good at fixing things and she was bad at filling the hole I would have in my life once she'd changed."

"You're right. That is a weird philosophy. Did it ever occur to you that with her life straightened out, maybe she was just uncomfortable staying with someone who'd seen her at a low point? It's easier to distance yourself from mistakes when you're not face-to-face with someone who watched you make them."

At least, that's what her dad had once said when he'd gotten out of prison the second time. Their reunion had been rocky because seeing Bree again had just brought home how much time they'd lost, how badly he'd screwed up. For a while, he'd decided it might be better to avoid her. It had taken several awkward holidays together before they'd repaired their relationship.

"Thank you," Noah said. "I think I like your explanation better. She made me sound like some crusader who wasn't happy without a mission or project. That's never who I wanted to be, it's just how things worked out."

Bree drained the last of her wine, belatedly noticing that she'd finished the glass without yet touching her food. Oops. "I know what you mean. I told you my father and I had some bumpy periods in our past? There were days where I felt like I had to be the responsible parent, talk him out of bad choices or monitor him to make sure he didn't go behind my back. And I hated him a little for that. I wanted the childhood my classmates had, or at least what I imagined they had."

She cut into her steak, needing to look at something besides Noah's open, understanding expression. The man had alluring eyes. And she didn't even want to think about his mouth. And, *damn,* he could cook. Stef was an idiot.

"This is fantastic," she said after she'd swallowed. "If carpentry doesn't work out for you, you could always open your own steakhouse."

"Shh. If the Hansons heard you, I could be banned from their establishment for life. Even Caleb was on his best behavior in there, for fear of alienating Mrs. H. and losing his barbecue supplier." He grinned. "But I'm glad you like it."

"This beats the tuna salad I would have ended up sharing with Mr. Darcy."

"Mr. who?"

"My cat. Everyone needs a best friend, mine just happens to be a plump tabby named after the hero of *Pride and Prejudice.*"

"I couldn't stay awake through every college lit class,

but that's by Jane Austen, right?" He paused, his fork in the air. "Wait a minute. That was a romantic story."

"So?"

"So you named your cat after a classic romance. Maybe you're *not* a complete cynic. Don't worry, your secret's safe with me."

She had bigger secrets than a whimsically named pet. "Noah, thanks for dinner, but you know it's not the main reason I came over."

"Is this going to have anything to do with how jumpy Sheriff Hardy made you?"

"I've never been in trouble with the law—only school principals—but my dad has. He's clean now, honestly. We both moved to Prescott to make a fresh start, to try to make up for lost time with each other, and to get him out of the sphere of some…former associates."

Noah steepled his fingers under his chin. "When Caleb and I were teenagers, I was convinced that if I could just get him away from some of his friends, things would be different. Now I know that only would have worked if Caleb wanted to change. And he didn't. I screwed up, too, but not wanting to do it again was what separated us."

"My father *does* want to change. Has changed. Trust me." Odd request, coming from her, but Noah seemed unfazed.

"So these recent break-ins are making you nervous because of your dad's past mistakes? I take it Sheriff Hardy knows."

"He knows, all right. Dad even went to talk to him, to keep everything aboveboard, and Hardy insinuated Dad had been rehearsing his alibi. Which is me, by the way. Now I have deputies showing up at the new job I worked hard to land. I can't let some burglar who's too incompetent to actually steal things mess up our lives."

"Nothing's been stolen?"

"No. Frank Garcia is a client of mine, an unfortunate coincidence, and confirmed that nothing's missing. I only got news of the Blevins break-in secondhand, but according to—"

"Blevins?"

"I think so. Steve Blevins. Does that sound right to you?"

Noah laughed as he ran his hand over his chin. "I don't believe it."

"You know him? Was he a friend of your brother's?" It didn't sound as if he'd been any friend to Noah.

"He was in my class, too young for Caleb to grace with his much cooler presence. I told you a couple of guys in my grade tried to carry on the legacy of the Dead Rebels? They approached me about joining them. Blevins, Garcia and one other guy…" He snapped his fingers. "Dave Holbrook."

"Does Dave still live in town? He's the closest thing to a connection I have so far." Had his place ever been robbed?

"I don't have a clue. I didn't even talk to them when I saw them on a daily basis. I could never prove it, so maybe I'm wrong, but I think they were the perpetrators of stunts that got *me* questioned. I guess you and I both spent time in the principal's office for stuff we didn't do."

Bree's face heated. "No, mine was deserved. I got accused of cheating or stealing lunch money one too many times and retaliated with fistfights on the playground. I had something of a chip on my shoulder and a decent right hook."

He unsuccessfully smothered a laugh. "Remind me not to make you mad, then."

A wave of disappointment went through her. She'd spent a lot of time in her life being mad at her father, but the truth of the matter was she'd made mistakes, too. "You didn't have the perfect childhood, either, and you turned out so well."

"You're not exactly a kleptomaniac making a living lap dancing on the outskirts of town, Bree."

"Maybe not." When had she poured more wine? she wondered as she lifted her glass. "But I'm bitter and skeptical, while *you're*—"

"Any comparison to Dudley Do-Right will get you thrown out of my house."

"Liar. You wouldn't kick a woman out into the night, especially when she's been drinking. You're too noble."

"You've had less than a glass and a half." He sounded annoyed. "And most of the thoughts I've had about you are more sexual than noble."

"Yeah?" She should change the topic back to the break-ins, to town politics, to anything less personal. But she wanted to hear more. Because he'd certainly inspired more than one fantasy since she'd clapped eyes on him, as well. Setting her glass on the table, she leaned back. "How sexual?"

For a moment, he didn't answer, gauging the challenge in her eyes.

Then he stood, leaning down so that his hands rested on the back of her chair, along either side of her. "We're not going there tonight. You called me upset and you *have* had that glass and a half of wine. When we have sex, I'd rather it be because you want me bad than because you have something on your mind you'd rather not think about."

She swallowed, drowning in the eyes that were so close. "You think I want you?"

"Let's find out." He lowered his head, his eyes open and staring into hers until that last heartbeat, when his lips brushed over hers, eliciting a sigh and a warm spiral of need in her midsection.

And she'd thought he could *cook?* Ha, that was nothing compared to how the man kissed! His mouth seduced hers with light, feathery touches that coaxed her to lean further into him, arching her back as she lifted to meet his kiss. Maybe her rampant appetite lately had only been a substitute for other needs she'd pushed aside. A different kind of hunger swamped her now, her body tingling with it as Noah slid his tongue into her mouth.

He helped her to her feet as she kissed him back, dragging her body up against his. Her nipples tightened, and little flames sparked in her blood. He felt so good. She rubbed her hands over the muscle of his arms, his back, down to the waistband of his jeans. A small, primal noise of appreciation caught in his throat, and she almost moaned her own response when he sucked gently on her lower lip.

Bree did whimper once in protest when he pulled away, breathing hard.

He didn't release his hold on her, though, sending her a level look. "We're going to have to finish that sometime."

Or, *now.* Now worked for her. Except the hesitant,

cautious, mistrustful part of her would have been furious with them both once the rest of her was satisfied. Noah was smart enough to know that.

"See?" She drew a shuddery breath of her own. "Noble."

When he opened his mouth, as if to argue, she slid a finger against his lips.

"But I like that about you," she added. He gently bit the end of her finger, and her body quivered. She liked that, too.

"Let's have this conversation somewhere else," he said. "How do you feel about the living room?"

At least it wasn't the bedroom. She doubted much talking would be accomplished there.

Abandoning the dinner dishes and remains of their wine, they went into the wood-paneled living room.

"I'd light a fire," Noah said, "but cleaning out the fireplace is one of the maintenance issues I haven't addressed yet."

"You've lit enough of a fire for one night," she told him wryly.

He grinned, pleased by this confession. Still, he sat far away from the sofa—choosing instead the cold hard stone of the hearth.

After kicking off her shoes, she tucked her feet beneath her, settling into the couch. "This is ridiculously comfy."

"Are you trying to lure me over there?"

"No." She smiled. "But I think I could make room for you, if you were so inclined. I just can't get over how…soothing this place is, for lack of a better word."

"Yeah. You wouldn't expect a place this creaky and

occasionally drafty to still offer so much warmth. It suited my grandmother, but I was expecting it to be a lot different without her."

"I'll bet she would have been so proud of the way you turned out," Bree said.

"Thank you. But that's not what you came here to talk about."

She inhaled deeply. "I was curious, since you grew up here, whether or not you spent much time with the Wrights, especially Jolie?"

"Not much. Michael had gone off to college by the time I moved here, and she was a grade—maybe two—behind me."

"There's quite an age difference between them, huh?"

"I don't know. Maybe seven years? Noticeable, but hardly shocking. From the little I know, they make a good match."

Bree balled her fists in frustration. "I just don't trust people who seem that perfect. At least *you* admitted to having a few dirty thoughts and one shoplifting incident." Whereas unyielding automatons like Sheriff Hardy, who seemed married to his pursuit of justice, were so far removed from her human experience that it might be a relief to find out he was on the take. "Everyone here talks about how Mayor Wright is one of the youngest in town history, how he can do no wrong, doesn't even have a single blemish on his track record, blah blah blah. It's people like that who suddenly show up on the front page with ties to organized crime."

Noah laughed. "Not to destroy your budding conspiracy theory, but I'm not even sure Prescott has much in the way of *dis*organized crime. I'll give you this much, though. In the past, there have been one or two wealthy town families who were able to pull some political strings behind the scenes. I just can't imagine Hardy being part of that, or his sister marrying anyone who would be."

"His sister?"

"Jolie. Jolene Hardy Wright. You didn't know?"

"No. I've finally learned my way around, but I haven't had a chance to brush up on everyone's family tree yet." She'd been wondering how useful it would be to try to get the sheriff to follow up on the mysterious-woman-in-the-stairwell lead. Now that she was ninety percent sure it had been his sister, she suspected trying to implicate Jolie in any alleged crime was the quickest way to get run out of town.

Bree needed some kind of plan B. Fast.

CHAPTER SEVEN

BREE WAS TYPING AT HER computer when her cell phone rang. Since talking to people was much less tedious than inputting listings onto the Internet, she was happy to take the call.

"Brianne McCormick, speaking. How may I help you?"

"Bree, I have a bone to pick with you!"

She frowned at her father's irate tone. "What's the problem?"

"The problem is that I just ran into a friend of yours down at Hanson's. Noah Tanner. And I gather there have been some facts you've conveniently forgotten to tell me?"

Well, she hadn't really thought kissing Noah last night was any of her father's business....

"Like a connection between the break-ins?" Larry prompted.

She blinked. "You two were discussing that?"

"Don't worry. We were discreet. I have had practice with conversations I didn't want noticed, you know."

Normally, it was that kind of reminder that made her cringe, but at the moment she was too confused. She and Noah had talked for an hour in his living room last night before she'd finally left. But she hadn't expected him to seek out her father and relay the details. "Since when are you and Noah buddies?"

"Um, never mind that. What I want to know is why you didn't tell me you were looking into this. That's the sheriff's job."

The sheriff she'd seen through the glass talking to the bookstore owner on her way to work this morning? If her father lost that job, she was going to...she tried to think of something really bad but still legal to do to Hardy. "Dad, I'm waiting to hear how you and Noah ended up having your little chat."

Her father sighed. "Well, it's possible that when I caught his name, I asked about his intentions. Toward you."

"What?"

"Well, you seemed interested in him after the off-the-road incident, and Lorna from the Cut Hut was in the bookshop telling some other woman that you'd been spending time with him...."

"Because I'm helping him sell his grandmother's place! And I'm twenty-eight. You don't need to screen men for me."

"Not like I had the chance back when you were in school. Guess I got a little overzealous about the chance to be fatherly. Forgive me?"

"I assume Noah wasn't bothered by your question?"

"He said his intentions were 'noble,' and oddly enough, I believed the guy."

At the word *noble,* a giggle threatened to erupt. She recalled the kisses they'd shared last night in his kitchen and the effort it had taken on his part to do the right thing, though he'd reiterated when he walked her to her car that they had unfinished business. But she didn't want to think about that during this phone call.

"Yeah, Dad. Noah's one of the good guys."

"Which is what you deserve."

"Don't start planning to give me away at my wedding just yet, okay? Romance isn't one of my goals right now. Even if it were, Noah's leaving town once he has his grandmother's farm ready to sell. He doesn't need to stick around for me to show it. Now, how did the…" She glanced out her open door. "Other topic come up?"

"I said something about the guy in my building, Steve, who was at his weekly poker game during the break-in, and Noah assumed you and I had talked about him. You've been doing a little detective work, huh?"

"Very little."

"Well, when you and Noah come up with a plan, make sure you keep me in the loop," her father insisted before saying goodbye.

You and Noah? When had they become a twosome? All she'd been trying to do was find out more about Jolie Wright. And she had. Apparently, Jolie was the youngest of the Hardy siblings. Rick, the oldest, had chosen to live in Prescott. A second brother, the middle child, served on the force in Austin. Jolie was the baby of the family, and apparently doing her own kind of civic duty. They'd lost their parents when the couple had some sort of accident on vacation, though Noah admitted he didn't know much about that since it had happened just as he moved to town, when he'd been coping with his own problems. The Hardy kids had moved in with loving grandparents and seemed to be a sterling family, which left Bree with a dead end.

Except for Dave Holbrook, the third troublemaker who'd gone to school with Garcia and Blevins. She drummed her fingers on the edge of her desk. Lots of people knew Garcia had moved, or was in the process thereof. And her dad had mentioned that Blevins played a weekly poker game—habits like that were easy to chart if someone was waiting for the apartment to be empty.

When her phone rang again, she wondered if her father had forgotten to tell her something or if it was actually a work-related call this time.

"Brianne McCormick."

"Hey, it's Noah. I just wanted to warn you that I ran into your father earlier and perhaps said more than you would have liked."

"No kidding. Dad called a minute ago."

"Ah. Sorry. He raised the subject, so I thought you'd spoken to him. By the time I realized you hadn't, he'd already deduced that you and I talked. But I have good news for you."

He'd changed his mind about being noble and wanted her to meet him at his place in thirty minutes?

With a sigh, she reminded herself that it had been *her* idea not to get involved with clients. Especially those on their way out of town. "What's that?"

"Before your father came in for lunch, I made some small talk with Debby Sue, told her that while I was here, it might be fun to call some of my old classmates. I threw out three or four names, including Holbrook's, to ask if any of them were still in town."

"And?"

"Well, unfortunately, Jessie Marino, the prettiest cheerleader in my graduating class has moved a—"

"Tanner!"

He chuckled into the phone. "Holbrook's still here. Debby Sue said he was in the same factory layoff as her Hank. As far as she knows, Holbrook's drawing unemployment and generally not doing squat with his life. There was, however, an unpleasant incident the last time Holbrook ran into Blevins at Hanson's. Debby Sue thinks that Dave might have been asking for a loan, and that Steve laughed in his face. Guess they didn't stay tight after high school."

So Dave Holbrook now had lots of time on his hands and had reason to be bitter? "Sounds like our culprit."

"You want to talk to the sheriff? I'll go with you, if you want, share all of this with Hardy."

"You think he'd listen to either of us?" From his demeanor the other day, the sheriff had tried and judged Noah long ago and condemned Bree because of her father's past. Her natural inclination to avoid the police kicked in. "I have a better idea...."

"I CAN'T BELIEVE I LET YOU talk me into this," Noah complained. "We could have at least used the truck. More legroom."

"I didn't talk you into it, you insisted on joining me," Bree shot back. "And it's *my* stakeout, so we use my car." No way was she sitting all night next to Noah in a vehicle that boasted one extra-long bench seat in the front. At least her car had a console full of CDs, maps and miscellaneous supplies safely separating the bucket seats.

"Fair enough. But do you really think spying on him is the answer?"

"I don't know. Maybe we'll get lucky and catch him up to something."

"Darlin', my idea of getting lucky in no way involves David Holbrook."

Her heart sped up, but she ignored it. Being this close to Noah for the next few hours probably wasn't her brightest idea, but this was her first investigation, after all. She was making it up as she went along. And he'd had a point—if Holbrook turned out to be some surly bad guy who happened to catch on to the fact she was following him, it didn't hurt to have backup with her on the op. Even a rookie knew that.

I've really got to stop watching so many detective shows and police procedurals.

It didn't look like she was going to get a chance to trail the suspect, anyway. All Holbrook seemed to be doing was watching TV in his front room. From their shadowed parking spot beneath the tree down the street from Holbrook's dilapidated house, she occasionally took a peek with her binoculars, but the only thing interesting about her night were the intermittent snatches of conversation between her and Noah before lapsing back into watchful silence. Every time he shared something, even if it was as small as a comfort food he'd liked as a kid, she felt the bond between them deepen. And every time he made her laugh, she wished he weren't leaving Prescott.

It was almost one in the morning when headlights flashed on the deserted road behind them.

"Uh-oh," Noah muttered. "Stow your binoculars under your seat as casually as possible, and don't freak out."

"Wh—" But then he was kissing her, and her question became irrelevant.

Oh, *yes*. She'd been daydreaming about this all night, the way he'd taste, the way he'd feel. His hand meshed in her hair as she rubbed her tongue against his. If only the damn console weren't in her way—

A knock at the driver-side door interrupted them just as Noah was sliding his other hand up her jeans-clad thigh. She almost jumped, but Noah seemed unperturbed.

"Mind if I ask what's going on here?" the young, fresh-faced officer asked when Bree rolled her window down.

"Sorry," Noah said, his tone anything but contrite.

The man sighed. "Someone in the neighborhood called and reported a car out here that looked as if it had people in it. I don't suppose you two could behave like adults and find a room?"

Noah laughed. "What do you think I was trying to convince her to do?"

The officer's lips twitched as if he were trying not to smile. "Better move it along. Sheriff Hardy frowns on loitering."

"Will do," Bree said, glad to finally have something to contribute, even if it came out breathlessly. Actually, *breathless* was probably perfectly suited to the situation. Once she'd rolled the window back up and pulled away from the curb, she cast a sidelong glance at Noah. "You knew it was a cop when he turned onto the street?"

"I thought I caught the reflection off a siren. If I was right, I wanted us to have our excuse ready before he got close. If I was wrong…well, it's not like kissing you was a hardship."

No, just a temptation. Even though she'd never had a fling before, would having one with Noah before he left town be such a bad thing? *Not if you weren't already falling for him.*

Why go out of her way to seek heartache?

NOAH WAS IN THE MIDDLE of a shower—a very cold one—when he caught the phone ringing. At two in the morning? It had to be Bree. She'd only dropped him off moments ago. Wrapping a towel around his middle as he moved, he hastened for the phone in the kitchen.

"Hello?" He ignored the water dripping in his eyes, hoping that she was calling because she'd thought of something and not because anything was wrong.

"Hey, little bro!"

Shock sent him into one of the kitchen chairs. *"Caleb?"*

"You got another older brother I don't know about?"

One is more than enough. "Is everything okay? It's after two." No telling what time zone his brother was calling from.

"Did I wake you?" The question was barely discernible over obnoxious background music.

"No."

"So it's not a problem, then, right? Look, I would've tried earlier, but we had a rush that didn't clear out until last call."

"You're in a bar, aren't you?"

"No, man, *the* bar. My bar. Won it in a poker game two months ago."

God help me. "I see." Caleb could turn around and lose the place playing cards tomorrow.

"I'm a businessman now. You understand why I couldn't come to Thanksgiving like we planned?"

"Oh, sure. Joe had aliens to blow up, and you had drinks to mix." Their grandmother would have disapproved of his petty tone, but something about the sarcasm felt viciously good.

"Hey." Caleb actually sounded wounded. "I'm making an honest living. Isn't that what you wanted?"

Noah plowed a hand through his damp hair. He didn't know what the hell he wanted. Maybe he hadn't for a while. He was good at his job, so he kept doing it, but he still felt… Had Stef been right? Was there some kind of "hole" in his life? While he'd been bewildered by their break-up, he hadn't exactly been overwrought, which made him wonder how badly he'd even wanted her.

I know the woman I want. But Bree had stated her main objections to being with him, and much as it pained him to admit it, they were reasonable.

"You still there, bro? Hell, man, say something once in a while. This phone call is costing me."

Noah laughed dryly, thinking of the long-distance minutes *he'd* logged just trying to track his older brother down, getting former roommates, girlfriends and employers who occasionally had an idea where Caleb might have gone next without bothering to inform his family.

"Joe's been worried," Caleb said. "No one's been able to get in touch with you. I called him when I couldn't reach you Thanksgiving night. He said you were going to Prescott without us."

"Seemed more rational than growing old and decrepit while I waited for the two of you."

"Sorry about missing the holiday. I thought Joe

would be there. And I'm really trying to make a go of this place. I hired the guy I won it from and if he ever beats his gambling problem, I might even take him on as a limited partner. Seems like the decent sort of thing you would do."

Noah honestly couldn't tell if he was being condescended to or complimented.

"We've been calling the farm," Caleb added. "But this is the first either of us were able to reach you."

"I've been in and out. There's not an answering machine here."

"What happened to your cell phone?"

"Left it in Dallas," Noah said flippantly. If Caleb were about to lecture him on responsibility…

But his brother just sighed. "I don't know what we were worried about. I mean, this is *you*. It might be unlike you to disappear off the face of the world for days on end, but still, how much trouble could you get in? You're the world's oldest Boy Scout."

The hell I am, Noah wanted to retort. Only, his brother had a point. Here Noah was, being responsible for all three of them. He had a business to run, too, yet he'd put his life on hold so that they could sell the place and split the profit in thirds. How was that fair?

If he were smarter, he would have stopped expecting fair after his dad died and his mom skipped out on them. Instead, he'd toed the line, done well in school, tried to make up for past misdeeds—both his and his brothers'—and waited for his disciplined efforts to be rewarded. Instead, Hardy still eyed him as though his mug shot should be up on the wall of the Prescott Post Office, while former truant Joe would make his first million by thirty and Caleb was running his own bar.

And their mother never had come back, no matter how good Noah managed to be.

"Caleb, I appreciate your concern, but I gotta go."

"Sure, probably getting ready for bed. I'll check back with you some other time."

Going to bed was the sensible thing to do, but once there, Noah just stared in the dark at the ceiling above him. He didn't feel like sleeping. What he *felt* like was being a little bad for a change.

CHAPTER EIGHT

AT THE KNOCK AGAINST HER partially ajar door, Bree glanced up, her heart skipping hopefully. Had Noah come to see her? He'd never made an unscheduled drop by at her office before, but after that kiss— "Oh, hey, Wanda. Come on in."

"I'm not bothering you, am I?" The teacher adjusted a heavy-looking shoulder bag.

"Not at all. Have a seat. Did you make a decision about whether or not you want to make an offer on the Peterson place?"

She nodded. "Yeah. But I could have called you about that. I was actually wondering if I could buy you lunch? I don't know many people in town yet, and all the faculty I've met from the high school are in class right now, plus I've been hearing about this barbecue place that's supposed to be really good...."

"I'd be happy to join you if you'll give me a minute to finish up an e-mail. But you don't need to pay for both of us."

Wanda flashed her a grateful smile. "Thanks. I'm excited about the move, but I forgot what it was like to try to meet new people."

"I understand completely." Bree was lucky she'd

been able to get together for the occasional evening out with her dad instead of just having Mr. Darcy for company. But between the staff at Hanson's, the many people she'd met through her job and the regulars at the bookstore, she no longer thought of herself as the new girl in town. Prescott was truly becoming home. Could she keep it that way, or would the sheriff's increasing inquiries ruin it all? The girls at the Cut Hut seemed to like her, but they liked gossip more....

The shrill of the phone scraped her raw nerves and she grabbed it quickly, shooting an apologetic glance toward Wanda. "Brianne McCormick."

"Bree, it's your father. Can you talk right now? About *you know what?* I've been doing a little detective work of my own. You inspired me."

Oh, God. She knew he meant well, but if her father wasn't careful, he could make the situation worse. At best, Hardy would resent the ex-con poking around in police business. At worst...

"I'm with a client right now, but can I call you later?" When he answered in the affirmative, she gripped the receiver tightly, as if trying to impress her words on him. "Just don't do anything rash until we've had a chance to discuss this further, all right?

He hung up before giving his promise. Bree was still worrying on the way to Hanson's. She gratefully accepted Wanda's offer to drive.

Bree had been moving at half her normal speed this morning, which she supposed was what happened when you were out past midnight on a completely pointless stakeout. In retrospect, she was surprised Noah hadn't tried to talk her out of the scheme. Instead, he'd been a gentleman, humored her and come along to make sure she didn't get hurt—as if she might actually have stumbled across a real criminal.

What if her father *did* cross paths with a real criminal? He could put himself in danger.

Inside Hanson's, Bree forced a smile for her new friend. "So, this is your first time here? You're in for a treat."

They sat in Debby Sue's section, which reminded Bree that she should mention the Cut Hut. Nothing would acclimate Wanda to town faster than a quick trim and a rundown of who's who in Prescott. They both ordered, Bree making recommendations between stifled yawns. She really should have asked for something caffeinated instead of ice water. At this rate, she'd never make it through this afternoon's workload.

"You okay?" Wanda asked. "You don't seem your usual energetic self today."

"Sorry. Noah and I didn't get much sl— I mean, I was busy last night and didn't get home until late."

"A-ha!" Wanda's exclamation came out so loudly she ducked her head. "Sorry. Good acoustics in here. You're talking about that man I saw you with, right? The one you said isn't your boyfriend."

"He's n—"

"Hey, darlin'." Noah appeared from around the corner, stopping at Bree's table to plant a kiss on her lips. "I was looking for you and figured this was a logical place to check. Hi, I'm Noah."

"Wanda." The woman shook his hand, shooting a *you-were-saying?* look at Bree.

"Uh…" seemed to be the closest Bree could come to

a coherent response. What was he doing here? Why was he acting as if they were a couple?

"I don't mean to interrupt, but could I talk to you for a moment?" he asked Bree.

Since Wanda was all but making shooing motions, Bree agreed to follow him outside.

"Hop in the truck," he instructed.

"Am I being kidnapped?"

He raked his gaze over her. "Tempting. But no. I want to make sure we aren't overheard."

Once she'd joined him, she realized he hadn't shaved. And his shirt was untucked. His hair was more rumpled than she'd seen it before, too. All in all, he looked pretty damn sexy.

"I've had a radical notion," he told her.

"Okay."

"Let's break into Dave Holbrook's house."

"What?" Even though he'd warned her it would be radical, she hadn't expected anything of that magnitude.

"Tonight. I've discovered his regular Friday routine is to drink himself senseless at CB's Roadhouse, then get poured into a cab. What if he's been the one ransacking places? He knew both men, he recently exchanged harsh words with Blevins, and, in high school at least, he didn't seem to be someone overburdened with a conscience. Maybe we might get a look at what he's found."

"What makes you think he found anything at either place? Everyone says nothing was missing." The words came out automatically, but she wasn't thinking about the robberies so much as wondering when Noah had lost his mind. Some time between now and when she'd last seen him, she supposed.

"Maybe whatever he took from one or both of them isn't the kind of thing they wanted the cops to know they had in the first place. You know, there's something else to consider. Fifteen years ago, those three were thick as thieves—pardon the expression. What if one of them has something, and someone else wants it back?"

"You mean like, Garcia didn't have it at his place and it wasn't found at Blevins's, so maybe Holbrook has it? I don't know. If it's something that's tied to all three of them, wouldn't they talk about it? Move whatever to a safe location, or talk to the police? This all just seems kind of flimsy, Noah." But intriguing. The impulse to act so immediately, *tonight,* and possibly head off her father doing something equally rash… With his past and the wrong judge, if Larry got in trouble with the law now, he could end up in prison for the remainder of his life.

Still. "It's been a long time since high school," she pointed out. "You're sure Holbrook's the connection?"

"They all three stayed in town, and we don't know what secrets they've kept these past fifteen years. I heard my brother talking to his friends one night at Trehan Point, and I swear something in his voice made me think he'd take a bullet for those two." Noah balled one fist against the steering wheel. "Yet he barely manages to keep in touch with his own brothers. Sometimes the teenage bonds people form are beyond logical explanation. Think about it, three guys are friends, guilty of all kinds of trouble together. Now, two of them have had their homes broken into less than a week apart, with nothing reported stolen. I think the third guy is our best bet for learning why."

Speaking of why. "What's your motivation for this?

You don't even live in town, do you really care that much about a couple of burglaries where no one was even hurt?"

"I care about you. Wouldn't it be better for you and your father if the real guilty party is discovered?"

Yes, preferably before one or both of them lost their job because of the sheriff's suspicions. But as much as that should matter to her, she was preoccupied with Noah's admission. He cared about her?

Well, there were many types of caring, and he went out of his way to display most of them, even in kindness toward strangers. Maybe his ex had been right and he really did need to find problems to solve and heroic missions to fill some kind of emptiness.

"I can do it without you," he said. "But it'll be easier with an alibi. We go to CB's tonight, where we act hot and heavy. I've had at least five people in town ask if we're an item, and that cop last night saw us kissing. We make sure Holbrook is there, then we leave, giving the impression that we're off to have sex on the nearest flat surface."

Her breath caught. Even though he was describing their cover and not their actual plans for the evening, the mental image sent need shivering through her.

"What you think?" he asked. "Do it with me?"

"Yes." She was either lust-addled or sleep-deprived, but worry for her father, who had *finally* managed to go straight, combined with the fact that she was tangentially connected to the first two robberies, made her antsy to have this riddle solved. Besides, there was something enthralling about doing something bad with a man she'd half convinced herself could be nothing but good. Lord knows between the two of them they'd both been accused of plenty they *weren't* guilty of; this seemed like karmic justice. Didn't the universe owe them one crime they got away with, especially when they were doing it for a good cause?

"Are you sure we can break in, though?" she asked. "Because I am not asking my father for any help or tips, if that was your plan. He can't know about this—he's already trying to come up with ways to crack the case on his own. I don't want to encourage him."

Noah made a dismissive gesture. "I can handle it. You saw Holbrook's place last night. We're not talking a guy with a sophisticated security system. He doesn't even have a dog. Call me after work, and we'll fine-tune the details."

She nodded, but didn't really feel her head move. It was as if she were watching herself from a distance, curious to know how this would play out. Would she get a taste tonight of how her father had let himself be seduced into so many wrong decisions? Would Noah change his mind at the last minute?

When she returned to the table, dazed, Wanda laughed. "I'm guessing his kiss goodbye knocked your socks off. You don't still expect me to believe you're only involved with him as a client?"

"No." Bree felt herself blushing as she added, "We're more than that." By this time tomorrow, they'd be partners in crime.

DESPITE THE BOLD AIR she was trying to adopt, Bree didn't think she'd have the moxie to come to CB's Roadhouse by herself. As she walked across the gravel parking lot and surveyed the building, she decided it was one of those bars where you just wouldn't be surprised if a brawl broke out and one patron suddenly threw another through the front window. As she followed Noah inside, their fingers entwined, she noted that someone had tried to brighten the interior with neon. Lots and lots of neon.

She plastered herself to him as they navigated the modest but tough-looking Friday night crowd. When Noah had picked her up earlier, she'd wondered if their all-black ensembles would make them stand out, but black seemed to be the attire of choice tonight, alternating with blue jeans and one memorably short leopard-print skirt worn by a woman on the virtually empty dance floor. Considering the way she was gyrating to a rather easygoing country song, the redhead had clearly come on a mission not to return home alone.

Following Bree's gaze, Noah shook his head. "I think she may have once dated my brother."

"So did Lorna at the Cut Hut, from what I hear. What about you, did you leave a string of broken hearts in Prescott?"

He gave her a slow, wicked, dimpled smile. "Would you be jealous if I said yes?"

"I don't get jealous. I just make sure men can't remember the women that came before me."

Noah stroked the back of his hand over her throat and down toward the scooped neckline of her black bodysuit. "I like this outfit," he told her. "But I'm going to like taking it off you even more."

Bree swallowed. They'd agreed on the ride here that while they wouldn't make a point of speaking to be overheard, they'd be "in character" all night and not careful about who listened. It was best if they appeared to any witnesses as lovers, oblivious to those around them. Of course, why a man seriously on the make would bring his date *here,* Bree had no idea. But they needed to make sure David Holbrook was parked on his regular bar stool. If they broke into his house only to find him home with a cold, they were screwed.

"What can I get you to drink?" Noah asked, glancing pointedly toward the bar.

She hoped Holbrook hadn't changed so much in the past decade that Noah couldn't recognize him. "Whatever you're having is just fine with me."

He nodded. "Back in just a second."

Even though he was only a few feet away, she was very aware of being alone and catching the attention of those men not watching the leopardess on the small, scuffed floor. Bree considered ducking into the ladies' room. On a real date, she'd probably use the opportunity to check her hair and reapply lipstick. Then again—she studied the unabashed grime beneath the neon—perhaps the rest rooms here were best left unvisited.

Noah returned with frosty bottles of Shiner, giving her an imperceptible nod as he handed her one. Holbrook was here. *We're really going to do this.* She lifted the beer to her mouth, taking a slug of the distinctive brew.

Noah sipped his more slowly, probably for the best since he would be driving and, later, picking locks.

Neither of them finished their beers, however. Noah lazily traced ovals up and down her spine, creating an expectant, sensitized response beneath the soft cotton. When she'd reached the halfway point on her bottle, he gently took it from her.

"Dance with me?"

She nodded. He set their beers down, then led her to the floor. He locked his arms around her, drawing her close. Once his lips touched hers, this would simply be a vertical make-out session masquerading as a slow dance. She wasn't even sure her feet moved as she swayed against him, her lips nibbling at his. Bree momentarily forgot that they wouldn't go straight from here to the nearest bed, where Noah would make love to her all night. Hopefully, any onlookers would be fooled—*she* certainly thought they made a convincing pair.

Songs melted into each other, bringing them closer to tonight's purpose. Noah pulled his head back, a question in his deep blue eyes. Was she ready, was she sure?

"Let's get out of here," she murmured, her voice so husky she almost didn't recognize it.

"Race you to the door," he answered, sounding a bit strangled himself.

Bree may have bumped into a couple of people on their way out, but she barely took notice of anyone except Noah. He, however, had more wits about him. As they left the building, he paused once, looking over his shoulder. She was sure he was checking to make sure Holbrook was still happily engaged in pickling his liver.

Time to misbehave.

STANDING AT THE BACK DOOR of David Holbrook's house, a penlight in one hand and Bree motionless behind him, Noah marveled at the trusting nature of Prescott citizens. As they'd approached, Bree had pointed to an obviously fake rock sitting at the edge of the cement slab. Sure enough, there had been the spare key to the house.

Truth be told, he was a little relieved they wouldn't have to rely on his dazzling criminal skills, although he'd been present more than once when Caleb showed Josiah how to pick a lock. Noah had usually been the one loudly objecting while both brothers ignored him.

Moments later, he and Bree had slipped into the house, moving as silently as possible despite it being unoccupied. *Now what, Sherlock?* Adrenaline was coursing through him, and he doubted he had the steady nerves it took to do this on a regular basis. He'd much rather exercise his inner bad boy on the dance floor with Bree— or in a bedroom—than ever repeat this performance.

Inside, he exchanged the penlight for a flashlight that would help them get a better look. Other than that, all they carried between them were two sets of keys to his truck and Bree's compact digital camera. The back door led into a small, dingy kitchen where a fly buzzed across an overstuffed garbage can. Beyond that was the living room at the front of the house, where Holbrook had spent most of his previous evening.

"Why don't you stay by the front window?" he asked. "Let me know if any cars come down the street. And let me know if you happen to glimpse any of those safes that are supposed to look like a big dictionary, or something." In a house this shabby, a complex wall unit seemed unlikely, but after the glaringly obvious fake rock, Noah half expected a novelty safe. Unfortunately, those came as everything from soft drink cans to faux underwear, so he hoped whatever they were looking for was large.

The house wasn't big enough for a separate office, but there was a desk up against the living room wall. He was debating whether or not to rifle through that first, then move to searching the bedroom. Would they get out of here faster if Bree took the desk while he went into the other room? He felt safer having a lookout, though. Caleb had always had *two* other partners in crime, and he'd still managed to get caught on occasion.

"Bree—"

"Shh." She turned to him with wide eyes.

"Car?"

Shaking her head, she gestured frantically toward the back of the house. But he didn't hear anything, nor had the kitchen light come on. Suddenly, however, he glimpsed a small glow. Another penlight.

I was right, someone is looking for something one of the Dead Rebel wannabes has! The nanosecond of triumph was eclipsed by concern for Brianne. He wanted to get her the hell out of here and was rushing her silently toward the front door when a darkly clad figure passed into the room.

All three of them froze at once, and Noah used the element of surprise to try to buy Bree escape time by shining his flashlight full force into the face of the intruder.

Though partially obscured by a navy hood, the delicate features were familiar. His gasp echoed hers. But he recovered first.

"Good evening, Mrs. Mayor. What's a nice girl like you doing in a place like this?"

Jolie Wright's mouth dropped open, but as they all waited to hear what she had to say for herself, she burst into tears.

CHAPTER NINE

AND TO THINK, BREE HAD ONCE guessed her life in Prescott would be normal, verging on dull.

"I—I—I didn't know w-what else to do," the mayor's wife wailed.

Noah looked horrified—this might have been the first time in his life he'd made a woman cry. He scooted toward the blonde, making shushing noises. Bree honestly wasn't sure whether or not he was trying to soothe Jolie or just trying to keep the neighbors from hearing.

"If Michael or Rick ever found out—"

"We're not here to bust you," Bree put in quickly. "We just wanted to get to the bottom of this."

Jolie's eyes focused on her, and she took several deep breaths. "Y-you saw me. At the a-apartment building. You knew?"

"That you were breaking and entering? No, but I was curious. To tell you the truth, I'm still not sure what's going on."

"Blackmail," the other woman said simply. The single word seemed to restore her calm. She sniffed. "One of my former...*friends* has threatened to wreck my current life."

And people wondered why Bree was cynical. Still,

she had trouble imagining the soft-spoken first lady of Prescott doing anything horrible enough to make blackmail possible.

"You knew Frank and David?" Noah asked softly.

She nodded. "And Steve. The three of them didn't have many classes together, but outside of school, they were tight."

Yet they were all in such different places now. Steve living a steady but modest life, Frank relocating to New Mexico, Michael drinking away his unemployment check…and Jolie presiding over the mayor's mansion. You just never knew what paths people would take, Bree reflected, thinking about all the times and places her own life could have veered a different direction.

It could still end up in a place that results in the irony of Dad bailing you out of jail in the middle of the night.

"I want to hear the rest of this story," Bree said, "but somewhere else."

Noah and Jolie both nodded, although the woman glanced at the desk. "Could I just check the drawers first? If the Polaroids are in there… I've gone to so much trouble and risk to find them."

So pictures had been the goal this whole time?

"Bree can keep watch at the window," Noah said, "and I'll keep an eye out back. *Hurry.*"

A few minutes later, Jolie made a distraught keening sound that distracted Bree from studying the street.

"No luck?"

"No. But we should go. It's a blessed miracle I wasn't caught either of the last two times. With three of us here…"

"Yeah." The two women joined Noah, who already held the key in his gloved hand. With the door locked behind them, it was doubtful anyone would ever know they were there.

"Mrs. Wright, maybe you could join us for a cup of coffee," Noah suggested. "Explain what's going on. Who knows? We might be able to help."

She sniffed, looking perilously close to tears again. "Why would you do that? Neither of you really know me."

Bree couldn't help laughing. "He's noble like that. Don't worry, you'll get to used to it."

OF ALL THE PLACES BREE MIGHT have imagined being when the sun came up, knocking at Sheriff Hardy's front door was not one of them. But since Jolie Wright now had a death grip on Bree's hand, escape seemed unlikely. Behind Bree and Jolie stood Noah and a shell-shocked Mayor Wright. The last few hours had been surreal.

Over a cup of diner coffee she'd sipped maybe once and a slice of apple pie she'd ignored completely, Jolie Wright had told them how, as far back as she could remember, her parents had gone away once a year for a romantic week alone while the children stayed with their grandparents. Only one week when Jolie was a teenager, they'd gone away and hadn't come back.

"Because of a stupid gas leak. They told us it was painless, peaceful, but can you imagine? They were on *vacation*."

Rick was already in training to be a cop, and apparently the senseless deaths that couldn't be avenged drove him to pursue justice wherever possible.

"I think he's a good officer, a good brother," Jolie had been quick to add. "But, he was, um, even stricter than my grandparents."

"And you were angry about your parents being gone," Noah had said gently. He'd exchanged a glance with Bree—they were both familiar with that kind of bitterness. Hell, they could practically form a club of their own.

"Right. So I rebelled, hung out with Frank and his wilder friends. They considered me their good-luck charm, figured if they ever *did* get caught and I was with them, we wouldn't get in as much trouble because my brother had some pull. Looking back, I think we probably would have been in more. But we were never blamed for any of the stuff Dave thought up." She'd shot Noah an apologetic glance, no doubt aware that he'd been much higher on any list of suspicion. "Mostly, I was just trying to have fun during two years when I was miserable and feeling alone. My brothers coped in a completely different way, and I loved my grandparents, but the generation gap made it difficult to talk to them. I don't think I truly enjoyed one wrong thing I did."

"Yeah, being bad sounds a lot better than the reality often is," Noah had agreed.

"Once I realized that, I cleaned up my act. When Michael moved back to town, we fell in love. But I've always known I don't deserve him."

Bree disagreed. Everyone made mistakes and should only be judged by how well they overcame them.

"Can you give us more information on the blackmail?" she'd asked. Noah had more experience with riding to people's rescue, but she found she genuinely wanted to aid Jolie.

"Polaroids from a party in high school arrived in the mail, addressed to me. We thought it was hilarious back then to snap shots we knew couldn't be processed at a photo lab. There'd been a game of truth or dare that night. I was sitting in a black lace bra at a table where there were drugs. I swear I didn't take any, but that's not what the pictures looked like. Do you *know* how pure Michael's reputation is? He doesn't have many detractors, but the few he has would love to sling something like this at him. Some people just can't believe in someone so good, and this would reinforce all their ugly doubts."

That last had made Bree squirm, recalling her own comments about the Wrights. But she finally realized why Jolie had been so panicked. It wasn't the constituents in Prescott or the mildly naughty shot of her in a bra, it was the possibility of hurting the man she loved. Or losing him.

Jolie had underestimated him, though. After the diner, she'd begged Bree and Noah for moral support, bringing them home with her as she confessed the truth to her husband, who'd been furious someone was victimizing his wife. Bree had wanted to quietly sneak out and let the couple resolve the issue, but by then Michael was thanking them profusely for helping Jolie find the courage to face her past. As far as he knew, they'd spotted Jolie *before* she'd entered the third house. Bree was uncomfortable with the lie…but more comfortable than she would be with unlawful entry on her record.

Now they relayed the entire story again for Sheriff Hardy in his living room. His sleepy features quickly hardened with anger. Luckily, he was more moved by his sister's tears than Bree would have guessed, and Michael was there to defuse the situation.

"It may be Holbrook who has the pictures," the mayor said. "Since he lost his job when the factory closed outside town, it's likely he's looking for money. But what if it was someone else? Darling, you can't break into every home in Prescott. Perhaps there's a way to use this to help people, let teens know that mistakes happen, but that falling in with a bad crowd isn't irreversible."

Not to mention that if Jolie made her past public, no one could hold it over her head anymore. *Problem solved, more or less.* Bree exchanged a pointed glance with Noah, who halted his pacing and nodded.

"Well, I think Noah and I are going to leave, let you folks handle this however you see fit. Just to reassure everyone, neither of us are going to breathe a word—"

"Not a word," Noah agreed, striding toward the door.

But the sheriff insisted on walking them out. "Tanner, it was you my officer saw the other night, scouting the Holbrook place, wasn't it? Is that how you caught her? I, um, owe you an apology. It's no secret I've often thought badly of you and your brothers, but you're… a…good guy. Thank you."

With a startled expression, Noah accepted the man's handshake. Bree managed not to giggle until they were outside.

"I think that may have caused him actual pain," she said. "But I give him credit for saying it. Not everyone can admit when they're wrong."

"I can. Watch—going to Holbrook's was a damn fool idea, and I don't know what I was thinking. Except that maybe I wanted to see how the other half lived. And impress you."

"By being bad?" She raised her eyebrows. "That's not what I'm looking for."

He opened the truck door for her, letting his body brush hers. "So, you *weren't* turned on last night at CB's?"

Bree bit her lip. Of course she had been, but not because Noah was a bad boy. Simply because he was Noah. She couldn't tell him that, though. His house was almost ready to sell, the mystery had been solved, and they had reached the point in the story where the heroic cowboy passing through town rode into the sunset. Bree's dad had been unequivocally cleared, and Jolie had her happy ending.

What about mine? She reminded herself that cynics don't expect happy endings, particularly with men they'd known a week.

"Noah, this has been a really wild week. Fun, in a lot of ways. Exciting. It's like what you said about wanting to see how the other half lives. I'm attracted to you, but it's all been part of the... It's time to go back to my real life now. And for you to return to yours."

His expression grew shuttered, his eyes closing her out as he took a step away. "I see. Well, we should get you home. You've got to be exhausted."

She was. But once she'd arrived and curled up on her queen-size bed with Mr. Darcy purring his happiness at her return, she couldn't sleep. Her eyes were dry and hot with unshed tears, even though she knew it was stupid to cry over a man she'd known for such a short while.

It wasn't just Noah that upset her. Eventually there might come a man who wasn't leaving town and didn't come with a convenient goodbye—would she trust him enough to give him her heart? Or was her fresh start in Prescott simply an illusion to hide the fact that some things never changed?

NOAH SLEPT MOST OF SATURDAY, escaping from his sense of unease and the hurt that had cut deeper than expected when Bree pushed him away. By Sunday morning, he was left with no other alternative but to deal with it. *So, deal with it.* He'd bounced back no worse for the wear when his girlfriend of four months dumped him. How hard could it be to go back to Dallas and forget a woman he'd known only a week?

Except he didn't want to forget Bree. Hell, he wasn't even sure he wanted to go back to Dallas. Unlike his brothers, who'd always wanted to flee Prescott as soon as possible, Noah's problem had never been with the place. It had been with people who passed judgment on him—like the sheriff, who'd now apologized. It had been with people, he admitted to himself, who weren't coming back. How long was he going to let his family's past haunt him?

Noah liked living in a smaller community. He loved the wide-open spaces he could enjoy simply by stepping outside his front door. He'd miss Hanson's, that was for damn sure. But mostly he'd miss the sense of rightness, of belonging, he got in this house.

I don't want to sell.

It wasn't so much a decision as a realization, the click of the proverbial light bulb over his head. Only, in this part of Texas, it was probably a neon sign.

Noah was a responsible guy. If he'd really wanted to part with his grandmother's farm, he would have got off his butt and come down here months ago. His brothers had just been a handy excuse.

What time was it in California? He had some calls to make.

And once he was through with those, there was a lady he needed to see. *Needed.* Stef had been wrong—he didn't "need to be needed." Bree was a strong lady, and his thoughts when he was with her weren't always about taking care of her. He did, however, want to be with someone who made him happy, someone he could make happy.

If Bree didn't think they could offer each other that, then he'd accept it. But he was curious to know how she'd react now that he was removing her reason for pushing him away with her oh-so-pragmatic dismissal. Who said they had to be realistic? They'd just spent a night indulging in B and E with the mayor's wife. Anything was possible.

MONDAY MORNING, NOAH WAS running on caffeine and enthusiasm. As he'd tried to explain to his brothers what this place meant to him, the perfect idea had hit him, one he was even considering sharing with Mayor Wright. But Bree had to be first, and he was on his way to her office.

He'd been so eager to see her that he'd left early and now wondered if she'd even be in yet. If not, he could wait. Part of being the responsible one in the family involved cultivating patience and discipline. Besides, he knew how important her fresh start in Prescott was and how much she wanted to prove herself at work. If she wasn't there, she'd certainly be one of the first to arrive.

His prediction proved correct when he pulled into the realty lot and saw her car. She was a determined lady. If she would expend some of that determination on a relationship, on her own happiness and hoping for the best, they might create something magical.

"Hello?" he called out as he opened the front door. As quiet as it was, he could hear her suck in her breath. He met her halfway, walking into her office as she'd obviously been coming out to see him.

"Noah! This is…a surprise." She took a few nervous steps backward, ultimately deciding to lean against her desk.

He sat in one of the chairs, noticing how beautiful she looked this morning. Maybe a bit more vulnerable than usual, but still strong and acutely feminine. "I'm afraid I have to ask you not to put the farm on the market." It wasn't necessarily the opening he'd planned to go with, but her big brown eyes had thrown him off balance.

"You've decided to go with another agent? I suppose I understand—"

"No! I've decided not to sell."

"Really?" She glanced up, her gaze confused.

"I love that farm. I think I even love…Prescott. There are a lot of good people here, but troubles, too. Think about what you've been through, my own family, even Jolie's problems in her youth. The farm has always been a haven of sorts for me, and I was thinking about talking to the Wrights about making it a refuge for teens."

"You mean like a shelter? Or a work ranch? A place for weekend retreats?"

He grinned at her enthusiasm, her ability to share his vision. "I'm not sure yet. But I'm looking into it." Even though he took some satisfaction in carpentry, he had a feeling there were more important ways to use his drive to fix things.

"So." She swallowed. "Does this mean you'll be staying?"

Standing, he reached for her hand. "I'm staying. I'll have to go back to Dallas, of course, tie up some loose ends before moving down here permanently, but I'm coming back."

She searched his eyes, saying nothing for a long time. Then a smile broke across her face like sunrise. "You know, even with my rampant trust issues, I believe you."

"Sorry if my not selling the place affects your job. I know commissions are important and— What are you doing?"

Raised up on her tiptoes, she circled her arms around his neck. "Kissing you. And don't apologize for staying. Do *I* look sorry?"

Her lips brushed his, sweetly hesitant as though she was still absorbing the possibilities. Noah, who'd had all night to consider them, crushed his mouth to hers, need buckling inside him when she deepened the kiss. It was only as he caught himself sliding his hand over the curve of her breast, and feeling her tremble in response, that he realized they were in her place of business. Just because there was no one here yet didn't mean there wouldn't be soon.

He broke the kiss, but then leaned in to nibble on the smooth column of her neck. "How set are your hours? I mean, if you weren't exactly here at eight on the dot…"

"My hours are flexible."

"You real estate agents are supposed to know all kinds of facts about the community." He rested her forehead against hers. "Is Trehan Point still the make-out spot of Prescott?"

She laughed. "I don't know. But the romantic in me wonders if we couldn't create a special spot of our own."

"Fair enough." His hand in hers, he drew her toward the door and the future awaiting them.

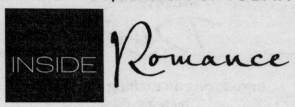

If you enjoyed what you just read,
then we've got an offer you can't resist!

Take 2 bestselling
love stories FREE!
Plus get a FREE surprise gift!

Clip this page and mail it to Silhouette Reader Service™

IN U.S.A.	IN CANADA
3010 Walden Ave.	P.O. Box 609
P.O. Box 1867	Fort Erie, Ontario
Buffalo, N.Y. 14240-1867	L2A 5X3

YES! Please send me 2 free Silhouette Desire® novels and my free surprise gift. After receiving them, if I don't wish to receive anymore, I can return the shipping statement marked cancel. If I don't cancel, I will receive 6 brand-new novels every month, before they're available in stores! In the U.S.A., bill me at the bargain price of $3.80 plus 25¢ shipping and handling per book and applicable sales tax, if any*. In Canada, bill me at the bargain price of $4.47 plus 25¢ shipping and handling per book and applicable taxes**. That's the complete price and a savings of at least 10% off the cover prices—what a great deal! I understand that accepting the 2 free books and gift places me under no obligation ever to buy any books. I can always return a shipment and cancel at any time. Even if I never buy another book from Silhouette, the 2 free books and gift are mine to keep forever.

225 SDN DZ9F
326 SDN DZ9G

Name	(PLEASE PRINT)	
Address	Apt.#	
City	State/Prov.	Zip/Postal Code

Not valid to current Silhouette Desire® subscribers.

Want to try two free books from another series?
Call 1-800-873-8635 or visit www.morefreebooks.com.

* Terms and prices subject to change without notice. Sales tax applicable in N.Y.
** Canadian residents will be charged applicable provincial taxes and GST.
   All orders subject to approval. Offer limited to one per household.
   ® are registered trademarks owned and used by the trademark owner and or its licensee.

DES04R   ©2004 Harlequin Enterprises Limited

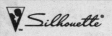

INTIMATE MOMENTS™

Don't miss the next exciting romantic-suspense
novel from *USA TODAY* bestselling author

**Risking his life was part of the job.
Risking his heart was another matter...**

Detective Sawyer Boone had better things to do
with his time than babysit the fiercely independent
daughter of the chief of detectives. But when
Janelle's world came crashing around her, Sawyer
found himself wanting to protect her heart, as well.

CAVANAUGH WATCH

Silhouette Intimate Moments #1431

When the law and passion
collide, this family learns
the ultimate truth—that
love takes no prisoners!

*Available September 2006
at your favorite retail outlet.*